The Dragonfly House

The Dragonfly House

Sam McAuliff

SAPPHIRE BOOKS

SALINAS, CALIFORNIA

The Dragonfly House
Copyright © 2020 by Sam McAuliff All rights reserved.

ISBN - 978-1-952270-14-7

This is a work of fiction - names, characters, places, and incidents are the product of the author's imagination or are used fictitiously. Any resemblance to actual persons living or dead, business, events or locales is entirely coincidental.

All rights reserved. No part of this publication may be reproduced, distributed, or transmitted in any form or by any means, including photocopying, recording, or other electronic or mechanical methods, without written permission of the publisher.

Editor - Tara Young
Book Design - LJ Reynolds
Cover Design - Fineline Cover Design

Sapphire Books Publishing, LLC
P.O. Box 8142
Salinas, CA 93912
www.sapphirebooks.com

Printed in the United States of America
First Edition – October 2020

This and other Sapphire Books titles can be found at
www.sapphirebooks.com

Dedication

For Lara LD. Without your stories, there wouldn't be a Dragonfly.

Acknowledgments

First, I want to thank Chris at Sapphire for adding me to the Sapphire family. It's been a great experience and I hope to make more books with you.

As always, I have to thank my betas. Their collective eagle eye for detail and keen insight keep my stories honest, consistent, and accurate. I rely on them to not just find the mistakes I've made, but more importantly, to tell me when something is out of character or when the story has veered off a cliff. They always tell me what they think, even if I won't like it. And my story is always better for it. Thank you, Lara, Sarah, and April, for your honesty, keen eye, patience, and time.

Also, a shout out to my hometown of Staunton, IL, which, though unnamed, served as the backdrop for Jame's hometown. I tried to describe the town as accurately as possible, from the size of the Main Street, to the Catholic school, the one grocery store, the one brick street still left, and even the bar. The bar described, Trinie's, was based on my grandmother's bar of the same name. The building is still there, but the bar has a different name and is owned by someone else now. And, like Jame, I also spent a lot of time at that library.

Chapter One

"Come in." A voice from the other side of the office door called out in answer to Jame Annis's tentative knock. Jame took a deep breath, then entered with her head high and with perfect posture. Posture was important. The boss hated slouching but never had to say a word to correct it, for her women respected her upraised brow and slightly cocked head enough to know of her disapproval and would quickly stand taller. When she saw them make this correction, she would give a slight smile but otherwise wouldn't note it. Jame made sure not to have a smile on her face, as this was a serious meeting. She walked across the room and stood in front of her superior with her hands crossed in front of herself, just behind the two chairs facing the desk. The owner of the voice sat facing her with a relaxed smile.

"You wanted to see me, Jame?"

"Yes, Ma'am."

"Have a seat." There was a small smile playing at her lips as she said this. There always seemed to be.

Jame took a seat and crossed her legs, trying to keep her Oxfords from bobbing nervously, and used her hands to flatten invisible creases in her trousers. She stopped just short of straightening her perfectly straight tie. "Thank you."

Jame's employer sat back in her chair and folded her hands over her stomach and looked bewildered.

"So, what's up?"

Her casualness helped to put Jame at ease, and she did smile now. There was no tremble in Jame's voice when she said, "Yes, well, I've just noticed... well, not *just* noticed, but there's been something that I've needed to talk to you about for a while."

Now she looked concerned. "You know I'm here if any of you women have a problem. You can always come to me. Is something wrong?"

"Not wrong, per se..." Jame trailed off and looked to the side.

"Jame, talk to me. What's going on with you?"

Jame cleared her throat, and now she did straighten her tie. "Well, it seems like...there's been some talk. About you...and me...by the women." Jame couldn't meet her gaze and looked at her hands instead.

Her smile turned from one of politeness to amusement. "Is that all?"

"Yes."

"So, what are they saying?"

"They're saying that...they're saying that I'm your favorite." Jame said the end of her sentence softly and looked aside again.

To Jame's surprise, her boss laughed. "Is that all?"

"Basically, yes."

"Oh, my sweet Jame, for you to be bothered by that...that amuses me."

Jame relaxed a bit at seeing her Mistress's amusement. She returned her smile, though cautiously. Jame uncrossed her legs and sat a little more comfortably. "I just don't want them thinking I'm not earning my keep around here. I mean, I meet with as many customers as they do."

She gave Jame a secret smile and said, in her most seductive voice, the one the women all vied to hear spoken to them, "I know. Oh, sweet Jame, you *are* earning your keep. And they *should* be jealous of you." She leaned forward in her chair again. "Because they're right...you *are* my favorite. Does that bother you?"

Jame gave a nervous laugh and straightened her tie again. "Ma'am, I'm sure you say that to—"

"To all the women? No, just you. Is that so hard to believe?" Ma'am stood and slowly walked around to Jame's side of the desk. Her clothes belied her self-made wealth and the power she had over the women who worked for her. She was dressed now as she so often was in old jeans and a button-up men's shirt. Her long reddish-blond hair hung loose to her shoulders, and she wore no makeup. She made no effort to hide her age or imperfections. She was in her late forties, and she wore it well. She stood facing Jame now, forcing Jame to look up at her. They were mere inches apart. Ma'am leaned down to caress Jame's cheek, and it instantly flamed under her touch. Ma'am gave her a warm smile. She said softly, "My sweet Jame." Then she caressed Jame's tie, letting it slide through her fingers, while she held Jame's gaze. Then, she took hold of the tie and pulled Jame forward, and Jame came easily enough, still looking at Ma'am with reverence. She pulled Jame to her until Jame had no choice but to stand or kneel, and one light tap on her shoulder told Jame which choice to make.

Jame went to her knees, her feet pressed against the chair and her hands behind her back. Ma'am let go of her tie and let her fingers caress Jame's short-cropped hair. "Do you know *why* you're my favorite?"

"No, Ma'am."

For a moment, she didn't answer, she just continued to smile and stroke Jame's hair, then she sighed. "You're my favorite, *Liebchen*, because...because...oh, sweet Jame, there's no one like you. You're my sweet Jame. That's all there is to it." She tapped Jame on the shoulder again, and Jame stood, leaving her arms behind her back. Her gaze never wavered. "You may sit." Jame unclasped her hands and did so. Ma'am sighed and walked back around her desk and resumed her seat. "What am I going to do with you?" A bemused smile played on her lips as she looked Jame over.

"Do with me, Ma'am?"

"Yeah. What am I going to do with you? You are my favorite, but it would be wrong to let on to the other women that their fears are true. I don't want them to think I think less of them. But, oh, the things I want from you..." She trailed off, not finishing that thought. Then, a new thought struck her, and she suddenly asked, "What would you do if you were me?"

"What would I do, Ma'am?"

"Yes, what would you do?"

After giving it a moment's thought, she said, "Well, I would remember that I'm the boss, and I could do anything I pleased."

"That was very bold of you to say." She nodded her approval. "And a very good point. I *am* the boss, aren't I?"

"Yes, Ma'am."

"And I can do what I want, can't I?"

This time, instead of answering robotically, Jame returned her smile and said, "Oh, yes, Ma'am."

She laughed. When she spoke again, her voice

had dropped a bit until it sounded like smooth jazz. It was satin and smoke and with it, she could bring a girl to her knees without lifting a finger. "Oh, I like that. Almost as much as I like you. Stand up." Jame stood. She leaned back in her chair, and Ma'am's gaze moved over Jame slowly, taking in the deep purple tie, the white suspenders, the gray trousers, and Jame's impeccable black shirt. "You are delicious."

Jame's cheeks flamed again. "Thank you, Ma'am."

Still using her smooth voice, she said, "Do you know what I want to do?"

Jame tried to restrain the grin that was working its way to her mouth, but she couldn't. She let it come, and when she did so, she noticed Ma'am's eyes crinkled with affection, but also something more, something she was often careful not to let show around the women: lust. Jame said, "I think so."

"Do you?"

"Yes."

Ma'am looked at Jame with challenge in her eyes and said, "Prove it."

Jame inclined her head and said, "Ma'am," then slowly walked behind the desk, letting her finger trail on the desktop as she walked and kept eye contact with her Mistress.

For her part, Ma'am smiled and watched Jame's progression around her desk. She leaned back and put her hands on the arms of her chair. When Jame was mere inches away, she said, still in her honey-dipped voice, "I like that smile you have, sweet Jame. Kind of sly. Makes me wonder what you're up to."

Jame chuckled somewhat mischievously and leaned down and put both hands on Ma'am's chair.

"I'm in charge now, *Madam*." Jame leaned in suddenly and gave her Mistress a hungry kiss, causing her to whimper and moan. Ma'am brought her hands up to pull Jame to her, but Jame pulled back from the kiss and grabbed Ma'am's wrists and held them to the arms of the chair. There was mocking in her tone when she said, "Ah, ah, ah, not yet, sweetie. What did I just say? Hmm? Now sit back and enjoy the show." Jame loosened her grip on Ma'am's wrists, but before she did so, she ran her finger lightly along and up Ma'am's arms, making her shiver, then she stepped back. Jame smiled at her and brought her hands up to her suspenders, hooking her thumbs behind each one, running them up and down a moment before she pulled them down to her sides. Then, her hands went up to her tie, and she untied it slowly. As she did so, she looked at it curiously, then looked to the woman sitting in front of her. "What shall I do with this? So many options. Thoughts?"

"Oh, so many thoughts."

Jame wound each end of the tie around a hand and pulled it taut. "I could...use it to tie your hands together. I could...use it to tie one wrist to the chair. Or I could gag you. So many options. Do you have a favorite, *Ma'am*?"

"Do whatever you like. I'm yours, sweet Jame."

"That's my girl." Jame looked at her in consideration, then said, "Stand up." Ma'am did so with a small smile and complete trust. "Turn around." Ma'am complied. "Give me your hands."

Ma'am shook her head and said pleadingly, "Please don't do this."

Jame unwound one of her hands from the tie and used it to trail a finger along the back of Ma'am's neck, then leaned in and put a feather kiss there. She whispered, "*This* is what you pay me for. Hands, please." Ma'am presented her hands behind her back, and Jame tied them together, then turned her Mistress around. Ma'am was looking at the floor. With sternness, Jame said, "Look at me." Ma'am met her gaze with a mixture of fear and defiance. Jame caressed her cheek, coming to rest on Ma'am's chin, then Jame pulled her to her, and Ma'am came willingly. Jame placed a kiss on her lips. It started quick and greedy, but Jame ended it slowly and softly, lingering with Ma'am's bottom lip for a moment, sucking it into her mouth. As Jame let her go and stepped back, Ma'am leaned into her, wanting more. Jame chuckled. "Tsk, tsk, patience." Jame grabbed her by the front of her jeans, keeping her at arm's length. She propelled her back in front of the chair. "You may sit." As Ma'am took a tentative step backward, Jame leaned forward around Ma'am and held the arms of the chair. Ma'am sat and Jame held her place, leaning over her but not touching her. Jame leaned in as if she was going to kiss or nibble on Ma'am's neck but then pulled back at the last moment, just as Ma'am was moving to accommodate her. After the third time doing this, Ma'am groaned in longing, and Jame chuckled again.

"Are you going to touch me?"

Jame stood. "Eventually." Jame slowly pulled her shirt loose from her trousers, keeping her gaze on Ma'am the whole time. As Ma'am watched, Jame's fingers went to the top button, and she undid it slowly, then the rest. When she reached the last button, Jame took the shirt off and draped it on the desk, on top of the day planner Ma'am had open. Jame knew it held the appointments for all the women, including her own. But she didn't care who her next client was. Right now, it was all about her Mistress. She stood in front of her naked to her trousers, walked up to the chair, and straddled Ma'am, who leaned back. Jame smiled. "Good girl, waiting your turn." Jame ran a finger along Ma'am's jaw, then trailed it down her throat, making her way around Ma'am's neck, where she put her hand in her hair and got a good grip, but she didn't pull.

Several emotions played out at once in Ma'am's eyes; one of them was anger, but lust was still there. She said evenly, "You know I don't like my hair messed with."

Jame leaned forward and put a nipple in Ma'am's mouth, then put her hands in her hair. "I know. Now do as you're told." Ma'am closed her eyes and eagerly sucked on Jame's nipple while Jame loosened her hold on Ma'am's hair but kept her hands in the same place.

Ma'am flicked her tongue over Jame's nipple until she had brought it out, then she sucked it into her mouth with fervor.

Jame put her head back and moaned, then cried, "Harder."

Dutifully, Ma'am increased her pace, sucking the nipple in faster, occasionally grazing her teeth over it but stopping just short of biting. Jame pushed Ma'am into her more, and this time, it was Ma'am who cried out.

Abruptly, Jame pulled Ma'am's head back and put her mouth on hers. Jame let her tongue play with Ma'am's, and she could feel Ma'am try to move her arms, but the tie held them fast. Jame knew the moan Ma'am made was just as much pleasure as it was frustration. Jame chuckled. "You want to move your arms, don't you?"

"Oh, god, yes."

"Should I let you?"

"Please," Ma'am begged.

Jame sat up and seemed to consider the question. Then she shook her head slowly. "Nah, not yet."

Ma'am groaned again.

Jame stood and said, "Get up." Ma'am stood, and Jame grinned at her but only said, "Turn around."

Ma'am turned around, and Jame untied the tie from around Ma'am's wrists.

"Okay, turn around and put your hands in front of you."

Ma'am complied, but she was smiling now.

Jame looked at Ma'am's outstretched hands. "Too bad I don't have handcuffs. But I think the tie is working just fine." As she said this, she retied the tie around Ma'am's wrists but not before gently rubbing her thumb over one wrist. "Does it hurt, my darling?" Jame asked with concern.

"No. You've been very gentle."

Jame smiled at her and brought Ma'am's hands up to her mouth, kissing each wrist in turn. Then, with sternness, Jame said, "Now lean over the desk. And you might want to hold on."

Ma'am leaned over with a smile, her breasts brushing against Jame's black shirt. She could feel the buttons push into her. Since her hands were now bound in front of her, she could move them more, and she grabbed the front edge of the desk.

Jame stood behind her and ran her hands over Ma'am's denim-covered ass. She whistled appreciatively. "You are one gorgeous piece of ass, you know that?"

Ma'am chuckled. "I hope I'm more than that."

Jame stood against her and ran her hands up and down Ma'am's legs. Ma'am put her head down. Jame reached around until she found the button on Ma'am's jeans and undid them, then found her zipper and pulled it down slowly. She eased the jeans down Ma'am's hips and let them fall to the floor. She let her fingers travel again until one found Ma'am's clit, and she rubbed it slowly while she brought her other hand around and put it under Ma'am's shirt, reaching around until she found a nipple. Once her fingers moved over it, Ma'am did a sharp intake and groaned again. Jame chuckled as she moved the finger that was on Ma'am's clit down until she found her wetness and dipped her fingers in. Ma'am pushed against her. "You like that, don't you?"

"Yes," Ma'am whispered.

Jame removed her fingers from the wetness and tapped Ma'am instead on her left ass cheek. "Spread your legs."

Ma'am did as told.

"That's my girl, you're ready for me, aren't you?"

All Ma'am could do was moan.

"That's what I thought." Jame entered Ma'am from behind, slowly at first, but she picked up intensity as she went, getting faster and faster, until Ma'am was gripping the side of the desk with such force that her knuckles were turning white, and she whipped her head back. Jame put her free hand on Ma'am's back to steady herself, which pushed Ma'am more into Jame's shirt.

"Oh, yes, oh, yes, oh, god, yes!"

Just as Ma'am's cries were reaching their peak, Jame slowed her pace and gently rocked back and forth against her.

Ma'am groaned. "God, yes...oh, just like that. Don't stop. Mmm." Ma'am rested her head against the desk, looking almost peaceful.

Without warning, Jame pulled her hand back and slammed it into Ma'am hard, and Ma'am cried out louder than before.

"Oh, fuck me! Yes, yes, yes!"

Jame obliged, getting faster and harder without being asked until Ma'am's cries rose in passion and became wordless moans. Jame pulled her hand out slowly as Ma'am collapsed against the desk. But Jame wouldn't let her have a moment to catch her breath; she pulled on the back of Ma'am's shirt and said, "Stand up now."

Ma'am did so on trembling legs. There was a dreamy expression in her eyes, and her face was at peace.

Jame placed a small, sweet kiss on Ma'am's lips, then reached down and untied her tie and freed Ma'am's hands. Ma'am made to reach up to touch Jame's face, but Jame backed away. Ma'am looked confused and almost hurt. Instead, Jame took Ma'am's hand, brought it to her mouth, and kissed it, then let it go. She took a step back, dropped to her knees again, inclined her head, and put her hands behind her back. "It was a pleasure to serve you, Ma'am, thank you."

Ma'am sighed contently, control back in her voice when she said, "You're welcome. Now get dressed." Ma'am backed away to pull up her pants, and Jame stood and retrieved her shirt and tie from the desk and quickly returned to the other side of it to put her clothes back on. While Ma'am resumed her seat, Jame stayed standing with her arms clasped behind her back and her head inclined. "Was there anything else you wanted, sweet Jame?"

Jame looked back up. "No, Ma'am."

"Good. I feel we settled this matter, don't you?"

"Yes, Ma'am."

Ma'am leaned back in her chair and smiled. "And if you hear the women talking again, pay it no mind, it's what they're going to do. As long as they mind their manners and do their job, then there's no problem."

"Yes, Ma'am. Shall I go?"

"You can go."

Jame nodded, then turned on her heel to leave, but just as she put her hand on the doorknob, Ma'am called out, and she halted in her tracks.

"Oh, Jame?"

Jame turned around. "Yes?"

"Thank you," Ma'am whispered.

Jame's cheeks flamed again. "Always my pleasure."

"I know." Ma'am smiled. "And mine."

Jame said nothing more, she just smiled and inclined her head, then left, self-consciously straightening her tie as she did so.

Chapter Two

"What did you say your name was again, sugar?" The question came from Maria, one of the new women in the house. She was still on door duty. It was her job to escort the new people around and let them see what their options were. She, like all the women, was dressed in her own clothes. Ma'am wanted her women to be comfortable as they waited their turn and knew that if she tried to make them dress in something that didn't suit them, it would make them feel uneasy. Maria was wearing a simple dress that wasn't low cut, but it showed off a good deal of her legs, one of her best features, and she always felt sexy when she wore it.

"It's Sarah. Just Sarah." The customer seemed a little nervous as she walked through the house, looking at all the women. Her gaze fell on each in turn but never stayed on anyone too long. She saw a redhead on a sofa reading a magazine. She had long hair and nails, much like Sarah herself. The woman was very pretty, but she was too girly for Sarah's taste. There was another woman sitting at a piano, playing a soft classical piece Sarah didn't know. She was dressed in a tight, conservative black dress, her hair done up in a bun, Sarah guessed for those who liked the naughty librarian type. She bit her lip and tried not to laugh.

Maria gestured to another woman who was wearing jeans and a T-shirt, hair back in a ponytail, looking like the proverbial girl next door. "As you can see, we have someone for everyone's taste. Just let me know when you see the one that strikes your fancy, and we'll get everything set up."

Sarah smiled but didn't reply. So far, she really hadn't seen anyone who grabbed her. But she was determined she would find someone; she didn't want to have made the trip for nothing. She felt like she was looking at a live version of some exclusive catalog, and all she had to do was turn the page and there would be another beautiful woman with a blurb next to her describing her best features and a price attached. She had never shopped for sex before, and it was all a bit overwhelming. As they passed into a sitting room, she spotted a well-dressed figure sitting in a comfortable-looking chair in a corner near a lamp, reading a book. The woman was a gorgeous dapper butch, replete with tie and suspenders and shiny black shoes. Sarah inadvertently licked her lips. Maria didn't miss the gesture.

Maria asked smiling, "You see someone you like?"

Sarah laughed nervously. "Yeah, but I doubt she's on the menu."

"Everyone's on the menu here. Who do you have in mind?"

Sarah inclined her head in the direction of the dapper butch. "Her."

Maria's face lit up in a bright smile. "Oh, that's Jame, and she's *totally* on the menu."

"Really?"

"Mm-hmm. You want her? I can set that up for you."

Sarah blushed at the thought. "Um, okay," she

stammered, and felt silly.

"No problem, come on." Maria took Sarah by the hand and guided her over to Jame, who immediately put her book down and stood. "Jame, this is Sarah. She would like to spend some time with you." Maria released Sarah's hand and took a step back.

Jame smiled warmly and took Sarah's hand, brought it to her lips, and kissed it, then she met Sarah's gaze. "It would be my pleasure. And hopefully yours."

Sarah couldn't help it, she giggled and blushed. Her hand was still in Jame's, and Jame was still smiling at her. She wasn't sure how to proceed.

"Well, I'll leave you two to get acquainted." Maria waved and left.

Jame dropped Sarah's hand and put her hands behind her back. "Would you be more comfortable sitting out here a bit and talking, or would you like to see my room?"

"Wow, um, I'm not sure. What do people normally do?"

Jame smiled but not unkindly. "Everyone is different. Everyone has different needs. Maybe we can start there. What do you need?"

Sarah gulped. "Um, I never thought of it like that. I'm not sure what I need."

Jame put her arm around Sarah's shoulders and escorted her out of the room and down the hall. "Okay, here's a different question: What do you want? There are no wrong answers here." Jame guided Sarah to a room down the middle of the hall and, with her free hand, swung the door open and tapped Sarah on the shoulder to encourage her to go in ahead of her. Jame walked in behind her and closed the door.

Sarah sat on the edge of the bed and looked around the room. It was elegant, and everything looked expensive. It looked like a man's room, a rich man's room, though Sarah had no personal reference for what that would look like. The rug on the floor contained an ornate pattern, the furniture looked to be from another century, English or French in origin, with dark wooden legs and overstuffed chair backs. There was another chair much like the one she had seen Jame reading in, set up in the corner between two built-in bookcases that were stuffed with books. On the far wall was a large mirror in a gilded frame. It made Sarah feel watched, even though all she saw was her own reflection looking back at her. Sarah's gaze fell again on Jame, who was standing in the middle of the room, letting Sarah take it all in. She stood with her hands clasped in front of herself, the same soft smile playing about her lips. It put Sarah at her ease, and she returned the smile.

When Jame could see that Sarah seemed more comfortable, she gestured to her bedside table. "On the table there is a black box with a button on it, do you see it?"

Sarah turned to look. "Yes."

"That's a panic button. That's for your safety, as well as mine. I tell you that, not because I think either one of us will need to use it, but to let you know that you are safe here. Also, anytime you're uncomfortable or want to change directions, tell me. I will stop or do something completely different. You're in charge, Sarah. Your wish is my command." Jame bowed in an old-fashioned way, with one arm behind her back, and it made Sarah giggle.

"Oh, wow, I've never had someone at my command before. This will be fun."

"Oh, that it will be, I promise you. Would you like a drink first? We have room service. Champagne, wine, something...harder."

Sarah bit her lip. "No, I'm good. So, how does this work? I just tell you what to do and you do it?"

"Yes. I can fulfill your fantasy, maybe try that thing you've always wanted to try but haven't yet. Or we can do all your favorite things, whatever they are. Or you can leave it up to me to serve you the best way I can. Either way, my job is to serve you and make you happy. And that is what I love to do, to make *you* happy." Abruptly, Jame took a step forward and went down on one knee in front of Sarah.

Sarah squealed delightedly, then laughed. "Wow, okay."

Jame took Sarah's hand and kissed it as she had done in the sitting room. "Tell me what I can do for you, beautiful one."

"I don't know what to tell you."

"How about a fantasy I can make come true?"

"My mind's a blank right now, nothing's coming to mind. But you're doing really good with this chivalry thing."

Jame smiled and stood, only to sit beside Sarah on the bed. Then, Jame brushed a hair off Sarah's face and leaned in to place a light kiss on Sarah's cheek.

Sarah said, "Oh, you're good."

Jame said nothing as she moved her lips from Sarah's cheek to her ear, nibbling there a moment.

Sarah leaned her head back and said, with no trace of humor this time, "You're very good."

Jame continued to move her lips softly down Sarah's neck. When she came to the hollow between

Sarah's neck and shoulder, Jame's lips sucked the skin there just enough to make Sarah moan but not enough to leave a mark. She pulled back, looked softly at Sarah, and brushed her thumb over Sarah's lips. Sarah looked Jame in the eye and kissed the thumb, and it made Jame smile as she leaned in for a kiss. As the kiss went on, Jame cupped Sarah's face in her hand. Jame seemed content to just sit there and kiss her, and at one point, Sarah moaned. After some time, Jame pulled back. "Have you thought about what you want me to do for you?"

"You were doing very well just now."

"Has anyone ever adored you properly before?"

Sarah looked down. "Um, maybe. Occasionally."

Jame took Sarah's chin in her hand. "Then that's not enough. If you like, I will spend our time together doing just that. As I said before, if you ever want me to stop or do something different, just say the word. This is about you, Sarah. As it should be."

Sarah blushed and looked back at Jame demurely. "Am I allowed to touch you?"

"Oh, yes. My body is yours. But let me touch you first, and we'll get to me momentarily. But is that what would please you?"

Sarah smiled and nodded. "Very much."

"Okay. But first things first." Jame got down on one knee again and gently ran her hands down Sarah's right leg until she came to the black flats she was wearing and slid off first one, then the other and set them aside.

"I feel like a reverse Cinderella." Sarah giggled.

Jame smiled. "I will do my best to be your Prince Charming, but I can't promise you'll get home by midnight."

Sarah laughed. "Doesn't matter now, you already have my shoes."

"Quite right." On both knees now, Jame slowly ran her hands up Sarah's legs, stopping at her waist, then she rose up enough so that she could reach Sarah, who met her halfway with a kiss, and Sarah put her arms around Jame's neck. She tried to pull Jame on top of her, but Jame resisted.

"Is something wrong?" Sarah asked, suddenly worried that she had done something she wasn't supposed to.

"Not at all. We can do as you wish if you like, but I was hoping I could finish undressing you first. I want to see you splendidly naked before me so that I can adore you better."

"You are really good at your job." Sarah laughed somewhat nervously.

Jame inclined her head. "You deserve the best. Let me give it to you."

"Okay."

Jame stood and took Sarah by the hand and pulled her to her feet. Once standing, Jame placed another kiss on Sarah's lips but pulled back before it could become intense. Then she put both hands on Sarah's blouse and unbuttoned it. Sarah looked down at Jame's hands almost in wonder. Once the blouse was unbuttoned, Jame slid it off Sarah's shoulders but made sure it didn't fall to the floor. She placed it on top of her nearby dresser, then she returned to Sarah and placed another kiss on her lips and put her arms around her. Sarah responded in kind and put her arms around Jame's neck. While their lips were pressed together, Jame unhooked Sarah's bra, then gently brought Sarah's arms down so that she could slide the garment off. The bra took its place with the blouse, and Jame came back to Sarah. Instead of unbuttoning Sarah's slacks right away, Jame stood in front of her and looked reverently at Sarah's breasts and smiled. The attention made Sarah blush profusely and brush a strand of hair off her face. Jame said nothing as she came forward and put her hands on Sarah's waist and bent her head to Sarah's chest, placing a kiss above her heart, then slowly moving her lips down to brush over a nipple. Sarah inhaled suddenly, and Jame's tongue came out to replace her lips, and her hands went to Sarah's hips. Sarah put her arms around Jame's back and ran her fingers through the other woman's short-cropped hair. Jame released the nipple and went to her knees, kissing her way down Sarah's stomach, and brought her hands up to the button on Sarah's slacks and undid them, then eased them down, along with the lacy underwear she wore. Sarah braced herself on Jame's shoulders as Jame pulled the pants the rest of the way off her. When Jame came back from placing the pants neatly on top of the rest, she looked Sarah over as she would a fine work of art, and her face held appreciation and wonder. "Do you know how beautiful you are?"

Sarah blushed again. This time, the blush extended to her chest, and she stood there, not knowing whether to accept the compliment and go on or quickly ask for her clothes back and leave. It was all a bit too much. All she could say was "thank you."

"You are more than welcome. Now before we continue, would you like to make any requests? Anything you want me to do, anything you don't want me to do? Something you would like to add to our fun?"

Sarah thought about it before she answered,

then a gleam came to her eyes. and she grinned. She suddenly grabbed Jame by the tie, apparently surprising her. "Yeah, I know what I want you to do now."

Recovering quickly, Jame asked, "What can I do for you, beautiful one?"

"Get undressed and give me your tie. And two others." Pulling on Jame's tie to bring their faces closer, Sarah whispered, "Now!"

Jame inclined her head and smiled. "It would be my pleasure." Jame retreated to her closet and came back with two ties, both, like the one she was wearing, silk and in solid, bold colors. She handed them to Sarah with a smile, then untied the one around her neck and handed that over, as well.

"Thank you."

Jame said nothing; she just smiled and inclined her head again, then proceeded to get undressed. She let her clothes fall to the floor. Once naked, she put her hands behind her back. "Where would you like me?"

Sarah smiled and chewed on her thumbnail, then pointed to the bed. Her voice sounded confident, however. "There, on your back, in the middle."

"All right." Jame did as told, centering herself in the bed, then put both arms up and grabbed the railing. "Is this what you wanted?"

"Oh, yeah. That's perfect." Sarah walked over and sat on the side of the bed and tied first one hand, then the other to the bed, testing each knot to make sure it was tight but not uncomfortably so. When she was done, she held the last tie in both hands. "You know what this one is for, don't you?"

"I think so. Can I make one request before you put it in place?"

Sarah smiled charmingly. "Yes."

"May I have another kiss?"

"Aww. Of course, you may."

Sarah leaned in to grant Jame's request, and Jame made it last as long as she could, taking advantage of the opportunity to play with Sarah's tongue and sucking in her bottom lip.

When they pulled away, Sarah said, somewhat remorsefully, "I'm almost sorry to be doing this... but that won't stop me." With that, Sarah placed the tie around Jame's mouth and head and tied it in place. "Now let me ask you, has anyone fulfilled *your* fantasies, Prince Charming?"

Jame shook her head.

"No? Well, maybe it's about time someone did, don't you think?"

Jame slowly nodded. You could see the smile in her eyes.

"Granted, you can't tell me what your fantasies are, I've made sure of that, but I think I'll just make do with making you scream. Does that sound like a good idea?"

Jame nodded again.

"I thought so. I think I'll start by doing this." Sarah straddled Jame, then put her lips to Jame's ear and whispered, "Can I mark you?"

Jame shook her head.

"Pity."

Sarah trailed her lips down Jame's neck, doing the same thing Jame had done earlier, sucking the skin between her teeth but stopping just in time. Jame's breathing increased. Sarah traveled farther until she reached Jame's nipple, where she stayed for quite some time, giving both nipples equal attention and making Jame squirm underneath her. An evil chuckle escaped Sarah's throat as she realized what she was doing to her captive. Her hair had long since fallen over Jame's stomach, and Sarah was sure it tickled her. That thought made her chuckle more as she trailed wet kisses down and across Jame's stomach, stopping just below her navel. She looked up and locked gazes with Jame and smiled. "Should I pull the gag down so I can hear you scream?"

Jame nodded emphatically, but Sarah shook her head, thinking better of it.

"No, better not." With one final smile, Sarah bent her head back down, kissing down to Jame's clit and pulling it into her mouth and sucking on it as if it were a nipple. Jame bucked underneath her and made a repressed scream into the tie covering her mouth. Sarah grabbed her hips and held on as Jame continued to move. She ran her tongue down the lips and up again, darting over Jame's opening and back to the clit. She spent most of her time there, as she knew it would drive Jame out of her mind.

And it did. Jame moaned against her gag and pulled on her bonds, crying out in frustration. But her cries were muffled around the silk, and she looked down at Sarah's head, though Sarah couldn't see, with admiration in her eyes. Then, her gaze strayed to the mirror on the other side of the room, and she looked into it and held her own gaze as she squirmed under Sarah's touch.

Sarah's licking intensified, and so did Jame's moans and squirms, until after several minutes, Jame let out a muffled scream and Sarah looked up, face gleaming in Jame's juices, and smiled. "That was lovely. But I think you have more in you." Sarah climbed back up Jame's body and pulled the gag down. Before Jame could say anything, Sarah attacked her with a fierce kiss. Jame responded hungrily, straining against her bonds again to try to reach her. Not being able to touch her, Jame moaned into the kiss. When Sarah pulled her mouth away, their lips were connected by a glistening trail. Smiling, Sarah pulled back enough to break the connection and without a word, trailed her fingers down Jame's body and entered her.

"Let me touch you. Please," Jame cried.

"I like it when you beg. It sounds good on you. But no. Now shh, let me work." Sarah put a soft kiss to Jame's lips, then slowly moved her hand back and forth, forcing her thumb to rub over Jame's clit every time they made contact. She slowly picked up speed, going faster and faster and inserting more fingers. Jame pulled and pulled against her restraints until she cried out.

"Yes, harder, harder. Fuck me harder, please."

Sarah laughed evilly. "As you wish." Sarah picked up speed, slamming into Jame harder. The harder she went, the more Jame moved and cried out, and it gave Sarah an evil kind of pleasure to see it, until finally, Jame cried out so loud it almost frightened Sarah. When she removed her hand from inside Jame, it was covered in Jame's pleasure. She placed another soft kiss on Jame's lips and then reached up and untied the bonds that held her. Once released, Sarah put her head on Jame's chest as Jame indicated, and Jame put her arms around her and kissed her on top of the head.

"Thank you, beautiful Sarah. That was lovely."

"I'm glad you enjoyed it. It's not often I get to be in charge."

"You should change that."

Sarah looked up at Jame. "With you?"

Jame smiled and brushed a strand of Sarah's long, unruly hair off her face. "Are you sure there's nothing I can do for you? I could make you scream just as much as you did me."

Sarah giggled. "Oh, I bet you could. But not today. Maybe next time."

"As you like."

Sarah sighed. "I suppose I should go. This was… an experience. Thank you." Sarah placed a quick kiss on Jame's lips, then stood from the bed and went to retrieve her clothes.

Jame sat up and rubbed her wrists a little and smiled. "It was for me, too. I hope you do come back, Sarah."

Sarah finished getting dressed, then walked over to Jame, who was now sitting on the side of the bed and took Jame's face in her hands. "You are worth so much more than I paid. So much more."

Jame blushed but said, "Don't say that too loud, or my price might go up next time."

Sarah laughed, then kissed Jame again but stepped away from the bed before Jame could put her arms around her. "I should go. I'll see myself out. Bye." Sarah smiled and waved, then walked out the door.

Jame smiled to herself and looked wistfully at the closed door. "I love my job."

As Jame stood from the bed to retrieve her clothes from where she had thrown them earlier, a disembodied voice filled the room. "Jame, can you come in here, please? And bring the ties. Oh, and don't bother getting dressed."

Jame looked at the mirror on the other side of the room and smiled, then bowed. "Yes, Ma'am," she said and did as told.

Chapter Three

The women were milling about the sitting room, trying not to look nervous, though most were failing miserably. Some were biting their nails and tapping their feet, some were pretending to read. Jame sat quietly in her favorite chair, her hands clasped in front of herself, her head leaned back, her eyes closed. No one could tell whether she was nervous or not, but some of the women on the other side of the room were glancing in her direction and whispering about her.

"Of course, *she's* not nervous, we all know *she's* doing well." Stacey scoffed and rolled her eyes for Meghan's benefit.

Meghan nodded her agreement. "I know, right? I wouldn't be surprised if she got a raise or something." The women nodded together and looked at Jame in disgust.

A hush fell over the room as Ma'am entered from the hallway. In owing to the seriousness of the occasion, she was wearing a white button-up man's dress shirt, untucked with the sleeves rolled up, over her jeans. That was about as formal as Ma'am ever got. When she walked in, she stood near the doorway, near where Meghan and Stacey were sitting. She looked down at them, Stacey on a footstool and Meghan in the chair next to it, and said, "Ladies."

They replied in unison, "Ma'am." They could

not meet her gaze and instead looked at her mouth. This made her smile.

Ma'am said to the room at large, "Before we continue with the interviews, I feel I should make an announcement." She put her hands on her hips as she looked down at Meghan and Stacey, then her gaze fell on everyone in the room in turn. "I've heard whispers among you that you think some of your coworkers are making more money than you are, and you're unhappy with this. Let me make one thing clear: everyone here was given the same deal when they signed their contract. The same flat rate, plus a sixty percent commission against all sales. Meaning, the more you work, the more you earn. And you know, how much you work is up to you and what the clients want. So, do some of you make more than others? Absolutely. Is that because I've renegotiated anyone's contract? No. And that's not going to change. Now I don't want to hear any more about this because it's a nonissue." She looked at Meghan and Stacey pointedly, then said, "Okay, Jame, you're next."

Jame stood and followed Ma'am out of the room, her hands behind her back, gaze forward. When they entered the office, Jame closed the door behind them and took her seat in a chair in front of Ma'am's desk while Ma'am resumed hers. Jame said nothing, just waited patiently for Ma'am to lead the conversation.

Once Ma'am was settled, she looked at Jame and smiled. "So, how are you, Jame? Anything bothering you or anything on your mind?"

Jame shook her head. "No, Ma'am. Things have been going well, I've gotten a lot of work lately, as you know. I've been able to save quite a bit, which is nice."

Ma'am looked at her curiously. "What *are* your

future plans? If you've told me, I've forgotten."

Jame squirmed a little in her seat. "I want to finish my education. I want to be a doctor. That takes a lot of money."

"That's right. I hope you'll forgive me, but I've forgotten what kind of doctor."

"I want to be a psychiatrist, Ma'am."

"You'll be good at that."

"Thank you."

"So, how many more years do you think you'll need to save for that?"

"I figure two more years working here. Then I should have enough. That is, if business stays as good as it has been."

Ma'am nodded thoughtfully. "And you'll be able to live and pay for school with what you're making here?"

"I've made some investments."

"Good, good." A silence fell between them while Ma'am looked Jame up and down thoughtfully. Jame met her gaze unflinchingly. Finally, Ma'am said, "You know, most women only stay here no more than a year, some as little as six months."

Jame shrugged. "We all have different goals."

Ma'am chuckled. "True. Though, often, when a woman leaves, it's not because she's met her goals, but because she's tired of being on her back. Why are you different?"

"I love my job. I like pleasing people. I should say, I appreciate that you've only given me female clients. Thank you." Jame inclined her head.

"You're welcome, though it hasn't really been difficult. You're not exactly someone men ask for." She smiled.

Jame returned her smile. "No, I suppose not."

"But you do seem to enjoy your work a great deal, I've noticed. The clients have noticed, too. You have at least four regular customers on the schedule for this week alone. Two have asked for weekly appointments. No one else has a schedule like that. You're my favorite because you make me money. What's not to love?" Ma'am flipped the pages of the planner that was always on the desk in front of her. "I got a call from the woman you saw yesterday, Sarah. She's one of the ones who asked for a weekly appointment."

A smile threatened to pull the corners of Jame's lips up, but she resisted.

Ma'am saw it and eyed Jame with curiosity and sat back in her chair. "How do you feel about that?"

"I'm glad that she was pleased."

"Are you?"

"Yes, Ma'am. I want all my clients to feel that way."

"Yes, yes, so you do. What I mean is, how do you feel about this particular client wanting to see you every week?"

Jame chose her words carefully. "I'm always glad for repeat business, that means I'm doing my job well. As far as her specifically, we got along well enough. I'll be happy to continue to meet with her as long as she wants."

"You did get along, didn't you? I noticed that." Jame instantly blushed. "Why are you blushing, sweet Jame? You know I watch all the women at one point or another. You also know it wasn't the first time you were watched."

"No, but it was the first time you asked for me

afterward."

"Well, she inspired me, what can I say?" A devilish smile played about her lips.

Jame's blush deepened. "You were rather... inventive and energized yesterday."

Ma'am threw her head back and laughed. "Oh, you have such a way with words, and you blush so nicely."

"I'm glad it pleases you."

Ma'am gave Jame a look that couldn't be mistaken for anything other than what it was: an invitation to play. She dropped her voice to the register she knew made women squirm in the best possible way. "Everything about you pleases me, Jame."

Jame inclined her head. "I'm happy to hear that, Ma'am."

Changing back to her professional demeanor again, Ma'am sat back in her chair and crossed her hands over her stomach and looked thoughtfully at Jame. "When you came to me, you only mentioned two reasons for wanting to work for me: the money and you enjoyed pleasing people, which I know you do, but I can't help but wonder...it's got to be something else that keeps you here. There are other ways to earn money, a smart girl like you."

Jame was suddenly uncomfortable. "Not as quickly."

"No, no, that's true." Ma'am looked at Jame thoughtfully, then asked, "How do you feel about pleasing me?"

Jame tried to choose her words carefully. "You mean as my employer or...?"

A smile played at Ma'am's lips. "Both."

"Um, well...in both capacities, my goal is to

please you. If I can bring you repeat business, I'm happy to play my part. If I can pleasure you, then that is my greatest joy." Jame smiled.

"I see, I see," Ma'am said thoughtfully. "You know what would please me now?"

"No, Ma'am, but I would like to."

"Hold that thought." Ma'am stood from her chair and came around her desk. Jame followed her with her gaze, but she didn't go up to Jame; instead, she left her office and closed the door.

Jame stayed where she was, as she hadn't been dismissed. She wondered where Ma'am went, what she went to get. Was it some favorite device she wanted Jame to use? A restraint or a toy? Something to inflict pain? Though pain didn't seem to be Ma'am's niche. She had never asked Jame to hurt her, and Jame knew she had a low pain tolerance. Once in the beginning, Jame had bitten down too hard on her nipple, and Ma'am had cried out, then smacked her, though not too hard, just enough to get her point across. And she had. Jame had never done that or anything else that would have caused pain again.

Jame didn't have long to sit and contemplate her fate; Ma'am came back a moment later with Meghan and Stacey. "Ladies, stand behind Jame."

Wordlessly, they did so. Jame followed Ma'am with her gaze again as Ma'am made her way back around her desk.

"You know what would please me now?" Ma'am asked again.

Jame shook her head. "No, Ma'am."

A devilish smile played about Ma'am's lips. "Oh, I think you do. I think you do, but you're afraid of being wrong. You're not wrong. You know what I'm thinking."

Jame looked between her two coworkers, who looked at each other, then down at Jame. They looked confused, but Jame was starting to understand. Jame looked at Ma'am and asked incredulously, "*Both* of them?"

"Yes."

"Wait, what?" Stacey asked.

"You gotta be joking."

"No, Meghan, I'm not. I want both of you to understand why Jame makes more money than you. Why she has repeat business and steady customers and neither of you do. And maybe you'll learn a thing or two."

"That's not fair! She sleeps with women. We have a completely different client list."

"Yes, Stacey, you're right, she *does* sleep with women, so you should trust that she knows what she's doing."

Meghan crossed her arms over her chest. "And if I don't want to?"

"As always, that's your choice. I was hoping you would take this as a learning experience."

"I don't see what *pointers* I could learn from Jame. I don't sleep with women," Meghan retorted.

Ma'am raised an eyebrow and replied, "You might be surprised."

"So what, you want us to go to one of our rooms or something and have Jame 'work us over'? What's that going to prove?"

"No, stupid, she wants us to do it here, in front of her. Pay attention."

"Fuck you, Meghan, I'm not stupid."

"Jame, how do you feel about this?"

"If this is what you want, Ma'am, I'd be happy to do so."

The women said nothing, but Meghan rolled her eyes. It did not go unnoticed.

"Jame, you can do what you want, but I think you should start with Meghan."

"Yes, Ma'am." Jame stood and turned to Meghan.

Meghan, to her credit, stood her ground and kept her gaze on Jame, her chin raised in a bit of defiance.

"What would you like me to do for you?"

"Nothing. I don't want anything from you. And I think this is just really ridiculous bullshit."

"I can't, just…no. I'm sorry," Stacey added.

"You're refusing to continue?" Ma'am asked.

"I can't, this is ridiculous. I mean, she's like my best friend, I just can't. And putting on a show for you like you're some, some…"

"What? Like some what?" Ma'am asked.

"Like some sultan and his harem or something. This is just sick."

"Stacey, you have to know that at some point, a client is going to ask for you to please him with another woman at the same time. Why not do it now, call it practice?" Ma'am smiled. Before Stacey could respond, however, she continued, "And who says you're *not* part of a harem?"

"I am *not* part of a harem."

"Then what are you? You tell me, what are you, Stacey?" Ma'am looked at her expectantly.

"I'm…I'm…" Then, very softly she replied, "I'm a whore. I'm just a whore."

Ma'am stood and pointed her finger at Stacey and said with vehemence, "No, you're *not* a whore, and that's not what I meant. I don't think of any of you like that, and neither should you. And I don't want to hear that word spoken in this house again, you hear me? I won't let the clients say it, and I won't let you say it, either. We understand each other?"

"Yes, Ma'am," Stacey muttered as she looked at the floor.

Ma'am turned to Jame and Meghan. "What about you two?"

"Yes, Ma'am," they said in unison.

"Okay then. Stacey, I'm not going to insist you participate."

"Thank you."

"What I wanted you to get from this is the fact that this is the pleasure business, and it's not about what you want. Of all the things Jame could teach you, that's the most important. If you can't learn that, then don't expect to ever have repeat business. You may go."

Ma'am began writing and crossing something out in her date book. Stacey turned to go, several emotions playing out on her face. Ma'am called out to her. "Oh, and, Stacey?"

"Yes, Ma'am?"

"Don't slam my door on your way out." Ma'am still hadn't looked up.

Stacey, trying to visibly control her anger, left, closing the door quietly behind her.

"Ma'am?"

"Yes, Jame?"

"Do you want us to continue?"

"I think I've seen enough. Meghan, you may go now."

Meghan left, and Jame looked back at Ma'am in

expectation.

"So, was that my performance review or theirs?" A small smile played at the corners of Jame's mouth.

Ma'am laughed. "How do you think you did?"

Jame let the smile come. "I think I did well."

"Good, I think so, too."

Jame dropped her head a bit but looked up at Ma'am with a look not unlike the one Ma'am often gave when she dropped her voice to the velvety rich tone other women have so loved in the past. "So, you were pleased? Or can I do more for you?"

"Oh, Jame, you can always do more for me." She held Jame's gaze for a moment, but then said, "But not right now, I have several more of these to do today."

"As you like." Jame stood to go.

"I didn't say you could go."

"You want me to stay?"

Ma'am held her gaze for a moment, then smiled. "No, but come to my room later."

Jame smiled. "Yes, Ma'am."

Jame turned to leave, and Ma'am watched her go, an unreadable expression on her face.

Chapter Four

Jame sat back on her bed, laptop open, pen and paper on the bed next to her. On the screen in front of her was the eBook version of her behavioral psychology textbook. One thing she hadn't mentioned to Ma'am during the performance review the week before was that she was already taking classes. The University of Nevada had an online master's program that she had started before she came to the house. She was one year into a three-year program and would leave when that degree was done in two more years, with enough money saved for med school.

She wasn't sure why she hadn't mentioned her schooling to Ma'am, but it just seemed private somehow, her thing. Ma'am controlled so much of her life, most of which she didn't mind, but this was her thing, and she wanted to keep it that way for as long as possible. She read steadily for three hours, taking notes when necessary. She only had the one window open, and nothing else distracted her as she read. Finally, she closed out the eBook and opened a computer file, one that was backed up on a cloud somewhere but not on a jump drive. It was hidden in a file labeled simply *Notes*. Each document in the folder bore only a date as the title. She had started a file with today's date earlier but had stopped after a little while to do her homework.

More and more every day, I see Ma'am as nothing but a cult leader. Last week, when Stacey mentioned 'harem,' it made me think: What is a harem but a sex cult run by a leader who wants you to do his or her bidding? There is no dogma here, no religion to follow, but we have a guru nonetheless. And if she is displeased? You can be dismissed without prejudice. She sits behind her desk like a queen on a throne, thinking we all worship her and want to kiss her ring, but she has no idea how we really feel, and I don't think she cares. She sees what she wants to see. She is a narcissist—textbook case. She also thinks she has total control of the women because she has a two-way mirror in each of our rooms, but we all find little ways to rebel. I have found out some of their secrets, but I won't betray them, not even in here. Everyone deserves their privacy, and we have so little here as it is.

Ma'am thinks I have feelings for her, I know she does. She looks at me with such affection and trust, it's almost painful. I don't want to hurt her, but she doesn't seem to realize that I'm just doing my job...what she pays me to do. That's not love. How could it be? Do I enjoy my work? Enough to stay as long as I need to, sure. So far, it hasn't even been distasteful. I stay on Ma'am's good side because I don't want male clients, though as she said, it's not really an issue, but there's always a first time. Dealing with the women's distrust and jealousy of me is difficult, but I didn't come here to make friends, though they're not all bad. They leave me alone for the most part, and I'm okay with that.

There are often little fights over nothing among them, and I'm happy to be away from that drama. On my days off, I leave here and spend my days in parks and coffee shops, enjoying the sunshine or the buzz of strangers' conversations that are easily ignorable. If I'm in a café, I'll get a bottomless cup of whatever's on tap and maybe a sandwich, some hipster version of a ham and cheese that they've given a clever name to, which they think is reason enough to charge eight dollars for, and stay all day. Sometimes, I'm working, other days, I'm observing the flotsam and jetsam of the patrons, thinking I can figure out a lot about a person by their coffee order. It's like my favorite party trick. The more adjectives in their order tell me that they're fussy and pretentious, like to pretend they're more health-conscious than they are, follow trends more than they should, and waste their money. While the guy who just orders his coffee black has OCD and imagines himself writing the great American novel and hears it that way in his head. He considers himself casual and uncomplicated, yet his clothes are expensive but made to look like they're not.

 I'm sure I'm wrong about most people, but I have great fun pretending I'm right. Ma'am is the one I get to study most of the time, of course, and I see so much of the cult leader personality in her that it often makes me leery about staying another two years, but I know it's the best way to get the money I need. I have often told myself that I won't fall under her influence, that I'm smarter than that, that I can stay here and do my job and still leave in two years. But they have an expression for that kind of thinking in my field: self-serving bias. I know I'm not immune to influence. It would be naïve to think I am. I must remain vigilant if I want to keep my individuality.

 I saw Sarah earlier today. She's very sweet, and I like to see her personality emerge. This is only her second visit with me, and she's becoming more confident in her dominance of me. I'm glad. I hope she continues to come and see me as I'm interested to see how she progresses in that. Maybe her confidence with me will have a positive influence on the rest of her life somehow. I like to think that, anyway. I like to think that my role is something of the sex surrogate, helping my clients regain confidence in themselves so they can have better relationships with others. Maybe it's something I should explore for real, instead of behavioral psychology. Though it's not exactly a respected practice, and I wouldn't be taken seriously. They don't exactly give tenure to sex therapists. Though considering how many professors sleep with their students, one could say they already do. I know I shouldn't joke about such things as I know how damaging that can be to the students.

One drawback to only sleeping with women is that they can become attached. I have four regular customers, and they all think they're special to me in some way, that they are the one I don't think of as a client but a potential girlfriend. That she and she alone is going to save my soul and drag me away from all this. Even women suffer from the white knight syndrome. I would say maybe women suffer from it more, so given to romance as many women are. When men think of knights, if they do, I'm sure they think of the great battles and being the hero, the woman only serving as the spoils of war, instead of a heart to be won and saved. I think Sarah's the same as them all. I know she wants to save me; I see it in her eyes when she looks at me with such affection and caresses my cheek. They almost tear up, and I can tell what she's thinking: poor Jame.

Meanwhile, poor Jame made a hell of a lot of money last year, saving most of it and spending very little. I also lied about that, or not really lied, but left out just how well off I'll be when I leave. I won't just have enough to pay for school and live on, I'll also have enough to buy a nice house. Not a mansion by any means, but a nice one in a good neighborhood. With plenty of room for books and a home office. I have simple needs. I don't need a swimming pool or a three-car garage or even a second story. Just a simple house with room for books, a roomy kitchen, and a nice front porch, perfect for reading and reflection. A house to raise a family in someday.

I could probably fall for someone like Sarah if I had met her under different circumstances. She seems sweet and she laughs a lot, and I think she might have a good heart. I don't want her to lose her heart to me, though. No good can come from it. I can't or won't date while I'm here. It's not good for business, and it's not good for her, whoever she might be. I can't stop working until I reach my financial goal, and if I were to fall in love, I wouldn't want to work here anymore. I couldn't ask a lover to accept this as just another job.

I have enough to worry about here at the house without the complications a lover could cause. Ma'am always asks for me now right after a session. I'm usually spent and don't think I can go on anymore, but she insists. She's inspired by whatever she sees in my room, she says, and has a major case of "I'll have what she's having." So, I drag myself into the small room behind my mirror. Ma'am is usually already naked when I get there, often having started without me. Her legs spread apart on the luxurious sofa she thinks is her due, her fingers in herself, her head back on the arm of the couch and her eyes closed. A moan will escape her throat, and I know what she wants me to do. I dutifully get down on my knees and let my tongue replace her fingers. Her hands stop what they're doing and grip my hair. When my tongue reaches her, she'll arch her back and inhale sharply and then usually moan out a throaty, "Yesss!"

I must admit, I do love making her come, though not for the reason she probably thinks. I'm not attracted to her and I'm not in love with her, but I like it for one simple reason: control. I don't normally have to be in control, that's not really my nature, but I must admit that I get great pleasure in seeing my boss, my harem leader, totally under my control. Moreover, begging me to be in control. I get the psychological dynamics at play in role reversal, and it's true for both of us. I know this. But that doesn't mean I can't enjoy it. To see her beg for more, to see her humiliated, not just by the things I'm doing, but also by the fact that she enjoys it so much. She is the only one I feel that with. With my clients, I will be what they want me to be, what they need me to be. It really is my joy to please them, to play the subservient one. I've always been a people pleaser, so why not make a living at it?

Before she left, Sarah said something that had me thinking for the longest time. "You are going to become my favorite bad habit." Then she smiled and kissed me. It stayed on my mind because it's just an intriguing thing to say. Calling me a bad habit is equating me with other bad things, like smoking or drinking or drugs, addictions, in other words. But saying it with a smile as she did makes it seem frivolous and joyful, like spending the day in sweatpants, eating a whole pint of ice cream, and not doing anything useful. Almost like how you might want to spend a Sunday. So, I was left wondering what she meant and if she thought I was going to be destructive to her somehow, or if she thinks we're going to grow old on a porch swing together. Of course, I know I'm probably overthinking things and romanticizing a bit, but I can't help either of those things. Just because I work in this house, having sex with several different women a week, that doesn't mean I don't want to fall in love someday.

I dream about it the same as most people do. I wonder what that woman will be like, where and when we'll meet. Will she be in line behind me at the coffee shop, ordering a simple cup of chai tea and a muffin, wearing a sundress and sandals, her long honey-colored hair flowing freely behind her, a book of poetry under her arm? I'll strain to see the title simply because it's a book and I like to know what people are reading. She'll see me looking and smile and hold the book out, and it'll be someone I'll have read or still want to read or even someone I've never heard of, and we'll strike up a conversation about it. We'll fall into step to a table for two and keep talking, neither of us doing what we came there to do but maybe what we were meant to do. It will be the start of something wonderful.

Or will she be someone in one of my doctoral classes, a fellow student, someone on the same career path, but who will be a proponent of Watson while I'm leaning more toward Tolman and we will butt heads constantly? This, in turn, will lead to much heated debate in the classroom, which our professor will enjoy and encourage. One day, we will continue to argue after class is over and start to leave the building together, deep in debate, finding a bench on the quad to continue our conversation. Eventually, we will find common ground on a mutual dislike of Skinner and start to laugh together.

Or 1,001 other possibilities. An ex told me once

that I was too much of a romantic to be a scientist. I told her that any good scientist should be a romantic. I said to appreciate the wonders and mysteries of the universe, one must first appreciate the great wonder that is the human heart and never underestimate the power love has on one's behavior. She had scoffed and said, "Maybe you should make that your research topic." She had been an academic but not a psychiatrist. Her specialty was mathematics, and she saw the world in black and white terms and didn't believe in variables. For her, K was always constant, and that's all there was to it.

So, I'm a romantic, sue me! I do want to be in love, but I don't want to mix business with love. What kind of relationship, what kind of healthy relationship, could start here under these conditions? Sometimes, I get the feeling that Ma'am thinks I'm going to one day be at her side and run the company with her. I don't feel that as a feeling of love on her part, though. It's control. Oh, I don't think it crosses her mind that way, but it is. But I can play the part, just as a rat in a maze learns which lever to push for food, I too know which buttons to push to remain Ma'am's favorite. I know where my food comes from.

Jame saved the day's entry and closed it out, then shut down her laptop and set it next to her on the bed. She put her arms behind her head and looked across the room and smiled. She knew Ma'am wasn't in the little room right now, she wasn't even in the house. It was Tuesday, the one day Ma'am kept for herself. No one knew what she did or where she went. Jame wanted to follow her one day just to satisfy her curiosity, but she hadn't dared to just yet. For now, she just enjoyed knowing that she wasn't being watched and her privacy was her own. She almost wished Ma'am was there because she suddenly felt in the mood to play. She closed her eyes and imagined lying there, unbuttoning her shirt and putting her hand inside, playing with her nipple until it peaked, then running her fingers down her stomach and under the waistband of her pants. Just once, she wanted Ma'am to come out of the little room and into hers and start going down on her for a change. Maybe she should make that her new goal. She looked at the mirror now with a Cheshire cat grin and held up her hand and curled her finger in a come-hither gesture. She mouthed, "Come here now." But she was thinking, *Said the spider to the fly*, then she laughed out loud.

Chapter Five

September was slowly slipping into fall, so Ma'am decided to enjoy the day. She left her car in the garage when she went out to run her usual errand. It was only a couple of miles, and there was a slight breeze that ruffled her reddish-blond hair, which made her smile. She walked casually, without hurry. Anytime she came upon someone walking a dog or flowers that were invading her passage on the sidewalk, she stopped and appreciated both. She hadn't always been that kind of person, but the older she got, the more she realized she was lucky to have made it this far with the choices she had made in life.

She was not someone who lived in regret. Not all the choices she made had been good ones, but they often led to better things down the road, as long as she was patient enough to wait them out. If anyone ever asked her if she had regrets, she always said the same thing, "No. I don't regret one damn thing. If I had done just one thing differently, I wouldn't be where I am now. So, I can only be grateful." And she was. If pressed further, she might say, "No. I made mistakes, but I own that shit." And she did. She once told the one she was on the way to meet, "Learn from everything, even when you think you've made a mistake because that moment will teach you the most of all." She had learned a lot in her forty-seven years, and none of it was a waste, she felt.

As she turned down Sixth Street, she briefly wished she had brought her music with her. Some blues would have been quite meditative in her ear on the journey, but she didn't want the headphones getting in her way when she sat. Plus, she reasoned, there was nothing wrong with enjoying the sounds of the world around her. Life didn't always need a soundtrack.

When she entered the restaurant, which wasn't exactly high class but the best their town could do, she felt a little out of her element. She was in jeans, as always, and a billowy blouse with a busy pattern, a style she never wore around the women. She saved this side of herself for one person who deserved to see her at her best. She told the woman at the door who she was there to see, and the young thing who wasn't much bigger than a matchstick, dressed all in black, smiled and escorted her to a table in the back where her lunch companion was already waiting and stood when she came closer. They hugged and exchanged hellos, then sat.

After the waitress took her drink order and left her there with the menu, Ma'am looked across the table at the man she came to see. She smiled warmly at him. "How are you? It's been two weeks."

"I know. Vacation, remember?" The gentleman was in his mid-twenties, tall and broad-shouldered and dark-skinned. He had black, short wavy hair and rich brown eyes and a dimple in his chin. He was handsome, in other words, but he seemed unaware of this fact.

"Yes, I remember. Have you ordered?"

"No, I was waiting on you." He smiled at her, then looked down at his menu.

Ma'am did the same. "I'm not sure what I'm in

the mood for today. Maybe the fish. Or a nice soup."

"Why don't you get what you always get when we come here?" There was teasing in his tone.

"Are you saying I'm predictable?"

"Maybe. I know you, you don't always like trying new things."

She turned the page in the menu, and her gaze fell on a delectable-looking dish involving lamb and figs. "Well, in that case, I think I'll try the lamb and figs."

"You hate lamb. Don't get something you hate just to prove a point."

"Correction, I hate lamb the way my mother makes it. Maybe I'll like it this way."

He closed his menu and set it aside and looked at her somewhat annoyed. "Why do you always refer to her that way?"

She looked up at him confused. "What way? She *is* my mother, I didn't make that part up, though I wished I had." She shrugged. "Oh, well, can't change history. How would you have preferred I refer to her? I refrained from the usual 'that evil bitch who was the reason I was in therapy for twenty years.' I was holding back out of deference to you." She smiled at him.

"Gee, thanks. You could have also referred to her as my grandmother. That would have been acceptable."

"Why do you have to make me feel like I'm losing on a game show or something? Are you punishing me?"

"I'm not punishing you, Mother. I just don't like how you talk about Grandmother sometimes."

Before she could respond, the waitress returned, and they placed their order. Then she crossed her hands in front of herself and looked at him across the table. She tried to keep her voice level. "Ian, your grandmother and I…you know we have a difficult relationship, we always have. But I don't want that to have anything to do with you and me."

"How could it not? I've always wanted to ask this, and since I just turned twenty-five, I'm more than old enough to know: If you had such a troubled relationship with her, why'd you give me to her?" He said it casually, almost as if he didn't care what her answer was.

She sat back and grabbed her drink and took a sip with a trembling hand. When she finished, she looked at him and asked, "You want to do this now?"

"Don't you think I've waited long enough? Whatever it is, Mom, I can take it. The truth is better than not knowing."

"I've never hidden from you what I do for a living. It was not the right environment—"

He cut her off. "Then why didn't you leave? You could have. We could have been together." He could no longer look her in the eye, and he lowered his voice when he said, "But you chose them over me."

"Ian…you got it all wrong."

"Then how is it different?"

"Don't you see, I was putting you first."

"What kind of twisted logic is that?"

"Ian…"

"Mother."

She exhaled, exasperated. "Fine, what do you want me to say? You want to hear that I was a strung-out hooker, addicted to crack, living in a flophouse?"

"I don't think flophouses are really a thing." A smile played at his lips.

She pounded the table, making their glasses and

silverware rattle. "Damn it, don't make me laugh." She smiled briefly, then started talking again. "Because no, that's not what was happening. I mean, there were drugs, but I stopped them when I was pregnant. And I was never actually strung out. But I was still working for every dime and saving for the future. At least I managed to put you through college."

Just as their order arrived, Ian mumbled, "Yeah, I've always wondered how many blowjobs that was worth."

The waitress quickly put their food down and walked away without a word.

"Ian Christopher Berry, don't make me punch you! You're a grown man now, it wouldn't be child abuse. I understand that you resent me and what I did, what I did because I thought it was in your best interest. Fine, maybe I can never get you to see my side, but I come here every week because I am damn determined to try. I have made mistakes, but I'm proud of what I've achieved. And I'm glad that you have become a successful young man." He started to speak, and she raised a finger. "Through no doing of mine, I get it. But is this your plan? To punish me for the rest of my life because you didn't have a nuclear childhood? Because your mother was an escort?"

He chuckled as he picked up his glass. "Escort."

She pointed her finger at him accusingly. "It's one thing for you to resent me for your childhood, but don't you dare judge me for something you know nothing about. Yes, I admit it, for more years than I'd like to count, I earned my money on my back, but I also saved everything I could. I did that for you as much as for me, whether you believe it or not. And I've built a business I'm proud of."

"By exploiting young women for your profit. You can't justify that."

Ma'am shook her head slowly. "All those years, your grandmother has been whispering in your ear about how horrible I am, and that's all you know. I do regret that. I wish you didn't hate me so much."

"Leave Grandmother out of this. And I don't hate you. I just disagree with what you do. They're people, Mom."

"I know. And I'm not out there recruiting vulnerable young women, wearing a velvet and fur coat with gold chains and walking stick. I mean, I hate fur and velvet, and I prefer silver." They exchanged a smile. "Ian, these women come to me looking to make the quickest money they've ever made. Most stay less than a year. In exchange, I give them a salary, plus commission, the best health insurance anyone could hope for, and a luxurious place to stay. Everyone is free to go when they please. I call it a business because it is a business. I have employees, and we sell a service. I don't have to justify it because I'm not doing anything wrong, and I have nothing to be ashamed of."

"Maybe so. Maybe I'll never understand what motivates a woman to want to do that. I was raised to treat women with respect. I don't know what kind of mother she was to you, but she was good to me."

"I know. I'll always be grateful for that. And I love women, I treat them with respect, too. But I'm also the boss, and sometimes, I have to be the boss."

"I'm curious, in all this time running a house of women, you've only fallen for that one?" He gave her a teasing smile.

"She who shall not be named."

"Right."

She took a sip of her drink, smiling into her glass. "Besides, you shouldn't be asking your mother these things."

Ian rolled his eyes. "Please, I surpassed innocent years ago. It's not like I asked you who was the best or to give me all the details."

"True. And if you want to know that, you have to find out for yourself."

"Mother!"

She laughed at him. "Don't tell me your grandmother raised a little conservative."

"She did not, though not for a lack of trying. I tell her I'm a Republican, but I'm not. She tried to get me to put some pro-life bumper sticker on my car once, and I told her I don't like bumper stickers. Now I guess I can't have one until she dies." He gave her a small smile.

"You lie to your grandmother?"

"Only about things I don't want to be lectured about."

"So, where does she think you are right now?" She cocked an eyebrow at him.

He tried to fight the grin, but it failed. "At work."

"You little sneak." She held her glass aloft. "We should toast to tradition. To lying to your grandmother!"

He clinked his glass with hers. "To lying to Grandmother!"

"Oh, sometimes, I wonder if you really are my son, then I see little glimpses. You make me proud, though I wish I could take credit for it."

"Well, you did make me. Grandmother always says, 'blood tells,' every time I do something she doesn't approve of. So, what did you tell her you were doing when you were, um...uh..."

"Working to put you through college?" She grinned.

"Yeah."

"All kinds of things. Usually nothing too complicated, you know? But I ran away, so it was easier to lie that way."

"I suppose that's true. You know, that's one story you haven't told me. Why'd you leave?"

"Maybe I'll tell you about that someday. Today is not that day."

It appeared as if Ian wanted to say more on the subject, but he let the matter drop. They finished their lunch with more laughter, which several times drew the attention of other diners. When lunch was over, Ma'am hugged him and said, "I love you."

"I love you, too, Mom."

When they pulled away, she asked in the style of Mae West, "Why don't you come up and see me sometime?" She laughed at his bemused expression.

"Oh, Mother, what'd I tell you about propositioning your son?" That drew more stares, which caused them both to laugh.

"Only on Tuesdays?"

He grinned. "Yes, that's what I told you. I gotta run, see you next week."

She watched him leave, then left a hundred-dollar bill on the table, more than enough to cover their meal, and walked out into the pleasant fall day.

She had missed being there when he grew up, but by then, she was starting to make her way in the business, and she had felt that was what she would have been better at. She had no confidence in her ability to be a good mother, yet she didn't have it in her to give him up. She and her mother saw the world in completely different ways, and there were some things she could never forgive her mother for, but she had also felt she'd had little choice.

All through his childhood, Tuesdays had been their day. It was the only day of the week she could get away, and she tried to make it special every time. In consequence, she knew she went overboard at times, taking him on day trips and buying him things, even though in the back of her mind, she knew she couldn't buy his love. She reasoned with herself that she just didn't want him to hate her, and he didn't seem to, even if he did have questions that she couldn't or wouldn't answer. Like his father. Ian had said to her once, in an angry moment, "I bet you don't even know who my dad was. I bet he was just some john to you."

All she could say was, "No, I knew him." But she ignored his pleas for more, despite how much it pained her not to fill in those gaps for him. There were some things she just had to keep to herself.

She walked back the way she had come, only this time, she stopped off at the little park that was halfway between home and the restaurant and found a bench to sit on. It was near a duck pond, and she used to bring them bread after every meal with Ian, but she read somewhere that bread was bad for birds and stopped doing it. It didn't stop them from trying, however. Two of them came up to within a few feet of the bench, and she put her hands out helplessly. "I'm sorry, I don't have anything." One quacked angrily and ruffled its feathers, then waddled away, taking his friend with him. She kept telling herself she needed to remember to bring birdseed for them but always forgot.

She sat back on the bench and spread her arms out and basked in the sun. She was wearing a pair of over-large sunglasses that made her feel like Elton John from the seventies. She loved sunglasses and owned several pairs. She couldn't help it; they were her favorite impulse buy. Out of her whole collection, however, it was the Ray Bans that were her favorite. She liked to pull them down her nose when she looked at someone, feeling like Tom Cruise in *Risky Business*. The irony was not lost on her. They went with the leather jacket she had hanging in her closet that had been part of her normal uniform when she had been in her twenties. Back when she had been coming home to her identity and trying to find a place to land that felt comfortable. She still wore it occasionally, and it still fit her perfectly. Only now it had aged with her and had creases the same as she did, but slipping it on was always like slipping into a part of herself. She needed to find more reasons to wear it.

She chuckled to herself, imagining what the women would think if they saw her dressed that way. A few of them had seen her leave the house that way, but most of them were new and hadn't seen her wear it yet. She wondered what Jame would think. Would it make her ask for alone time with her? She hadn't yet done so. Jame came when Ma'am called her, but Ma'am would rather she came on her own, instead of having to be summoned.

Another duck came up and quacked at her, and Ma'am looked down at it and smiled. "What do I have to do to get that girl's attention, anyway?" The duck cocked its head at her but made no further noise. "Yeah, I don't know, either." She sat back again and looked up toward the sun and closed her eyes.

Chapter Six

Sarah sat on one end of her comfy couch, one leg tucked under, in pajama pants, a baggy T-shirt, and one of her favorite pairs of fuzzy socks. Her hands were wrapped around a steaming mug of coffee that she blew on to drink it faster. She smiled at the woman sitting across from her. "What are you looking at me like that for?"

The other woman smiled back. "Because you look like you're up to something, but I'm not sure what."

"Well, if I am, I would be horrible at keeping it a secret if you could tell what I was up to."

"Sister dear, you *are* terrible about keeping secrets."

Sarah squealed with laughter.

"Every year, you spill the beans about what you buy me for my birthday and Christmas. And when you don't tell right away, your body language gives you away. So, what's up with you?" The other woman sat curled up in the big chair that matched the couch, a favorite of Sarah's ex-husband and where he was often found asleep when he wasn't working his long hours.

"Nothing…"

"Uh-huh. I believe that like I believe I'm going to win the lottery I don't play. There's something. You usually grin like that when you…"

Sarah's grin grew wider.

"No! No way! Since when?" Danni slapped the side of the chair. In doing so, some of her coffee spilled on her leg. "Shit! It's okay, it's all on me. None got on the chair."

"Must you always make messes when you come over?" Sarah asked, amused.

"Apparently. What are little sisters for?"

"In my experience, to make messes I have to clean up and to annoy the piss out of me. Sometimes, at the same time."

"It's a gift."

"Too bad you can't put that on your résumé, you'd have tons of offers."

Danni scoffed. "If only. Now stop deflecting, spill."

Sarah burst out laughing again. "But you already did that."

"Oh, ha ha. You know what I mean, who's the guy? And don't tell me there isn't one because I know that look."

"There actually isn't a guy." Sarah held up the first three fingers on her right hand. "Scout's honor." But she couldn't stop the giggles.

Danni pointed at her. "Liar!"

"Actually, I'm not. I haven't been with a man since Patrick and I divorced. But I was with someone, you're right about that."

"The only choices left are woman and young boy. Have you become a cougar? You're the right age for it."

"No, I have not. Too much trouble to teach them."

"You were with a woman?"

Sarah nodded.

"Wow, it's been awhile, huh? I thought that was just a college thing."

Sarah shrugged. "Not really. I mean, I've always been bi, I just never found a woman I wanted to date for a long period of time. And then I got pregnant. Things happened."

"So, was this something casual, or are you dating someone now?"

Sarah chuckled. "I'm definitely not dating someone. It's just for fun. I missed sleeping with women, but I'm not ready for a commitment right now. So, I have something that's no strings attached."

"Is that even possible?"

"For me or as a general concept?"

"Both."

"Okay, well, let me speak for everyone here… yes, yes, it's possible. Trust me, she's not going to get attached to me."

"Clearly, you don't know women if you think she's not going to get attached. Women can't help getting attached." Danni shook her head knowingly.

"Oh, really? Tell me, sister, how do you know so much about dating women?"

"Uh, because I am one. I know what I'm like in relationships, casual or otherwise. I can't tell you how many times I've gone in with every intention of keeping things easy, breezy, casual and then turned into a jealous psycho bitch."

Sarah laughed. "The first step is admitting you have a problem or are the problem."

"Oh, I know exactly who I become."

"Yes, but not every woman is like you."

"Ha! You clearly have been with men too long. They're all like me. Trust me, she'll be fine keeping things casual in the beginning, may even mean it, too, but eventually, she'll get jealous and start wanting more from you and sending you crazy texts and calling all the time. If you want to date a woman, more power to you, but may the gods have mercy on your soul." Danni gave Sarah a pointed look.

"Geez, you make it sound so appealing. But I'm pretty sure that's not going to happen."

"We'll see. I give it three months before she starts wanting more from you. Three months." Danni held up three fingers of her own.

Sarah laughed. "Okay, you're on. In three months, if she hasn't asked me for a commitment or started stalking me, you'll owe me something."

"Okay, like what?"

"I don't know yet. I'll let you know."

"What you're going to end up getting is an 'I told you so.'" Danni smirked.

"We'll see."

"So, who is she, how'd you meet her? What makes you think she's not going to want a commitment? Is she in jail or something? Only sees you on conjugal visit day?"

"Something like that."

"Oh, god, I was kidding. Please tell me you're not dating a convict. I blame *Orange is the New Black* for making that seem like a viable choice." Danni looked horrified.

Sarah laughed. "I've never even seen that show."

"Oh, my god, you haven't? You totally should." Danni smacked the arm of the chair again, this time being more careful not to spill her coffee.

"I'll keep that in mind."

"So, anyway, go on."

Sarah sighed. "Well, she's not a convict. She's… something else entirely."

"What, like a hamster?"

"A hamster? Of all the possible things to choose from, that's what you come up with? How would that even be possible? Never mind, I don't want to know, and if you know, I really don't want to know." Sarah waved her hand in a dismissive gesture.

"It was the first thing to come to mind, I don't know."

"God, you're weird." Sarah leaned forward and put her now empty cup on the coffee table and pulled her other leg up under her.

"Okay, I've let you stall enough…"

"Let me?"

"Yes, let you. I haven't yet attacked you with relentless questions. You know I'm capable." Danni smiled at her.

"Oh, I'm aware." Sarah exhaled in finality. "Okay, I'll tell you, but this has to stay between us."

"I promise."

"I mean it! This is kind of personal and very much embarrassing." Sarah looked away.

"Oh, I'm intrigued. But yes, you have my word I won't tell anyone."

"The person I've been seeing is a…she's a… prostitute. Or escort or whatever."

"Seriously?"

Sarah put her head in her hand, and an expression of embarrassment that looked like pain crossed her face. "Yes. From the house on the east side of town."

"Shut up! Big sister, when you decide to hire a prostitute, you go top dollar. That's something, at least. Wow, I can't believe it." Danni grinned.

"Yep. No skanky hos for me."

"What made you want to go that route?"

"Well, they don't really have a Grindr for lesbians, you know? I just wanted sex without complications. I didn't want to hear someone's life story or have to care about them. I'm not ready for a relationship so soon. And I hadn't been with a woman in forever, so it was a natural choice. Just my luck they had a hot butch. Oh, my god, ties and suspenders, shiny shoes, the whole bit." Sarah smiled and put her hands to her chest and looked wistful. "She's gorgeous and respectful. Submissive if I want her to be." She put her hands on her cheeks and felt them. "I've said too much."

"Well, I think this is awesome. Very sex positive. I hear that's a good thing to be these days. Good for you, knowing what you want and going after it. How many times have you seen her? Is it going to be a regular thing?"

"I've seen her twice. And yeah, it is. I gotta spend his alimony on something, don't I? Why not spend it on something he never gave me, like an orgasm?" The sisters burst out laughing.

"Hell yeah!" Danni raised her hand in a high five, and Sarah obliged.

"Besides, it's nice being with someone who is just happy to do what I want and will take care of my every need. It's kinda like TLC, and I really need that right now."

"Aw, I know, hon. I'm glad you found a way to get that. So, uh, is she good?" Danni asked mischievously.

"Would I continue paying her if she wasn't? Besides, don't think I'm going to give you details, that's just gross and wrong. We don't share that much."

"I tell you everything about my sex life, when I have one."

"Yeah, I know, and I've never asked you to."

"See how much I care enough to volunteer?"

"Is that what you call it? I call it oversharing."

"You love it." Danni grinned.

"I love *you*, I do not love hearing about the blowjobs you give your boyfriend or how you found out how anal sex *is* everything it's cracked up to be." Sarah smirked.

"Ha! My sister made an anal sex pun! Love it!"

Sarah couldn't help but laugh. "You're a bad influence on me."

"That's why you love me. I make your life interesting."

"That's one word for it."

After Danni left, Sarah poured herself another cup of coffee, then lay back on the couch with one arm behind her head and the other balancing the cup precariously on her stomach. She smiled to herself. She hadn't meant to tell Danni about her weekly visits to see Jame, but Danni was right, she had always been terrible about keeping secrets. Especially from Danni. Danni had been her coconspirator. They gushed to each other anytime they were dating someone, even if Danni often overshared. Sarah suspected it was because she was still trying to play catchup with her big sister, but there were many things Danni had done that Sarah had never attempted nor wanted to. But paying for sex, Sarah knew, was one thing Danni hadn't tried yet.

A smile crossed Sarah's face as she thought about some of the things she and Jame had done together. She had seen her just the day before. This time, she had let Jame make love to her, and she screamed so loud, she was sure others in the house had heard, and it had made her embarrassed, even though Jame had assured her that it was not a sound that was unusual there. Afterward, Jame had held her in her arms and stroked her hair. It had felt so peaceful and right and had been easy to forget for a moment that they weren't really lovers, just enjoying themselves in the afternoon. She had looked into Jame's eyes and saw, or imagined she had seen, a mixture of emotions. Satisfaction from a job well done, a look she recognized from Patrick in the beginning when they had still enjoyed touching each other and he was always so proud of himself, thinking he was the king of the world. But she also thought she saw something else, something more in Jame's eyes, but she couldn't name it.

Sarah sat up enough to take a sip of her coffee, then licked her lips as the sweetness lingered. It made her think of Jame's lips and how swollen they'd been after Jame had gone down on her. The wetness that shined on Jame's face gave Sarah such satisfaction to see. To know that a part of her was now on Jame, and when Jame came up for a kiss, she tasted herself on Jame's tongue. She had wanted to stay with Jame longer, but she knew she couldn't. It was just so cozy there, even if there was a large mirror on the other side of the room that made her feel watched. One of these days, she would ask Jame about that mirror, but she was afraid to at the same time. What if her suspicions were right? What if someone *was* watching them? Sarah suddenly grinned. "I guess I'll have to put on a better show next time then."

She giggled to herself, thinking of all the things she and Jame could do together. All the things she had yet to try. Maybe she would feel safe enough with Jame to try them. Patrick had never made her feel safe. Hell, Patrick really hadn't turned her on, but he thought he did. According to Patrick, since she was faithful to him, it had meant she was satisfied and happy. But really, she had been bored and often sad, and the baby hadn't filled in the missing gaps in their marriage. He had eventually noticed the gaps, too, but instead of trying to fix them, he found Ciara, a woman from his work who thought Sarah was one of those women who gave all her attention to her baby and left none for her poor husband. Ciara had been more than willing to help. Afterward, Sarah had said to Danni, "You can't give what you don't feel."

Sarah reached over and put her cup on the coffee table and curled up on her side with her hands under her head. It was almost time to pick P.J. up from school. Sarah sighed. "I need a new hobby. Besides Jame." Then she chuckled to herself as she put her feet on the floor and stood.

Chapter Seven

Ma'am chuckled to herself as she watched Jame through the two-way mirror with her current client, thinking, *Some clichés really are true*, as the head librarian pleasured Jame. Susan had asked Jame to keep her suit on from the waist up, as she was only interested in going down on Jame and had been doing so for the past half hour. She was nothing, if not thorough. Ma'am muttered, "Easy, girl, save some for the rest of us."

Ma'am was sprawled out on the sofa in the little room behind the mirror, also naked from the waist down, her own fingers exploring, her head lolled back in the corner. After having her eyes closed for several moments, she rolled her head over and looked in at Jame again. At that moment, Jame opened her eyes, as well, and searched out a spot in the mirror until her gaze fixed on Ma'am's. Ma'am chuckled to herself. Jame had been in this room many times and knew where the sofa was. Ma'am knew that Jame was looking from memory, that she couldn't actually see her, but still. She locked gazes with Jame and held it steady while she gave herself another orgasm. Wishing her fingers were those of Jame's, or better yet, Jame's tongue, is what had sent her over the edge. In her bliss, she couldn't help but close her eyes again. When she reopened them, Susan was sitting up on the side of the bed and Jame was looking like a spent ragdoll. Jame grinned at her in the mirror before she turned her attention to a now clothed Susan, accepting Susan's goodbye kiss, licking her lips. Ma'am imagined the licking was because Jame could taste herself on Susan's lips, but Ma'am wasn't sure whose benefit Jame did it for. Perhaps all of them.

Once Susan left, Jame turned back to the mirror and arched an eyebrow. Ma'am knew she was asking if Ma'am wanted her to come into the room behind the mirror, but Ma'am said nothing. After waiting for another moment, Jame shrugged, stood, and walked to the other side of her bed and opened the door there that led into her private bathroom. To Ma'am's disappointment, Jame closed the door. Ma'am sighed. It was probably just as well. There were things she had to see to in her office. There was a very boring side to her job, the business side. Though most people probably wouldn't think about it, a brothel was still a business, and someone had to order supplies for the house and pay the taxes. She didn't trust anyone else to do those things for her, though she often wished she felt comfortable hiring someone.

After a sigh, Ma'am stood and put her clothes back on, then took one final forlorn look at Jame's room. Jame still hadn't emerged from her bathroom, and Ma'am figured she was taking a shower. As much as she would love to watch Jame while she bathed, she wasn't about to invade the women's privacy everywhere. Ma'am left the room and entered the upstairs hallway. She passed Mercedes, one of her new women, as she was walking a client back to her room. Mercedes was wearing a plaid skirt and knee-high socks, per the client's request, Ma'am knew. As they passed, Ma'am smiled at them with a nod. "Father."

Father O'Neil looked at her a moment, then gave Ma'am a hasty nod before he turned away from her to focus again on Mercedes, dressed to look like one of the girls at the local Catholic school.

Ma'am shook her head. She was in no place to judge anyone. She made her way back to her office, passing several women on her way, bestowing on them a small smile and curt nod, not stopping to talk to anyone. She felt that a few of them were passing judgment on her as she walked by, as they knew where she had just spent the last hour. No one dared say anything, however. They knew better. Ma'am suspected that they were still just jealous of Jame. They knew she never asked for any of them anymore nor watched any of them while they worked. They just didn't hold the same allure for her that Jame did. They were generic pages out of a catalog to her, there to be appealing to the male clients who weren't that imaginative. Grown women looking like underage girls held no appeal for her. But men's fetishes and perversions kept her in business, and she made damn sure all the women she hired were of age. She provided a place for fantasy; it was just a fantasy she no longer wanted for herself.

⁂

Jame closed the door behind herself and smiled. She hadn't been that thoroughly enjoyed in quite some time. The librarian sure knew what she was doing. Her clit was still throbbing and swollen, the insides of her thighs damp. She sighed, pleased with how the session had gone, and began untying her tie and unbuttoning her shirt, letting them fall to the floor. She couldn't help checking out her profile in the mirror. She knew she wore a smirk. The smirk was for the thought of what Ma'am must have thought of the events of the past half hour or so. The whole time, she could feel her gaze on her, as if she was in the room with them. She had sought out a spot in the mirror where she imagined Ma'am's eyes would be, zeroed in on her like a target in crosshairs. She knew she had grinned, she couldn't help it. She knew Ma'am was loving the scene. She knew what she liked. She also knew that while Jame was lying back in contented bliss, Ma'am was probably doing the same, looking at Jame the whole time, wishing Jame's fingers were the ones inside her, instead of her own.

"I got you right where I want you," she assured her reflection. Chuckling to herself, she went to the tub and turned on the faucets, adjusting the temperature to just below the hottest setting. Once it was to her liking, she climbed in the tub and pulled the curtain closed, then adjusted the showerhead. The hot water felt luxurious as it fell like rain down her body. She mused to herself that it was almost too bad that one of the house rules stipulated that they weren't allowed to bring clients into the bathroom for safety reasons for both parties. Since there was no camera in there, once the door was shut, the activities couldn't be monitored by prying eyes. Which was too bad, really, as there were several things that could be done in that room. But on the other hand, it meant it was the one room in the house she was assured privacy, and she relished her privacy.

With the gilt-edged mirror on the far wall of her bedroom, it often felt like living in a fishbowl. She sometimes felt watched when she was doing nothing more than reading, which was ridiculous, because why would Ma'am bother to watch her read? How boring would that be? But still. Sometimes, when she was reading for pleasure, she would take her book downstairs to one of the sitting rooms. Even though the other women in the house were always wandering about, they usually left her alone, rarely engaging her in conversation. She felt unseen among them, more so than she did in her own room most days. She could sit in a quiet corner and read, unnoticed and unmoving until the cook, Marie, announced that it was dinnertime or there was an unexpected client who was asking for her. Those were referred to as "walk-ins" by the other women of the house. Like Sarah had been.

Since most of the clients were men, Jame didn't get tapped for walk-ins very often. Most of her clients were by appointment only, which she preferred. Made her work in the house feel more like she imagined her psychiatric work might be someday. Seeing clients on an hourly schedule, getting at the heart of their issues in a fifty-minute hour, making good coin. Only not having to take her clothes off or shower afterward.

Jame turned off the shower after a good, thorough scrub-down and stepped out onto the bathmat and reached for her towel. Once dry, she picked up her clothes from the floor, then opened the bathroom door, leaving her only sanctuary, confident Ma'am was no longer watching her. She knew that once Ma'am had nothing to look at anymore that she would leave the room behind the mirror that was a converted walk-in closet and that Jame could walk through her room, completely naked, without the possibility of unseen eyes watching her every movement.

After depositing the clothes in her hamper in the closet, she proceeded to get dressed, this time in casual clothes. She had no more clients scheduled for the day, and she wasn't required to advertise herself like a prized heifer, though you wouldn't know that by some of the women downstairs and how they always seemed to be dressed as if in costume, like the house was just an elaborate, never-ending cosplay of clichéd hooker fashions.

Now dressed in men's slacks and a short-sleeved collared shirt, Jame picked up her current book, Machiavelli's *The Prince*, and headed downstairs, hoping her favorite chair wasn't taken.

⁂

"That's a pretty house. Mom, why can't we live in a big, pretty house like that?"

Sarah glanced out her window to see what P.J. was referring to. At that moment, on her left, they were passing The Dragonfly House, where Jame lived. Sarah barely glanced at the Victorian marvel with its big front porch and the blue painted metal dragonfly holding pride of place above the front steps. She bit her lip a moment, then met her son's gaze in the rearview. "You're right, it *is* a big, pretty house. But I kinda like ours, don't you?" She smiled at his reflection and the way his brown mop of hair never seemed to comb out right, much like his father's.

"I guess so. It's kinda small and boring, though. And that one has lots of people. There's always people outside."

Out of the mouth of babes, she thought. "Yes, there are." She said nothing more as they drove by.

They passed the house every time she took P.J. to his father's house, and the boy was right, there *were* always people outside. The house had a big front porch with several chairs and swings, and the women of the house were often sitting out there, reading or chatting amongst themselves, enjoying the weather on nice days. Advertising, her cynical mind reminded her. She hoped to see Jame out there, but she had yet to do so. Though Jame didn't strike her as the porch-sitting type. She imagined Jame spent most of her time indoors, coffee shops probably, her nose in a book. She seemed the type.

She had seen an older woman on the porch once, sitting in a white wicker rocker, her denim-clad legs propped up on the railing, revealing her cowboy boots, her head back. It looked as if she was sleeping, but it was hard to tell as she had been wearing sunglasses. It had only been a quick glance. It was another day she had just been passing by, not a day when she had stopped in. It made her wonder who the woman had been. She seemed at peace, as if she belonged there. She also seemed too old to be working there, in Sarah's estimation.

Afterward, she had been curious enough to ask Jame about her the next time she had seen her. She had been lying in Jame's arms. Jame always gave her time to cuddle if she wanted to, something she greatly appreciated. She had been lying with her head on Jame's chest, her hand on Jame's stomach while Jame lay there quietly, just holding her, occasionally caressing her. "I have a question," Sarah said suddenly.

"Hmm?" Jame asked.

"Is there an older woman who works here?"

"A couple, I guess. Why do you ask?"

"Is there an age limit on...what you do?"

Jame glanced down at her, clearly confused. "Um, not that I'm aware of. Though, I'm sure, there must come a point in a woman's life when she decides to stop. What an interesting question." Jame became lost in thought.

"Sorry, I wasn't speaking philosophically, I was being literal. Damn it, words!" Sarah sat up, frustrated with herself. "What I mean is, I saw an older woman on the porch the other day and wondered if she worked here. I thought she looked too old to...you know...do what you do."

Jame sat up, glancing at the mirror before she replied. "Oh! I think I know who you saw. You probably saw my boss. We call her Ma'am."

Sarah crinkled her nose. "Ma'am? Like in Madam?"

Jame nodded.

"That's kinda gross. Like that's a real title or something? In the real world, bosses have actual names."

Jame glanced at the mirror again. "Well, this really isn't the real world."

Sarah noticed that Jame kept glancing at the mirror and realized her initial instincts had been right, they were being watched. "No, it's *her* world."

Jame shrugged. "Well, yeah. It *is* her house."

Sarah pushed Jame back down and rolled on top of her with a sly grin on her face. "Well, it might be *her* house, but it's *my* show."

Sarah shook herself out of her reverie before she could remember just how much Jame had screamed in pleasure at her ministrations. Now was not the time or place for thoughts like that. Feeling like the worst mother ever, she turned the corner onto her ex-husband's street and pulled up in front of the house he shared with his new girlfriend. With false cheer, she said to her son, "Okay, we're here."

Sounding less than enthusiastic, P.J. replied, "Yea."

"What's wrong, sweetie?"

"Why does *she* always have to be here? Why can't it just be me and Dad?"

Her heart breaking for him, she replied the best way she could. "It's her house, honey. Just be good, okay?"

He rolled his eyes at her and drew "mother" out. "Mother, I'm always good." Then, he grinned beatifically at her.

He made her laugh. "Come on, time to get out of the car and give your ol' mom a hug."

"Okay." He sighed as if put upon. Nevertheless, he did give her an enthusiastic hug goodbye.

She braced herself for the confrontation at the door, but the handoff went smoothly, and she was back in her car within a couple of minutes with a quick reminder to Patrick about making sure P.J. took his allergy medication while he was there.

On the drive home, she passed by The Dragonfly House again. This time, there was no one on the porch, which was a shame. They would have had a spectacular view of the sunset if they had been.

꧁꧂

Too old to do what Jame does? Ma'am chuckled to herself. "Oh, honey…I'm not old, I'm experienced. I'd shake your world to its foundation. Old. Hmpf."

Ma'am smirked as she watched Jame stick up for her. "Damn right it's my world. Jealous?"

Ma'am had momentarily stopped touching herself to have a one-sided conversation with a woman who couldn't hear her. She remembered the day Sarah was speaking of. She had been sitting in her favorite rocking chair, her feet up on the railing, basking in the sun and listening to the birds that often visited the feeder Ian had made in junior high, which she had dutifully hung from the tree in the front yard. She often thought of him when she sat there, remembering him as a little boy. One day when he had been visiting, a blue dragonfly had landed on his shoulder while he sat on the steps. He had laughed and tried to pet it, but it had flown away. Thereafter, he called her house The Dragonfly House, and the name had stuck.

Damn it, the last thing she wanted to do right now was wax poetic about her son. She focused once more on the action before her. When she tuned back in to what was happening on the other side of the glass, she saw Jame gripping the headboard with both hands, her head bent back, her eyes closed, and the vocal cords on her neck strained. And she was screaming in pleasure as Sarah's arm moved rapidly back and forth inside her. Intrigued, Ma'am leaned in for a closer look. "Why, you little minx. You *are* doing what I think you're doing." Ma'am smiled and continued to watch as Sarah pulled her fist out of Jame one last time, leaving Jame spent and soaked and unable to move or form much in the way of words.

In the room on the other side of the glass, Sarah was sitting up, asking if there was a place she could clean up. Jame gestured vaguely toward her closed bathroom door, telling her to leave the door open.

"Good girl," Ma'am replied approvingly.

When Sarah emerged from the bathroom, she proceeded to get dressed while a still unmoving Jame watched her vaguely from the bed. Jame sat up enough to kiss Sarah goodbye, then Sarah turned to leave, but not before she looked at the mirror with a grin and winked before closing the door behind herself.

"Oh, that's how it is, huh? We'll see about that, little girl." Instead of following her into the hallway, which had been her first instinct, Ma'am stayed where she was. She wasn't sure what she would have said to her if she had followed her. Or why she wanted to in the first place. She turned back to Jame to see her standing and dragging herself into the bathroom and closing the door, her legs looking a little wobbly. "My poor sweet Jame. Maybe you need to get fucked like that more often. Only next time by me." She sighed as she gathered her pants from the floor and put them on, then reached for her shoes.

Chapter Eight

The following Tuesday, Jame took her laptop out to her favorite café and found a table in the back. The first hour, she did her homework for her online course, then she pulled up Facebook and spent several minutes catching up with friends and family she hadn't talked to in a few weeks. When she had left her small town downstate, she had told everyone that she was taking a job as the personal assistant to a rich lady who she had met back when she worked in the coffeeshop in a nearby city. Part of that story had been true. She had met Ma'am in the coffeeshop in St. Louis when Ma'am had come into town on a shopping excursion, she had claimed. Later, Jame would wonder at that excuse, as Ma'am didn't seem the type to spend a lot of her free time shopping.

Ma'am had obviously been flirting with her, and Jame didn't mind. Ma'am was pretty hot for someone Jame realized was probably old enough to be her mother. Redheads had always attracted her, but it was more than her outer appearance. Everything about the older woman was a sensual turn-on, calculated to awaken every part of her. Jame read her right away. She could tell the woman, who gave her name simply as Renee, was used to having people be drawn to her. It was in the way she moved, purposeful yet casual at the same time, as if she knew you were hooked, and she didn't have to try too hard. It was in the smoky coolness of her voice, like a fine malt liqueur over ice. It was in her eyes, glacial blue but oft times seductive.

She came in every day for a week, always sat at a table near the window that gave her a clear line of sight to watch Jame's every movement behind the counter. Sometimes, Jame would catch her eye and give her a small smile. Renee would blush in return, and Jame didn't buy it for a minute. She could tell she was playing a game, wanting Jame to think that she was charming her, that she was demure but welcoming to whatever Jame had in mind. She was trying to control the moment, lure Jame to her so that Jame felt empowered and emboldened to approach her, sitting back and letting Jame make the first move. Clever. At the same time, Jame figured there was no harm in playing her game. Let her think she was catching her. She was only in town a few more days, she had already told her that. It could be a one and done and she would have a story to tell later about that time the rich lady came into her coffee shop and she let her think she had been seduced. They both leave happy and no harm done.

Except it didn't end that way. After they had spent the weekend having sex in every possible place in Renee's suite at the Chase Park Plaza, Jame had been presented with a contract and made a job offer. Not how her one-night stands usually ended. The contract seemed on the up and up. She had looked across the table at her on Sunday morning. Renee had ordered breakfast to be sent up, and they were now talking over coffee, as if the sex had been a prelude to a business meeting.

"Why me?"

"Why not you?"

Jame looked down at the contract again, reread the very generous offer before her. "I'm no one special."

"Oh, I beg to differ."

"What I mean is, I'm not exactly the type one expects to…to be…I mean…" Not able to find the right words, Jame trailed off.

Renee grinned. "You mean you don't think you're the type of woman men expect to find when they hire an escort."

"Yeah. About that…I only have sex with women. I don't think I'm who you're looking for." Jame lightly tossed the contract back on the table and looked back at Renee with an apologetic shrug.

"You've read that contract cover to cover at least three times now. Did it say anywhere in there about you having sex with men?" Renee arched an eyebrow, the corners of her mouth working their way up into a knowing smile.

"Well, no, but…"

"But what then? I have no intention of having you sleep with men. I'm diversifying my business. I've had women come to me and say they wish I had more variety. The key to having a successful business is knowing what the customer wants and giving it to them. You know what they say? See a need and fill it."

Jame grinned. "Is that what they say?"

Renee nodded.

"What I didn't see is a term of service. How long is this contract for?"

"Well, it's not like you're an indentured servant. You can leave whenever you like. It's a job like any other. You do your job, you get paid. You have health insurance, you pay taxes. On paper, you're my personal assistant. It just so happens that I need several assistants."

Jame reached for her coffee and took a sip. "And would I have to...personally assist you?"

Renee paused for a moment, considering her answer. "It's not an obligation. It might occasionally be a request. A request you can feel free to deny. I don't take advantage of my women. In my house, no one does anything they don't want to do. And that goes for me, as well as the clients. My top priority is your safety and your autonomy. Well?"

Jame still hesitated. Being a prostitute or an escort, whatever you called it, had never been on her radar. She wanted to be a doctor, but it was something she knew she would have to work hard for. She had no money, and her family couldn't help. The money she was being offered would pay for all of that in just a few years. Could she do it? Essentially step away from her life for a couple of years to allow her body to be used in this way? For money? She met Renee's gaze again. "What do I tell my family?"

"The same thing you tell the IRS. That you're my personal assistant."

"What'd you tell your family?"

Renee seemed caught off guard by the question. She broke eye contact and looked down at the table for a moment as if she was searching the wooden surface for the answer. Finally, she quietly replied, "My family is none of your concern."

"Fair enough." Jame took note of the weak spot in Renee's armor. There was something there, something about her family that suddenly put her on guard. It might come in handy to know what that something was. For now, she just eyed the beautiful, sensual woman sitting across from her, taking in her time-honed shrewdness, and considered the very generous contract before her. "Okay. But I want to wear suits."

Renee grinned. "Baby, you can wear whatever you want."

Jame hadn't thought of Ma'am's real first name in quite some time. No one in the house ever spoke it out loud. She wondered how many of them knew what it was. She still didn't know what the issue was with Ma'am's family. Ma'am kept no pictures in her office, and no one came to the house to visit her. Jame suddenly wondered if Ma'am was lonely. She didn't seem to have any friends except Marie, the cook, and Stella, the maid. A couple of times, Jame had gone down to the kitchen for a late-night snack and had found Ma'am sitting at the table with them, drinking whiskey and laughing together. They had stopped talking when she had come in, obviously waiting for her to leave so they could continue their revelry. Other than that, Ma'am still left the house every Tuesday like clockwork. Now with a small pouch of birdseed in her pocket that Jame had seen Marie give her. She supposed Ma'am took a walk to the park and fed the ducks. Again, she was troubled by the thought that Ma'am might be lonely. "Maybe she just needs a girlfriend," she mused to herself. A real one, one who wasn't on her payroll.

※※※※※

Ma'am sat on her favorite bench at the duck pond, throwing seed at all who approached. They stayed a respectable distance in front of her but nevertheless stood there waiting, knowing she would feed them. "See, I didn't forget you. I always keep my promises."

"Yes, she does. Hello, Mother." Ian sat beside her, placing a square zippered bag between them.

Ma'am looked at him and smiled. "Hello, son. Here, better take some of this so we can eat in peace. I've been negotiating for them to leave us alone."

Ian reached out his hand and took the birdseed. Two ducks immediately noticed the exchange and zeroed in on him as a new food supplier. He dutifully fed them. "Oh? How's that going?"

"I think I'm making some progress, but only time will tell." Once all the seeds were gone, she wiped her hands on her pants and turned to unzip the bag. "Thank you for bringing lunch. You're such a good boy." She grinned at him as she reached in to pull out a sandwich from her favorite deli.

Ian joined her by pulling out his own sandwich, and they sat in companionable silence for a few minutes, enjoying their meal and watching the ducks, who had gotten bored with the humans when they realized they had nothing more for them.

When she finished her sandwich, she turned to him and asked, "Did you mean it?"

"Mean what?"

"That I always keep my promises? I feel like I broke a thousand promises to you." She couldn't meet his gaze and instead turned away.

"You never made me nearly that many promises. You were always careful not to. Intentions are not the same as promises, not if you keep them to yourself."

"Why do I feel like you're always letting me off easy?"

"Well, that's an improvement. Before you said that you felt like I was punishing you."

"I guess it depends on the day."

Ian chuckled. "So, how are you?"

"I'm good. Business is going well, the weather's been good to us, and I'm having a great hair day, what more could I ask for?"

"Mother, since when do you care about bad hair days?"

"I don't really. I have hats for that. Just making conversation. You know, I was thinking about when you were a little boy the other day. Do you remember the dragonfly?"

Ian looked over at her. She appeared lost in thought as she looked out at the ducks. "I remember. It wouldn't let me touch it. It was beautiful, but it was just there for a moment. I always hoped to see it again, but it never came back. You know I named it?"

Ma'am turned to him in surprise. "Named it? You never told me that. What'd you name it?"

Now he looked shy, as if he didn't want to admit it. "Well…"

"Come on, out with it. Tell your old mom."

"Oh, I can't believe I'm about to admit this. Why did I start this?" He ran his fingers through his hair, now clearly embarrassed.

"It couldn't have been that bad."

Ian gave a sigh, then admitted, "I named her Penny."

"Penny? Why would that embarrass you? I mean, I've never been fond of the name myself, but it's not that bad."

"You don't remember?"

"Remember what?"

"Penny."

Ma'am looked at him, still at a loss.

"Penny used to…work for you. I thought she was pretty. Like one of Grandmother's favorite expressions, pretty as a penny."

Ma'am threw her head back and laughed. "Oh, you are a sentimental boy, I've always loved that about you. Sorry, I had forgotten all about her. She wasn't here that long, and it was a long time ago."

"Whatever happened to her, anyway?"

"She ran off and got married, if I remember correctly. That happens occasionally."

"Didn't happen to you."

"Well no, it didn't, not yet. I guess Julia Roberts has been too busy to come and rescue me."

"She was the prostitute in that movie."

"Oh, I know. A girl can dream, can't she?"

Ian stayed an hour, then he said he had to get back to work. She hugged him goodbye, holding him tighter than usual. She was sure he noticed, but he didn't comment on it. For the millionth time, she wished they were closer, that talking to him wasn't so strained. But at least he was trying, she had to give him that. She knew he could have chosen to shut her out once he was old enough to make his own decisions about whether or not to spend time with her, but he hadn't. And for that, she was grateful.

※ ※ ※ ※

Sarah sat across from Danni in Grayson's Deli, her favorite place on the square, opening a sugar packet and putting it in her coffee.

"So, you haven't talked to me in like a month.

I'm beginning to think you don't love me anymore." Danni took a bite of her sandwich, her expression not matching her words. Her eyes were filled with humor instead of reproach.

Sarah casually stirred her coffee and smiled. "Damn, I was hoping you wouldn't find out this way. This whole sister thing, it's been fun, but I'm over it now."

Danni shrugged. "That's fine. I kinda always hoped you were an older brother, anyway."

Sarah opened her mouth, incredulous. Recovering, she said, "Well, I wanted a puppy but got you instead. I guess we can't always get what we want."

"True. A puppy, huh? Is that why you made me drink from a bowl on the floor when I was four?"

Sarah burst out laughing. "I couldn't believe you did it! Oh, Mom was so mad! 'She's your sister, not a dog!' You were such a stupid kid."

"You were my older sister, I trusted you! God, you were such a brat. Still are most of the time."

"I let you drink from a glass now."

"My loving sister." Danni raised her glass as if in salute before she took a drink.

Sobering, Sarah replied, "Anyway, sorry I've been MIA recently, I've just been thinking about some things."

"Oh? What 'things?'"

"Just...life stuff. Like, going back to work now that P.J.'s in school and if I should sell the house. You know, life stuff." She tried to pass it off as no big deal, but Sarah had never been good at hiding her emotions.

Danni looked at her, concerned. "Those are some big things."

Sarah nodded.

"Why sell the house? I thought you loved that house."

"I've always liked the house, I don't know if I've ever loved it. That might be too strong a word. I was thinking of something bigger, maybe older. Maybe this one's too modern for me. It was built in the seventies, for crying out loud. Nothing good came out of the seventies."

Danni grinned. "Wait, weren't you born in the seventies?"

"1981, you toad!" Sarah threw a potato chip across the table at Danni, who promptly picked it up and ate it with devilish enjoyment.

"Oh, yeah, keep forgetting. It was so long ago."

Sarah shook her head in exasperation. "I could have had a puppy."

"You love me."

"Hmm."

"Anyway, well, while those are viable things to think about, that doesn't excuse you for ghosting me."

"I didn't ghost you!"

Ignoring her, Danni went on. "I think you've been ghosting me so you could spend more time with a certain…companion." Danni's eyes danced with mischief as she looked across at Sarah, who was squirming in her seat. "Got you!" Danni pointed her finger in accusation.

"So? I've picked up a new hobby, sue me. Besides, it won't be forever, just something I gotta get out of my system. I'm having fun. Maybe, instead of annoying me about this, you should get your own hobby."

"Oh, I've thought about it. So much so that I went over to that house of yours on the east side of town."

Sarah looked at her, alarmed. "What? You what?"

"Yeah, I did, I went over to that," now Danni leaned across the table and lowered her voice, "Dragonfly place just to see what was so special about it."

"Did you…did you…you know?"

"Look at you, you do this all the time, but you can't even say it out loud. Did I pay for a girl?"

Sarah nodded.

"Thought about it but didn't really see anyone who appealed to me. Well, I saw one, but I was told she was the boss, and she didn't meet with clients. Such a shame. She was kinda hot. Oh, I think I saw your favorite one, too. She didn't see me, though, had her nose in a book. She was cute." Danni nodded approvingly.

Sarah smiled. Jame with her nose in a book didn't surprise her. "Wait, since when do you like sleeping with women anyway?"

"You don't know everything about me. I've tried things."

"Oh, that I know."

"Some things I've tried more than once. I think I'm omnisexual or something."

Sarah looked at her, confused. "Since when? And how is that different from bisexual, anyway?"

"Since awhile now, it just never came up. And don't ask me to define the terms, it's all so confusing."

"That's why I just stick to bi. At least I know what that means."

"Yeah, I think it's passé to be bi now. But whatevs." Danni shrugged, obviously not caring for current convention.

Remembering something, Sarah suddenly asked,

"Wait, you think Ma'am is hot?"

"Who?"

"Sorry, the madam, I guess she is. Jame says they call her Ma'am, isn't that weird?" Sarah crinkled her nose in disgust.

"I don't know, a bit strange. And dictatorial if you ask me. But she's the boss, I guess she can be called whatever she wants. But yeah, I thought she was kinda hot, for an older chick. Your Jame was cute, just not my type."

Sarah shook her head. "Okay, can we change the subject? This is too weird to be talking to my baby sister about."

"Aww, you always start to squirm when we talk about sex, you're so cute."

"Shut up, toad." Sarah threw another potato chip across the table at her, but Danni deflected it amidst her laughter.

Chapter Nine

Ma'am watched, almost transfixed, as Sarah buckled the last buckle on the strap-on she now wore. Jame was on her knees on the bed, her ass in the air, gripping a pillow when Sarah entered her from behind. Ma'am had to chuckle. Never had she seen someone take over Jame as much as Sarah had. As she continued to do every time the two of them had a session. With the rest of her clients, Jame was the one in charge of the scene, being the dashing young seducer of their dreams, fulfilling all their desires. But it seemed that Sarah was there to fulfill Jame's. Every time, she left Jame crying out for more, screaming her name. And every time, Sarah became bolder and more of a showoff in Ma'am's estimation.

Now before she left, Sarah would blatantly look at the mirror, searching her out. When she had first noticed her doing so, Ma'am had been surprised that she had been found out, but now it amused her. None of her own women, Jame included, performed especially for her benefit, they just did what they were paid to do, and if she got off on it sometimes, good for her. But Sarah made her feel special. The week before, Sarah hadn't wanted Jame to touch her, nor did she touch Jame, other than a few sweet kisses. Instead, she had told Jame to pull her reading chair out of the corner and place it in such a way that Jame could see her but not block Sarah's view of the mirror. Jame had obliged. While Jame sat back in her chair, relaxed, with her hand fingering her clit, Sarah lay back on the bed, legs open wide in front of the mirror and brought herself to orgasm with a vibrator. Several times, her gaze had strayed to the mirror, searching, until they settled on a specific spot, then she would close them and bring herself to another orgasm, until finally, her legs began to tremble, and her hand went slack on the vibrator. When she had finished and sat up, she had looked into the mirror with a pleased, triumphant grin.

Now, to Ma'am's surprise, she realized Jame wasn't the reason she kept coming into the small room behind the mirror. Week after week, she found herself in there again, watching and waiting for what Sarah would do next. She felt like she had her very own peep show. Only there was no shade that came down after a couple of minutes. This show went on for an hour each time. And the performer paid her for the privilege of performing.

When Sarah finished with Jame, Jame lay spread-eagle across her bed, and Sarah turned to face the mirror. Her gaze fixed on a spot in the mirror as she held the dildo in her hand. She glanced down at it, then back up to the mirror with a slight smirk and a look of obvious invitation, as if she was asking Ma'am if she wanted to take a turn.

Ma'am chuckled approvingly. "Someday. If you're lucky," she muttered, grateful the two-way speaker was turned off from her side. "Someday, little girl, I'll show you what experience can do." Ma'am continued to watch as Sarah unhooked the strap-on, then took it into the bathroom to wash it off. The whole time, Jame barely stirred on her bed. Just before

Sarah came back out, Jame rolled over and looked into the mirror and grinned slyly. "Oh, yes, Mama loves the show. Good job." Ma'am was about to leave when she saw Sarah emerge from the bathroom, now fully dressed and the strap-on hidden away in a shoulder bag, her hair up in a loose bun, looking as if she was heading into the office. She walked over to Jame and kissed her goodbye, then turned to the mirror, grabbed her pants leg, and dropped a small, sarcastic curtsy, the whole time with a grin on her face. Then she backed out the door and was gone.

Ma'am couldn't help but laugh.

꙳꙳꙳꙳

After Sarah left, Jame showered, then settled herself on her bed to work on her homework. She knew Ma'am would have left the little room by now and her privacy was her own again. Before she opened her homework, however, she went to her journal file and started a new entry.

Sarah keeps surprising me. She's getting more and more innovative with her exploits. She's become quite the exhibitionist as of late. Such a change from the shy woman who first came to see me several weeks ago. Every week, she's running the show, and each time, she's doing something different. I can't complain, as it's always to my benefit. I've also noticed her playing to the mirror more and more. I think she's figured out that someone's watching. It seems to excite her. I think this is what she needed, someone to focus on her and find her sexually exciting and alluring. She must have been missing that in her marriage. She told me about her ex once. *He didn't sound like the type of guy who cared much about her or showed her much affection. That's where I come in.*

I do wonder what Ma'am is thinking of all of this, she hasn't said. Though, I think she's back there watching every time Sarah's here now, waiting, as I am, to see what she'll do next. I don't blame her. Sarah puts on a good show. Honestly, she could do well here if she wanted to. And she wouldn't have a problem working with male or female clients, so she could make a lot of money if she really wanted. She did say she's looking to go back to work, though I'm sure this wasn't what she had in mind. She would make so much more here than she could anywhere else. Maybe I'll drop some hints as to that possibility, see if she takes the bait.

This field research has become invaluable to my future plans. I realized the other day that my notes could very easily be turned into a book, perhaps used as research for a dissertation. I had previously just thought of focusing on Ma'am, as she is fascinating enough to fill volumes, but with as interesting as Sarah's becoming, I would be remiss if I didn't include at least one chapter about her. I thought of a great title the other day: Women of The Dragonfly House: An in-depth look at the two years I spent working at a Midwestern brothel. *A bit long, I know, but academic titles are like that. Maybe a chapter on jealousy would be appropriate, considering how some of the women treat me because of favoritism. Probably end it on a chapter about life beyond the brothel, what comes next. Yes, I think that would make a great book.*

When I came here, I had no intention of using this place for research, but I think it would be a waste of my time if I didn't take advantage of this situation. I know

Ma'am has some confused feelings for me she thinks are love, and Sarah might be developing the same type of feelings. In her case, it's typical transference. I'm giving her what she needs right now, and she's mistaking it for love. As for Ma'am, I'm not sure. Maybe the same thing. Though, since I'm here under contract and what I do with and for her is more for my terms of service, though I can technically say no, I'm not doing it out of any sense of affection. When I'm pleasing Ma'am, she's just another client. Making her feel special is my job, it's what she hired me for. If she confuses that, then that's on her. But emotions are a funny thing. It doesn't take much to stir them up, either way. The question is, how much do I want to stir the pot and how much do I want to just sit back and watch it boil? I think, to be true to my chosen field, it is best for me to be the observer of human behavior. But being the puppet master is almost hard to resist.

≈≈≈≈

Ma'am was enjoying the fall colors in the park. On a whim, she had brought her camera with her to take some shots of the trees and maybe stroll through the botanical gardens at the other end of the park and capture some pictures of the flowers in bloom. As she walked up the cobbled path that meandered through the flowers, her gaze fell on one particular yellow daisy, which was still holding on despite the early fall weather. Sitting atop the flower was a monarch butterfly. Very carefully, she aimed her camera and focused, making sure to get the butterfly and the flower in frame. Just as she snapped the shutter, the butterfly took off, but she kept shooting, hoping to get a shot of the insect in flight. She heard the sound of childish laughter as she removed the camera from in front of her face. She saw a little boy, not more than five or six, she guessed, standing with his mother a little farther on the path. A butterfly had decided that he was a good perch and was resting on his hand. He was staring at it, transfixed and smiling. When he looked up at his mother to show her, Ma'am followed his gaze up to a familiar face. Standing before her was a woman she knew better naked than she did clothed, though the other woman had never taken her clothes off specifically for her. She had a few seconds of uninterrupted gazing before Sarah turned and saw her standing a few feet in front of them and instantly blushed and averted her eyes.

Undaunted, Ma'am walked forward anyway with a casual stride. She smiled down at the boy when she came closer. The butterfly flew off as she approached. "It looks like you almost had a new pet."

The boy looked up at her and returned her smile, not sensing a threat from the stranger. "Nah, butterflies can't be pets, they just gotta fly. I tried to keep fireflies as pets once, but they all died. Butterflies shouldn't be in jars." He shook his head emphatically.

Sarah laughed. "Nope. They both belong outside."

"That's right. As you said, they just gotta fly." Ma'am met Sarah's gaze for a moment. It held a look of curiosity.

"More butterflies!" P.J. ran down the path, looking for more butterflies.

Sarah and Ma'am hollered after him simultaneously, "Don't run!" before both broke out into nervous giggles.

"Your son?" Ma'am asked as they strolled

casually in his wake.

Sarah nodded, smiling. "Mm-hmm."

"What's his name?"

"P.J. Patrick Junior," she amended.

"Ah. I like P.J. My son's name is Ian."

Sarah turned to Ma'am in astonishment. "I didn't know you had a child. I mean…"

Ma'am smiled softly. "He's not a child anymore, he's twenty-five. I named him after the other great Janis. *Society's Child* had always been a favorite. It resonated with me."

"You mean Janis Ian?"

"Yes."

"I thought she was popular way before that, like in the sixties." Sarah suddenly stopped talking and looked at Ma'am nervously. "I mean…"

Ma'am laughed gently at her. "She was, and the answer's no, I'm not that old."

"Sorry. How'd you know that's what I was thinking?" Sarah looked away from Ma'am and focused again on P.J., who had stopped chasing butterflies to crouch down on the path looking for loose rocks. Seeing that he was occupied and not moving, Sarah stopped walking.

"I could see the wheels turning. Well that, and you were starting to blush. You should blush more often." Sarah's cheeks instantly flamed again, and Ma'am chuckled. "Yes, like that."

Speaking almost in a whisper, Sarah leaned in to ask, "Are you flirting with me?"

Mimicking her posture, Ma'am leaned in to ask her own question, "And if I was?"

Sarah started to visibly squirm. "I don't know, it just feels…weird. Wrong somehow."

"Do you feel like you would be cheating on Jame?"

"What? No, it's just…it's just…what I do with Jame at your house is…is just something I do at your house. I leave it there. Does that make sense?"

Ma'am pulled back and spoke in a normal tone. "I think so."

"It's just…something I do for fun."

"It's business."

"I guess that's one way of putting it." Sarah took a step closer so that she could speak softer again. "Look, I'm sorry if my teasing let you think…"

Ma'am raised her hand part way and interrupted her. "It's business, I got it." Ma'am suddenly smiled. "You have a lovely son. Cherish these years with him. They go by way too quickly." Ma'am nodded, as if she were tipping a hat, then walked back the way she had come, leaving Sarah standing in the middle of the path muttering swear words under her breath.

≈≈≈≈

Ma'am sat at her desk, the memory card from the camera in the slot on the side of her laptop, going through the photos she had taken the day before at the park. Before she had reached the botanical gardens where she had run into Sarah, she had spent some time at the duck pond, standing on the dock, taking pictures from the railing looking out over the water and the trees that skirted the edge. She always loved the fall. The trees in the Midwest turned wonderful shades of red and orange and yellow, which showed up so well in photos. Photography had always been a secret hobby, one she engaged in occasionally when the mood struck her. The walls in her bedroom at the top of the house, her sanctuary, which none of the women of the house had ever seen, was covered with her photos, equal parts taken in nature, as well as candids of Ian through the years.

Of the photos in front of her now, she had two really good ones she felt were wall-worthy, one from the dock and one from the gardens. But there was an unexpected photo from the garden, one that had been captured as she was following the trajectory of the butterfly as it flew off the flower. Her camera had captured Sarah and P.J. just as another butterfly had landed on his hand. He was looking at the insect in wonder, and Sarah was looking down at him with such a look of maternal love, it almost ached to see it. Sarah's smile was only for that boy. The photo was better than one would expect, considering how quickly and how blindly she had been shooting. They were both in frame, their faces were clear, and the flowers and trees around them blended together in multifaceted hues of color. It was beautiful. Ma'am sat looking at it with her chin in her hand, contemplating what to do with it. It deserved to be seen, but she didn't have the right to add it to her collection upstairs; they weren't her family.

She didn't have any candids with her and Ian together; there had been no one around to take them. Her walls were covered with his school photos her mother had been kind enough to give her, from his kindergarten graduation up until college. There were also scores she had taken of him at various times, some during sporting events he briefly participated in, to the candid moments when she could catch him off-guard, enjoying a moment, as P.J. was in the picture on her screen. As he grew older, there were a couple of times he had bravely asked her for the camera and taken a few of her, her long hair hanging loose and partially obscuring her face, her shades on. Her go-to pose for pictures.

    She clicked to the next image to see that the camera had caught Sarah as she had turned her head slightly in Ma'am's direction, and she was able to see more of her smile and the softness of her eyes. This was not the face of the woman who seemed to live to tease her. This was not the face of the woman who dreamed up new ways to make Jame scream with desire every week. This was the face of the woman who loved her son beyond anything. This was who she really was. Ma'am rarely got to see this side of her clients. There was a reason for that. She didn't want to know them. She didn't want to know about their lives. She didn't want to know who they loved or who they might be cheating on or what their disappointments were. They were clients. She was paid to provide a service, a service to make them happy, at least briefly. That was what Sarah paid for. Sarah paid her so that once a week she could come here and feel safe to live out her fantasies, fantasies that brought her out of herself for one short hour a week. Then she was able to leave and go home, back to being P.J.'s mom and someone's daughter, someone's sister perhaps, someone's friend.

    It was a luxury Ma'am didn't have, not really. She envied Sarah that. She also envied the fact that Sarah had the luxury to be that boy's mother, a privilege she had denied herself. It was a decision she had justified as being what was best for him. It had seemed like the right decision at the time.

She sat on her mother's sofa, chewing the nail on her left index finger, a childish habit she hadn't done in years. Her mother was pacing in front of her, one hand on her hip.

"You move out of my house, move god knows where, telling me you were old enough to make your own decisions, not listening to or caring about a word I had to say, only to come back here and sit in my house, in front of Jesus," Cecilia Berry stopped to gesture to the framed painting above the fireplace, "and tell me that you're pregnant." Mrs. Berry stopped pacing and now stood in front of her daughter and asked almost triumphantly, "Now I wanna know, what do you expect me to do about it, Miss I-have-all-the-answers?"

Renee started to speak, but her fingers still obscured her mouth, and her words came out in an unintelligible mumble.

"Take your damn fingers out of your mouth and talk like you're supposed to."

Renee put both hands under her thighs, hoping to quell her childish behavior. She tried to meet her mother's gaze. "I need your help."

Cecilia scoffed. "I should have known. I should have known you'd come asking me to help you get an abortion. Well, you've come to the wrong place for—"

Renee interrupted her. "What? No! I don't want an abortion! I could never do that."

"Oh. Then what exactly do you think I can help you with? You want to move back in, I suppose."

Renee shrugged. "Not really."

"Not really, what does that mean, not really?"

"It means that I have a place to live right now, but when it gets closer to the time, and afterward, for a little while. A few weeks, that's all."

"And then what? You think I'll let you stay after that, that once I see the baby, I'll take pity on you and want you to stay? Because if that's the case…"

"Not me. Just the baby." Renee looked down at her mother's shoes. Her mother was wearing what she always wore, white canvas Keds with no socks. Renee could see part of her mother's calves revealed by her three-quarter pastel capris. She tried not to roll her eyes at just how much of a caricature she found her mother to be.

Cecilia stood up straighter, her face one of shock. "What do you mean, 'just the baby'? Are you really asking what I think you're asking?"

"Yes."

"Why, Renee? Why, in God's name, are you asking this of me?"

Renee stood and looked her mother in the eye, unflinching. "Because I want my baby to have a chance at a good life. I'm not in a position to promise him that. But you are. I can't let him go into the system. Mother, please. This will be the last thing I ever ask of you."

Her mother began to shake her head, though she seemed unaware of the fact. "I just…I just…Renee, do you know what you're asking?"

"Trust me, I have not come to this decision lightly. And I'm not being selfish, I promise. I know it's a lot to ask of you. Financially, I'll give as much as I can, always."

"It's not just that."

"I know. Mom, do you think I want to give up my child? Because I don't."

"Then why are you?"

Renee took a moment before answering. "Because I've done some things you wouldn't be proud of. Doing some things. And I'll be able to provide for him, but…it's just best if he grows up in a wholesome environment. Has a chance at a normal life. A mom who is home to bake him cookies and listen to his day. My life isn't like that."

"There are different kinds of mothers. And whatever you're doing, you don't have to do it forever. You can stop. Whatever it is, it's not a life sentence."

Renee looked at her mother, resigned. "I will, someday. But not yet. In the meantime, I want him to be safe. Mother, please. He's your grandson."

Cecilia's eyes moistened, and she reached up to touch Renee's face and smiled. "My prodigal daughter…though I suppose it's not the same, is it? He wasted his money on prostitutes." She chuckled at the thought.

Surprised at the imagery, Renee laughed, too. "No, not the same."

"Okay, I'll do this. But he will always be *your* son and my grandson. You will not disappear on him. You will see him regularly and be a part of every milestone. You will not leave that boy wondering who you are, you hear me?"

"Yes, ma'am. I intend to."

"Good. What about his father? Does he know?"

Renee bit her lip and shook her head. "It was a one-time thing. I haven't seen him since."

"I see. Do you know his name, at least?"

"It was Reggie. That's all I know."

Cecilia looked thoughtful. "Reggie?"

"Yes."

"Was he black?" She whispered the last word,

even though they were standing in her living room.

Renee exhaled through her nose and did her best to keep her tone steady. "Not that it matters, but yes."

"Don't take that tone with me, I was just curious. So, when he's born…"

"He might have a tan and kinky hair, yes. Where are you going with this, Mother?"

"Just trying to get a picture of what my future grandchild will look like. I'm sure he's going to be a beautiful boy. Was his father good-looking?"

"An Adonis." She was being more than kind. Reggie had been short, with an acne-scarred face and a small bit of stubble on his cheeks that looked more like pubic hair instead of the beard he hoped it would become. He had told her that he was still a virgin at twenty-four and finally wanted to do something about it. He had been sweet in his inexperience, so she had been gentle with him.

"Well, that's something, at least."

* * * *

Ma'am smiled, grateful Ian had taken after her side of the family. Though his skin and hair were dark, she saw more of her own father when she looked at his face than his own. He did have his father's sweetness, however.

She made a new folder on her desktop and labeled it "Butterflies" and saved the shots of Sarah and P.J. there before sending the other two shots to the jump drive so that she could print them. Then she dislodged the memory card and the jump drive and closed her laptop.

Chapter Ten

Ma'am walked into the kitchen to find Marie and Stella already there. Stella was at the sink, prewashing the dishes before she put them into the dishwasher, and Marie was wiping down the stove and work area. They both turned and smiled when Ma'am walked in.

"Hello, ladies. How's things?" She gave them a tired smile, then reached into the cabinet above the stove and pulled down a bottle of scotch. She held it aloft to the others, moving it back and forth invitingly, and grinned at them.

"Hell yes." Stella immediately turned off the faucet, wiping her hands on a nearby dishtowel.

"Thought you'd never ask, let me just wash my hands." Marie threw away the paper towel she'd been using to wipe the counter down, then went to the sink to wash her hands before joining Ma'am and Stella around the butcher block table that sat in the middle of the room.

Ma'am had grabbed three tumblers out of the cabinet before sitting and poured each of them three generous fingers worth, then held hers up. Stella and Marie joined her. "To old times and good times."

"And the few times they're the same," Marie joined in.

"Amen!" Ma'am declared, laughing. They clinked their glasses, then drank, each showing various faces of approval, but also surprise as the effects of the whiskey hit their throats.

"Damn, Renee, that is some fine-ass liquor."

Marie winked at her. "You're welcome." She bumped shoulders with Stella, and they both giggled.

Ma'am scoffed. "God, you two are disgusting. All this lovey-dovey crap. This is not the place for that." But her affectionate smile defied her words.

Stella waved her hand dismissively. "Whatever, you jealous old whore. You just wish you were as lucky as we are." She leaned across the table and chuffed Ma'am on the chin before leaning back and taking Marie's hand.

Still smiling, Ma'am took another drink before replying, "What do I have to be jealous of? I get all the sex I want whenever the mood strikes me. And with variety."

"Heard tell, you've been doing more watching than doing, you perv." Marie grinned across the table at Ma'am before taking another drink of her own.

"I swear, you two get more like high school girls every day. Love is rotting your brain."

"Well, I've read that being in love is like being high on cocaine or something. So, if you're calling us dopey schoolgirls, I'd say that's accurate."

"Maybe I'm also saying you shouldn't get your medical knowledge from memes."

"Well, not all of us are cut out for med school."

"Yeah, we're not all like your little hot butch." Marie raised her eyebrows in a teasing fashion at Ma'am.

"She is not *my* anything. Well, she's my employee, that's all."

"Uh-huh. Don't think I don't know where you

spend most of your time these days. You have a thing for her."

Ma'am eyed Marie across the rim of her glass. She was trying to choose her words carefully. "I don't have a *thing* for her. I don't have a thing for anyone." Ma'am shifted her gaze to the bottom of her glass, looking thoughtful before she took a sip.

She didn't see Stella and Marie exchange glances. Finally, Stella spoke. "Anyone?"

"What?"

"You said 'anyone.'"

"Yes, and?"

"I think what Stella's getting at is that you just sorta implied that Jame might not be the only one you…like." Marie shrugged, at a loss how to explain further.

"You two are some gossipy old broads, I swear. You've been reading too many romance novels, that's the problem." Ma'am nodded as if she had them figured out.

"Maybe, but you've been acting differently lately, I know that."

"What are you talking about?"

Stella glanced at Marie before responding. "Introspective seems to be the best word for it."

"Contemplative," Marie chimed in.

"In your feelings."

"Yes!" Marie pointed at Stella, as if they finally figured out the puzzle.

"Feelings? I've been in this business too long to have feelings."

"Bullshit! I call bullshit."

"Careful, or Marie won't want to kiss that dirty mouth."

"Please. Why do you think I kiss that dirty mouth?"

Ma'am put her hands out flat on the table and stood. "Well, this has been fun, but I'm going to bed. Thanks for having a drink with me." Ma'am picked up her glass and held it aloft again. "Ladies," she said, then downed the remaining alcohol before placing it back on the table with a satisfying clunk.

"Sure, leave when it's just getting interesting. Did we strike a nerve, sweetie?" Stella's mischievous tone and the playful glint in her eyes belied the sweetness of her words.

"Of course not, how could you? Didn't I just say I don't have any feelings? Good night." She gave them a smile and little wave as she left the room. Once her back was turned, Marie and Stella exchanged worried glances.

❧❧❧❧

Sarah walked out of the First Bank and Trust on the square and headed west to the far corner, where she had parked her car in front of the title and trust place where she had once worked part time before P.J. was born. She had been hired through unabashed nepotism, as the owners were her father's cousins. They had hired her on to do light office work, but she was let go when they sold the business. Now, every time she passed it, she gave it an involuntary sneer. She was just reaching her car when she heard someone say her name in a light, feminine, questioning manner, and she turned to see who sought her out. She was startled to see the woman she knew as Ma'am standing behind her on the sidewalk, dressed much as she had been that embarrassing day in the park, in jeans, a T-shirt, this time a yellow one, sunglasses that hid her eyes, and a cap, further obscuring her face. Sarah felt overdressed as she stood there in her best black slacks, owing to the chilly October weather, and dark purple blouse, as well as one of her favorite pairs of black heels.

"Ms. Burgess?"

"Oh. Hello." Sarah reached up and put a stray tendril of hair behind her ear, which had worked itself loose from the bun she had put it in before she left the house.

"I wasn't sure that was you until I caught up with you. You look lovely. Special day?" Ma'am smiled at her and removed her glasses, then promptly squinted in the afternoon sun.

"Um, thank you. N-no, not a special day, not really. Just a…just an interview."

"Job interview?"

Sarah nodded.

"Ah. Where at?"

Ma'am seemed happy to just stand there and make idle conversation with her, as if they were old friends. Sarah was not sure how to proceed. She gestured vaguely behind her with her thumb. "Just the…at the bank. Over there." Something about Ma'am made her uneasy in the light of day. It was one thing to play to a mirror, knowing she was more than likely being watched and liking it versus standing in front of the one person she felt no compunction about teasing once a week. How does one hold a normal conversation under such circumstances? She didn't even know what to call her.

"I see. How do you think you did?"

"I don't know. I mean, I haven't worked in a

while, so I don't have much in the way of experience, just an accounting degree."

"Well, that's more than a lot of people have."

"I guess." Sarah looked thoughtful, wondering if her degree might give her the push she needed to get the job.

"Well, I hope you get it." Ma'am smiled and inclined her head as if in a bow.

"Thank you. Again."

"I seem to always make you uncomfortable every time we meet. That is obviously not my intention."

Sarah knew she was blushing; she couldn't help it. Ma'am was doing nothing wrong. She was being perfectly nice, but the normalness of the situation just seemed too much for her. "It's not you, honestly. You've been…nothing if not polite. It's me. I'm making it weird." She tried to laugh at herself as she knew she spoke the truth. She *was* the one making it weird. Involuntarily, she took a step backward, her hip bumping against her car door, wondering why she did so, as Ma'am hadn't moved toward her. She chuckled again and tried to steady herself.

"You're not making it weird at all. I can see how it can be off-putting when worlds collide like this. I'm sure you never thought they would, even though our town is small enough that it was bound to happen." Ma'am smiled, still not moving from her position on the sidewalk.

"Yes, yes, I suppose so."

"Maybe there's something I can do to make it less awkward. Can I buy you a cup of coffee, perhaps? There's a café over there." Ma'am inclined her head to the Bottomless Cup Café a little farther down on the square.

Sarah followed her nod, even though it wasn't necessary. When she looked at Ma'am again, she said the first thing that came to mind before she could stop herself. "Why?"

Obviously taken by surprise by the question, Ma'am rocked back on her heels, as if Sarah's direct question had hit her chest with the force of a blow. Recovering, she replied with a slight chuckle, "Well, I've been told it's an acceptable form of social interaction two people can engage in when they want to know each other better."

Now curious, Sarah narrowed her eyes at her. "I'm still confused as to why." Now she took a step closer and lowered her voice. "I mean, I thought we discussed the business thing before. We have a business relationship, that's all."

"I think we both know it's more than business."

Now lowering her voice to barely above a whisper, Sarah went on. "I will not deny that I take pleasure in teasing you, but I have no intention of taking what happens in that room and moving it into the real world. Are you stalking me or something?"

Ma'am stood back and put her hands in the air much more defensively than she had when they left things in the park. "No, I'm most definitely not doing that. I'm sorry if I overstepped. I promise you, my interest is sincere. I offer only friendship."

"Why?" Sarah asked again, this time in her normal tone, but with more curiosity and a growing amount of irritation.

Ma'am shrugged. "Because I like you. Because you're not afraid to give me sass. Because you love your son. And because when you smile, especially when you're giving me sass, it does wonderful things to your face. You have a very expressive face. I could say more, but that would probably make you feel uncomfortable. And I've done that enough for one day."

Sarah exhaled, visibly relaxing. "Why are you trying to charm me?"

"I wasn't. I was just being honest. Charm only works if you're not afraid of me."

"I'm not afraid of you."

Ma'am held out her arm. "Then, Ms. Burgess, will you allow me to buy you a cup of coffee?"

Sarah looked at the extended arm, then up into Ma'am's eager face, and something occurred to her. "I don't have coffee with people unless I know their name. It's kind of a rule I have."

"Ah! Of course." Ma'am doffed her hat and bowed comically. When she stood, she replied, "Renee Berry. It's a pleasure to make your acquaintance." She extended her hand to Sarah, who shook it with a smile.

"How do you do? Okay, Renee, one cup. We'll see how that goes."

Ma'am returned her hat to her head and extended her arm, and Sarah took it. "So, does this count as one of those meet cute things? I've never had one."

Sarah laughed. "More like a meet…weird."

Ma'am considered her words. "Well, better than nothing, I suppose."

※ ※ ※ ※

Sarah sat across from the woman she now knew as Renee, absentmindedly stirring the spoon in her cup with her head askance.

"You're not sure about me." Renee gave her a

gentle smile.

"I'm…cautious about you. I'm still not sure what you want from me."

"I meant what I said…friendship. You would be surprised how hard it can be to make friends in my line of work."

Renee's attempt at humor was not lost on Sarah. She finally returned her smile. "I can imagine. What makes you think we can be friends?"

"I don't know, just a feeling I have. I think we have more in common than you think."

"Like our sons."

"Yes, like our sons. Though to be fair, there's a bit of an age difference between them."

"Not just them." Sarah took a sip of her coffee, trying to hide her face, at least for a moment.

"I suppose that's true." Renee sat back into the corner of her booth and stretched her legs out on the seat, the picture of contentment and relaxation.

Sarah laughed. "Make yourself at home."

"I like to be comfortable."

"I've noticed."

"You disapprove?"

"Not at all. Just an observation." Sarah was remembering the day she had driven by and had seen Renee sitting on the porch, though she hadn't known who she was then. She remembered how Renee had been leaning back, with her feet up and eyes closed, content in the moment to just sit still. Sitting still and being peaceful was a luxury she didn't have a lot of time for lately.

"I just turned forty-seven."

"What's your point?"

"Figured you were curious."

Sarah shrugged. "I'm curious about a lot of things."

"Well, whatever I can do to satisfy your curiosity."

Sarah narrowed her eyes at her. "Yeah, don't do that. It's weird."

Renee laughed. "That seems to be the adjective of the day."

"Just trying to keep it consistent."

"Well done. But seriously, if there's something you want to ask, please do so."

"Hmm. I gotta say, this was not the interview I prepared for today. I'm not sure what to ask."

"All right then, why don't I ask you a question while you think of something to ask me?"

"Okay, go ahead."

Renee put both feet back on the ground and leaned across the table, somewhat eagerly. "So, what brings a young mother like you to my house? I'm sure you could find any number of willing partners out in the real world."

"That's easy. I'm not looking for a partner, at least not right now. My marriage ended less than a year ago, and I currently have some time, as well as a little extra cash to play with. So," she shrugged and smiled playfully, "I'm playing with it."

"Yes, you are." Renee started to grin, but at a look from Sarah, she bit her lip. She couldn't help but chuckle, however. "Was I being weird again?"

Sarah held up her thumb and index finger about an inch a part. "Just a little."

"Oh, good, not that much then."

"Okay, I think I've thought of something."

"Go ahead."

"How did you get started in your line of work?"

Renee sat back in her seat and considered Sarah for a moment before she answered. Finally, she said, "Ah, my tragic backstory."

Sarah made a face. "Don't be an ass."

Renee looked chagrined. "Sorry." She cleared her throat, then gave a true, though cryptic answer. "Let's just say it was nepotism."

"Wait, like you were recruited by a relative?" Sarah's voice involuntarily rose an octave or two on the last word, but she couldn't help it. The very idea appalled her.

"No, not exactly. Just someone I knew."

"Hmm. Okay. How old were you?"

"The first time? Seventeen."

"How old were they?"

Renee exhaled and looked off to the side. "Mid-twenties."

"Mid-twenties? That's statutory rape!"

Renee put up her hand while nervously looking around the café. "No, it's not. I was old enough to consent, according to state law. It's okay." Despite herself, she couldn't help but laugh.

Sarah glanced around the café and noticed several heads turned in their general direction. She caught the stare of one particular woman across the way and curled her lip like a snarling dog. After giving her another look of disapproval, the other woman went back to her own meal.

Renee was enjoying a good laugh. "I should hire you for protection."

Glancing around at the woman again and taking in anyone else who had given them a look of disapproval, Sarah's next words were said at a volume meant for the whole room to hear. "Well, people just need to mind their own fucking business."

Renee wiped a tear out of her eye. "Oh, goodness. We definitely have to make coffee a regular thing."

Sarah turned back to her companion and gave her a radiant smile. "Oh, most definitely. And always here."

"Well, it has already been established that you like an audience."

This time, it was Sarah's turn to laugh.

"I do like to see you smile."

Jame sat in her favorite chair downstairs, reading her book and trying to ignore the occasional stares from her coworkers, as well as the clients who were occasionally walking through. The male clients never seemed to know how to talk to her or even if they should. And she preferred it that way. At least they left her alone. This afternoon, as she sat there reading, two of the other women, Amy and Rayne, came through in animated conversation and sat on the sofa on the other side of Jame. She kept reading, ignoring them, until she caught a piece of their conversation, and her ears perked up, though she continued to turn pages.

"So, they were having coffee together? Like a date date?" The two women sat, half turned in each other's direction, both wearing casual clothes and no makeup. They had already worked and were done for the day.

"Totally looked that way. They looked really cozy."

"I just can't imagine Ma'am on a date. And with

a client!"

"I know, it's so weird. And with that Sarah woman. She's like young enough to be her daughter." Amy crinkled her face in disgust, and the women broke into laughter.

Jame kept her head down and continued to pretend to read. Ma'am and Sarah? She knew Sarah took great pleasure in playing up to the mirror to tease Ma'am, but she couldn't see them dating. For her, it wasn't so much the age difference that made it seem odd, more so the idea that Ma'am would be interested in someone other than her. For months, Ma'am had been obsessed with her, always asking for her, giving her longing looks that Jame was convinced she wasn't supposed to see, to lately asking for her less and barely giving her a look. If it was true, if Ma'am and Sarah were dating, was Ma'am only watching them now because of Sarah? Was Sarah only meeting with her because it was part of some sex game between her and Ma'am? But that didn't make any sense. If Ma'am wanted Jame to join in, she would have just said so. Jame wondered just who was pulling the strings.

"I hear they totally made a scene at the café."

"Gross. What happened to being discreet?" Amy asked indignantly.

Rayne shrugged. "I don't know. I guess that only counts if you're a priest or the mayor."

"Double standard much?"

"For real." Rayne turned to Jame to ask her next question.

"What do you think about that, Jame?"

Startled to hear her name, Jame looked over at the smiling women on the sofa. "I'm sorry, what?"

"About your best client and Ma'am dating?

About not being Ma'am's favorite anymore?" Rayne asked with a touch of obvious malice.

"I have no opinion on what anyone does, I just work here." Jame marked her place in the book, then promptly stood to leave. Before doing so, however, she turned to the women and said, "I'd be careful of gossip if I were you. I don't think the woman who signs your checks would appreciate it too much if she heard you talking shit about her in her own house like this."

"Fuck off, teacher's pet!"

Without saying anything further, Jame gave Amy a small nod as she left the room, working hard to hide her smirk. Some days, it was like living in a sorority house, and Jame had never cared much for sorority girls. She needed fresh air. She returned her book to her room and quickly changed into clothes more suitable for walking, then grabbed a light jacket and headed outside. They were only a couple of miles from town, an easy walk, if she wanted to head in that direction. If, instead, she was to head east, she would find recently harvested corn and soybean fields, along with a stray horse or two. They weren't as far out of town as some townspeople wished they were, but they were nowhere near schools or parks or anywhere else that made parents nervous, so Jame knew Ma'am was left alone about her business. Which is the way it should be. Jame just wished the women of the house were as indifferent to what Ma'am did with her time as the locals seemed to be.

Jame headed west instead, not intending to walk all the way into town, maybe only half that distance. Ma'am's property was separated from her closest neighbor by a crudely fenced acre of overgrown

Kentucky bluegrass, which Jame had been surprised to see grew this far north. She stopped a few feet from the fence and saw her, one of the most beautiful creatures she had ever seen. Tall and beautiful, with a mane the same shade of dark brown as hers. She saw Jame looking at her and sauntered over to the fence. Jame, smiling, walked closer and reached out to pet her.

"Hello, sweet girl. I wish I knew your name. Horses don't exactly wear name tags, though. I hope your human named you something cool, like Whiskey or Mahogany. Okay, admittedly, I'm not good with horse names, but either way, you deserve a cool name. You're a cool horse. Yes, you are. You're so cool. And beautiful, of course. Next time, I'll try to remember to bring you some sugar. Would you like that? Would you like some sugar?"

"It's her favorite, but if you do that, she'll probably never leave you alone after that. You'll have to bring her some every time you walk by."

Jame turned and saw a young woman about her age standing on her left. She hadn't noticed her approach. She quickly took in the woman's sturdy boots and faded, dirty jeans and stained T-shirt, along with her sweaty blond hair pulled back in a loose but serviceable ponytail. She was cute, she supposed, in a girl-next-door, little sister kind of way. "Well, that wouldn't be too bad. There are worse things. What's her name?"

The other woman studied Jame for a moment before answering. "Her name's Godiva."

"Like the chick who rode naked on a horse? That Godiva?"

"No, like the chocolate."

"Like the...oh, that's funny!"

"It was either that or Dark Roast."

Jame wasn't sure if the woman was kidding or not, as she didn't crack a smile. Then, she saw the corner of her mouth move and realized she was trying hard not to. "You're joking, aren't you?"

"Wow, can't get anything by you. You must have gone to college or something."

"Well, yeah." Jame suddenly seemed unsure of herself and thought the woman might be threatened by her. She wasn't sure how to proceed.

"Relax, Ivy, it's cool."

"Ivy? My name's not Ivy. It's Jame. Why'd you call me Ivy?"

"Cause you look like Ivy League to me, the way I've seen you dressed most of the time. I just figured you weren't from around here."

"I'm not, I'm from the city," Jame replied, stretching the truth a bit.

"No, really?" She put her hand to her chest and pretended to look shocked.

"You're mocking me."

"You city girls sure are smart."

Despite herself, Jame was laughing. "Sometimes. Hey, what's your name, anyway?"

"I'm flattered to be remembered. It's Julie. I'd shake your hand, but..." She gestured vaguely to the barn behind her house that Jame hadn't taken the time to notice before. "...I wouldn't want to get you dirty."

Jame chuckled, thinking, *You have no idea.* What she said was, "Well, my mother always said I'm washable." Jame stuck out her hand, but Julie didn't take it.

"Nah, I don't think so. I gotta go. See ya later,

Ivy." Julie smiled before she turned and left.

Jame spoke as Julie was walking away, but as her words came out of her mouth, they didn't seem loud enough to travel very far. "It's...Jame." Shaking her head, Jame looked back at Godiva and gave her a small wave, then continued her aimless journey toward town.

Instead of the woman she just met, her mind drifted back to the conversation between Amy and Rayne. It still seemed hard to believe that Ma'am would be dating anyone, especially a client. The entire time she'd been at the house, she hadn't seen Ma'am date. Of course, she wasn't with her all the time. Ma'am still left every Tuesday, eleven in the morning, like clockwork, going who knows where. Which seemed odd. If Ma'am couldn't go to the café with Sarah without the women of the house talking about it, how could she get out on Tuesdays without anyone knowing where she was going? Unless they did. Maybe everyone in the house already knew where Ma'am went on Tuesdays, and that was the one thing about her they all agreed, collectively, not to gossip about. As if they were all complicit in some secret. But, Jame reasoned, that didn't seem possible, human nature being what it is. It helps people form and solidify the group dynamic. With ten women working in the house, it only seemed natural that they would start talking about what Ma'am did with her Tuesdays at some point. Or maybe they had been but had decided Jame didn't need to know. She kicked a dirt clod and shook her head. She was starting to sound paranoid. All these thoughts about gossip and paranoia just fed her ego, and she knew no good could come from it.

The farther she walked, the houses started to

come closer together, and the outer edges of the town took shape. One house, whose unseen owner Jame had taken to calling The Patriot, was of a more modern style than the Dragonfly and had a flagpole in the front yard, proudly displaying the Stars and Stripes, except on inclement weather days. Some days, she had walked past and seen the flag at half-staff, and if it wasn't Veterans or Memorial Day, it always made her wonder if some old soldier had died. Whenever she saw it, she would bow her head in a moment of solidarity.

She walked on. There was so much life happening in these houses. There was evidence of children in the yards of some of them, with various toys and bikes strewn about in a haphazard way, even though she never saw the owners of the bikes. She always thought it was a shame that kids didn't play outside much anymore, preferring to stay indoors, hiding from the sun. Growing up, her mother had made sure Jame and her brothers went outside and stayed out for a few hours, playing in the dirt and inventing their own fun.

Rick and Tony had always been protective of her, standing up for her when the older and bigger kids picked on her, preferring to be the only ones to have the privilege of teasing her or bopping her a good one. It taught her to stand up for herself, for which only later she would be grateful. They had both joined the Army after high school, and she hardly ever saw them, which made it easy to lie to them about what she was currently doing. They had never been to the town she now called home, so they didn't know Ma'am or the Dragonfly. They had no reason not to believe her when she told them that she was taking a couple of gap years off school to work for some rich lady who paid her well enough to cover med school. If they had their suspicions, they kept them to themselves. She saw them at Christmas, and they teased her about dressing better than them. She would rub their stubbled heads and tease them about also having better hair than them. She missed her family and hated lying to them, but she knew she could never tell them about this time in her life. They would never understand.

Maybe the same was true with Ma'am, who was always secretive about herself. Jame had only tried to ask about Ma'am's past that one time, the first weekend they were together. But after getting shot down by Ma'am's icy resistance, she had backed down and not asked again. She suddenly wondered if Ma'am missed her own family, if they knew how she had made her money and how her life had turned out. Maybe that was what she did on Tuesdays, saw her family. Maybe that's why, if the other women knew, they never spoke of it. They were all tight-lipped about their families. She knew she wasn't the only one who lied about her life to her parents. Maybe there was an unspoken code among the women in her profession against gossiping or pressing too hard about family matters, while gossip of other sorts was okay. Definitely something to think about. As Jame neared the park, the layout of the book she was intending to write about the women of the Dragonfly took shape in her head.

Chapter Eleven

"Grandmother asked about you this week."

Ma'am raised an eyebrow at Ian. They were at a new restaurant today, one a few towns over. Ian had heard good things about it and wanted to share it with her, he said. Ma'am knew the truth or thought she did. He was tired of the knowing stares from their fellow diners who knew who she was and what she did for a living but never had the courage to say anything to her face. She had long since gotten used to their judgment and was able to shrug it off, but it was harder for him, she knew. "Oh? What did she ask?"

"She misses you."

"She said that?"

Ian hesitated. "Well, not in so many words."

The corners of Ma'am's mouth lifted in an attempted smirk, but she squelched it. "So, what words *did* she use?"

"She just asked how you were and said she hadn't seen you in months. She sounded sad."

Ma'am very much doubted that her mother was capable of that emotion where she was concerned. Abject disappointment, maybe. Shame, absolutely. She took a drink of her coffee and tried to be charitable. "I see. Well, I don't have a lot of free time these days. And what I do have, I'd rather spend with you." When she smiled at him, it was genuine.

He returned her smile but with a note of levity.

"I'm honored."

"You should be."

"Besides, if local rumor can be believed, I'm not the only one you've been keeping company with." He raised a questioning eyebrow at her, amused, but she wouldn't meet his gaze and instead looked down at her menu.

"You shouldn't listen to rumors."

"So, it's not true?" He leaned across the table on his elbows, almost too eager to hear about his mother's potential dating life.

She turned a page in the menu, hardly glancing at it. "You really shouldn't be this eager to learn about my personal life. It's not healthy."

"Bullshit! You're evading the question."

"No, I'm not evading the question. It's simply a nonissue."

"I don't believe you."

"As you like." She nonchalantly turned another page.

"Well, for your information, wanting to know if my mother is happy *is* my business. I wasn't trying to pry, I was just hoping that someone was bringing joy to your heart. It's been too long."

The look Ian was giving her reminded her of the look she saw on Sarah's face when she looked down at P.J., one of pure love. It was a look she didn't see on his face often, but when she did, it always grabbed her. She found herself smiling and put her hand to her chest, taken aback. "Sometimes, you really are a sweet boy. Moments like this, I see your father in you."

Ian looked surprised. "You never bring up my father. Why were you thinking of him just now? I didn't think you knew him that long."

"I didn't, but you can tell a lot about a person when you…meet them the way I meet them. Your father was sweet. You definitely get that from him. No one has ever called me sweet. At least not twice."

"That's because they don't take the time to get to know you. They only see what you allow them to see, which is all hard edges and sharp points."

"You seem terribly complimentary, like you're trying to butter me up for something. Are you trying to talk me into going to see your grandmother? Is that what you're after, son of mine?"

Ian laughed. "Would that be terrible?" Before she could respond, he went on. "Also, I was hoping you would tell me who you're dating."

Ma'am sighed and closed her menu, having made up her mind, but also exasperated with him. "I'm not dating anyone." He started to protest, but she cut him off. "I'm telling you the truth. If these rumors are about what I think they're about, I happened to run into an acquaintance the other day, and we went for coffee. I can't help that the conclusions people drew from that were that I was dating someone. As you say, it's been awhile. Should that day come, you'll be the first to know. After all, I can't have you relying on rumor for all of your information."

"Fine, don't tell me." He smiled at her.

"Ian Christopher! You take your mother at her word, or I'll leap across this table and smack the black right out of you."

At that moment, their waitress walked up to the table. Her question died on her lips when she heard Ma'am's exclamation. "Hi! Ready to or…der?"

Ian, with a straight face, looked up at the startled young woman and waved his hand as if the whole conversation was of no consequence. "And she means it. I used to be darker than this."

The waitress looked between the two of them, not sure how to respond.

Ma'am threw her head back and laughed uproariously.

༄༄༄༄

"So, are you going to tell me where you're going?" Cecelia Berry stood in front of the window in what had been Renee's old room but was now being occupied by her newborn grandson. Renee was standing at his crib, rubbing his back, smiling down at him as he slept.

Renee whispered back in reply, "I have to get back to work. I've been gone too long."

"You didn't exactly answer my question, Renee." She turned to face her daughter, her arms crossed over her chest, a determined look on her face. "You haven't answered any of my questions. Is it so wrong to be concerned for my only child?"

Renee looked away from the sleeping miracle long enough to afford her mother a brief glance. "Of course not. There are just some things I'd rather not talk about. I wish you could understand that." She looked back down at Ian again, smiling in wonder at his perfect toes and his chubby legs and his curly black hair. He was beautiful. She still couldn't believe that she had been able to create such a perfect little human.

"Why do I get the feeling that what you're hiding from me is more than just a privacy issue?"

"I never said I was hiding anything from you,

Mother. Not in so many words."

"Not in so many words? Then what words would you use?"

"Do we have to do this now? In here?"

"I figured this was the perfect place to have this conversation. Maybe remind you of what's the most important."

"I already know he's the most important. Why do you think I'm leaving him here? Why do you think I'm going back to work? Everything I do is for him now. I'm not being selfish."

"Really? Because that's the word I would use."

"He's asleep, let's have this conversation in the other room. I don't want to wake him." She didn't wait for her mother's reply; she simply walked out of the room and headed downstairs to the living room. Her mother followed in her wake.

Once they reached the living room, Cecilia resumed her normal tone of voice. "I'm not stupid, you know?"

"I never said you were."

"I just figured you thought I was, that you thought you were keeping some big secret from me, but I've had my suspicions since you sat on my couch and told me you were pregnant."

"Suspicions about what?" Renee asked with trepidation. Though she had never thought her mother stupid, she had never considered that the truth would occur to her. The thought that she might have figured it out scared her.

"I was always good at math, you know. It was my best subject. Even I can put two and two together, and the answer I came up with was not a good one. Not a good one at all."

"And what did your math problem tell you?"

Cecelia shook her head, as if the thoughts inside were so distasteful she could dislodge them with the movement. "I can't even say it. Just the thought is too disturbing. If I say the words, put them out there, that'll make them real. And I'm really hoping I'm wrong."

"Would it make you feel any better if I said that I'm not doing anything I don't want to do?"

"No!" At her raised voice, both stopped talking for a moment and looked to the ceiling, waiting and listening. When they were satisfied Ian hadn't been disturbed, Cecelia resumed talking. "No, it would not be better. I'd prefer you not be doing it at all. I mean, do you actually like what you're doing? You couldn't possibly."

"Are you really concerned with my job satisfaction? Is that really your biggest concern?"

"Of course not, smart mouth. I just can't believe my own child would risk her own soul for…for…this life of sin."

Renee rolled her eyes. "Oh, geez, don't get all self-righteous on me." Before her mother could protest, she went on. "Besides, even Jesus was cool with prostitutes. If it's okay with Jesus, why can't it be okay with you?"

"That is a misinterpretation of scripture. If you had paid attention in church, you would know that. Prostitutes sought him out, it's not as if they were part of his disciples."

"Well, maybe they should have been."

Cecelia took a deep breath, exhaling slowly. "I don't want to argue the Bible with you. You obviously have strayed far from your faith."

Renee muttered, "That's an understatement."

"I just don't see why you can't give that up now and do something more befitting an unwed mother. Something your son can be proud of. Instead of... instead of..."

Renee crossed her arms over her chest and looked at her mother with challenge in her eyes. "A whore?"

They stared each other down for the longest moment before finally Cecelia broke the connection by saying, "If you go back to this life, I will never forgive you. And I won't associate with you unless it's regarding your son. Your son, who I will gladly raise, if it means keeping him away from the sinful life you're leading. Do I make myself clear?"

Renee breathed through her nose for a moment, before responding. When she did so, every word was clipped. "Crystal. Clear. Mother. I will send money every month, and I'll visit every Tuesday."

"Why Tuesdays?"

"Never mind, just accept that I will never miss a Tuesday. He has my word. And I promise not to bring shame on you by letting your precious congregation know how I make my living."

"Fine. When are you leaving?"

"I'll leave in the morning."

Cecelia said nothing, only nodded in response before turning to walk out of the room.

"I'm sorry, Mother," Renee whispered at her retreating back, but she wasn't sure if she had heard her or not as she didn't pause her stride.

Sarah stood in the hallway outside P.J.'s classroom with the other parents, awaiting her turn with Ms. Rosie, as the kids called their teacher. P.J. had pulled her over to a display of Halloween decorations to show her the pumpkin he had made, wherein he had carefully written his name in big, bold, black crayon. She had dutifully exclaimed over it, barely able to take in the rest of the display of orange and black and childish script, before he dragged her farther down the hall to show her more of his handiwork. She made sure to keep ahold of his hand amidst the crowd, which wasn't easy, as he was so eager to show her everything his teacher had painstakingly hung on the walls near his classroom. When he had nothing else to show her, she walked him closer to his classroom and stood a few feet from the door.

She noticed most of the other children seemed to have both parents present, though it was difficult to tell for sure, as several of the little ones were running about, playing with their friends. Normally, she would have let P.J. do the same, but she wanted him nearby when their time came so that she could get it over with. She was still steaming that Patrick had refused to come, claiming parent/teacher conferences were a mom's domain and that he had no place there. His whole attitude toward P.J. had changed since he moved out, and it pissed her off. Since then, he seemed more content to only interact with their son on his scheduled weekends and nothing else. Even though she had told him that, despite the custody order, he could see his son anytime he wanted. The divorce had nothing to do with P.J., and she didn't want to keep him from his son, but how was she going to convince her son of this if his own father refused to take more than a passing interest in him?

"Your first time?"

Sarah turned to the woman who was now standing on her left. She was another young mother, early thirties perhaps, with a short, serviceable brown bob of a haircut, dressed in slacks and comfortable loafers and a button-up blouse. Inwardly, Sarah thought of the woman's getup as "standard-issue soccer mom" and glanced down at her own attire of white dress with black polka dots, with a wide collar, reminiscent of the fifties. Every time she wore it, she paired it with red lipstick and heels and put her hair in a bun. However, considering where she was, she had toned down her lipstick and wore shorter heels, and she wore her long brown hair down on her shoulders. She just loved the dress, it made her feel classically sexy. Plus, P.J. loved the polka dots, so it had been an easy choice. Nevertheless, she felt a little overdressed. She smiled at the woman and asked, "That obvious?"

The woman chuckled. "A little bit. It's all right, it gets easier. Actually, that's a lie. These things are always awful, you just get less nervous. Trust me, a glass of wine always helps."

"Before or after?"

"During." They laughed together.

Noticing the other woman didn't have a child next to her, Sarah asked, "So, which one is yours?"

The woman pointed to a little blond girl wearing a pink tutu and unicorn tights. "The fashion victim over there. That's Chrissy, my youngest."

Sarah followed her finger to the girl in question and smiled. "She's adorable. She definitely has her own sense of style."

"That's one way of putting it. I'm Deanna Roberts, by the way." She held out her hand, and Sarah shook it.

"Sarah Burgess. And this is P.J." She smiled down at him as he turned to Deanna and politely said hello.

"Nice to meet you, P.J. You too, P.J.'s mom. That's who you'll be from here on out now, just so you know."

"I don't mind. I've been called worse."

Deanna looked her over briefly, then muttered, "I'll bet."

Sarah caught the change in Deanna's tone and wondered at the sudden snideness. She narrowed her eyes at her. "I'm sorry?"

Deanna cleared her throat. "Nothing."

Irritated now, Sarah turned to Deanna and demanded, trying to keep her voice level, "No, clearly, you meant something by that comment. What did you mean?"

Deanna averted her eyes and looked about the hallway as if looking for a way to escape the conversation. "I'm sorry, I really didn't mean anything by it."

"Clearly you did. I don't know you, yet you seem to have an opinion of me, based on what, I don't know. Is it because I'm divorced, is that it?"

"No, of course not."

"Mommy, there's my friend. Can I go say hi?"

Momentarily startled, Sarah looked down at P.J. and collected herself. "What?"

He pointed. "Over there. That's Tommy and his moms. Can I go say hi?"

"Okay, but nowhere else. Stay where I can see you." P.J. ran off down the hall toward his friend, and Sarah turned back to Deanna Roberts and crossed her arms over her chest.

"Look, this is a small town and people talk."

"And?"

Now clearly uncomfortable, Deanna stammered, "Sometimes, when you associate with…certain people…word gets around, and people make assumptions. That's all I'm saying."

"Certain people? What people?" Sarah thought she knew where Deanna was going with the conversation, but she wanted to make her say it.

"Just, you know, people with a certain reputation. People who…people who…live on the outskirts of town, if you know what I mean."

Sarah had to fight the grin that was building. She had a sudden urge to crush this soccer mom under the heel of her shoe. "Oh, I know what you mean. And if I'm being perfectly honest, I'd rather hang out with 'people who live on the outskirts of town' than an alcoholic soccer mom in sensible shoes." Before Deanna could think of something to say in her defense, Sarah went on. "Now if you'll excuse me, I have to go retrieve my son." She turned on her heel, her skirt swishing about her legs in a satisfying way, and walked the few feet down the hall to where P.J. was in animated conversation with a little brown-haired boy with his smiling parents standing nearby.

Chapter Twelve

Ma'am sat at her desk Wednesday afternoon going over the house's budget. The first of the month always meant salaries and household bills, tasks she hated. Over the years, she had learned how to do payroll and pay taxes and order things that were needed to keep the house running, even though she found it boring and wished she trusted someone enough to hire her to do it. Between the legal issues of her business, as well as the lack of trust she had for everyone in the accounting profession, she had long since decided she was stuck with the task. She sighed dejectedly as she pulled up another spreadsheet, this one displaying the names of all the clients who had honored her house with their patronage in October. She paused when she saw Sarah's name. There it was, every Wednesday, two in the afternoon. Sarah Burgess for Jame.

She glanced at the bottom of her monitor screen: 2:07. Sarah was downstairs now in Jame's room. Probably getting undressed at this very moment. Ma'am briefly wondered what new thing Sarah would do this week in the hopes of catching her attention. She sighed again but for a much different reason than before. She hoped Jame knew how lucky she was.

Ma'am dropped the window with the spreadsheet to the bottom of her screen and pulled open the picture file on her desktop. She scrolled the camera shots until she came to the one with Sarah and her son. Ma'am always went back to the smile. It was so genuine. It drew her in every time. She wasn't sure how long she sat there with her chin in her hand, smiling at the picture, partly feeling ridiculous, when her office door opened and Stella walked in with a cleaning bucket in one hand and a vacuum in the other. Ma'am quickly closed the pictures and pulled her spreadsheet back up.

"Oh, hey. I figured you'd be…well, you know." Stella smiled at her boss as she closed the door behind her and set the bucket on the floor.

Ma'am smiled back at her. "No time for fun and games today, it's the end of the month. Much to do."

"Uh-huh." Stella grinned as she reached under Ma'am's desk to the trashcan to grab the partially full bag, nonchalantly shoving aside Ma'am's legs without reverence.

Amused, Ma'am said, "Oh, I'm sorry. Don't let me get in your way."

Standing back up, Stella waved her hand in the air. "I'll work around you. Wouldn't be the first time I was under someone's desk with them."

"True, but that someone was never me."

Stella sighed mockingly. "Worse luck for me. But if it would get me a raise…Marie and I are trying to save for retirement, you know?" She gave Ma'am a playful wink as she crawled back under the desk to replace the trash can she had emptied.

Ma'am scooted her chair back to give her more room. "Sorry, love, I don't diddle my staff." Despite her words, she returned Stella's wink and gave her a playful pat on the bottom, which caused Stella to jump and bang her head on the underside of the desk.

Stella came out holding her head and cussing. "Staff, my ass, you used-up whore. That hurt."

Ma'am laughed. "You must be out of practice."

"It has been awhile. What are you doing up here mooning over pictures, anyway? I thought you had work to do. Unless bookkeeping is not what I thought it was."

"I wasn't 'mooning' over anything. I was doing the budget. See?" Ma'am pointed to the spreadsheet on the screen that displayed the previous month's appointments.

"Mm-hmm." Stella set about dusting the top of Ma'am's desk, but it was clear she was just going through the motions.

"I just finished payroll. Would you like to see, Mother, to prove I've been doing my homework?"

"Oh, no need. I know what I saw."

"What you saw was me being a good girl."

"Really?" Stella asked knowingly.

"Really."

"Then what's this?" Before Ma'am could move or speak to protest, Stella dove for the computer mouse and clicked on the dropped-down picture files. The first one to pop up was Sarah's. Stella looked back at Ma'am with a triumphant smile on her face. "Oh, my god, do my eyes deceive me, or do I see a blush on them cheeks?"

Unable to hide her grin, Ma'am replied, "Back off, short stuff. Go vacuum something. And get away from my computer." She shoved Stella aside playfully.

Stella dutifully stepped aside. When she spoke, she spoke with sincerity. "Honey, you don't have to hide this. You have a crush on someone, I think it's cute."

"I do *not* have a crush on anyone. Get back to work." Ma'am growled.

"Methinks the lady doth protest too much."

"If you're going to quote Shakespeare at me instead of doing your job, at least get it right. The line is, 'The lady doth protest too much, methinks.' Everyone always says it wrong."

Stella rolled her eyes. "That's it, Final Jeopardy, I'm out of here." Stella picked up her cleaning implements and the small bag of trash she had gathered from under Ma'am's desk, then turned on her heel, pretending to be in a huff.

"If you want that raise, come back when you don't smell like bleach." Ma'am grinned at Stella's retreating form.

Stella turned back around to make her reply. "Now we wouldn't want you breaking your rule about 'diddling the staff,' would we?"

"I can make an exception."

Stella huffed. "I guess the women don't count as staff."

Ma'am chuckled. "They're…employees."

Stella scoffed. "Whatever helps you sleep at night."

"Like a baby." Ma'am grinned.

Finally, Stella left, and Ma'am turned back to the picture that was still taking over her screen, then looked down at the time again. 2:15. Taking one last look at the picture, Ma'am sighed, then slammed her laptop closed and abruptly stood to leave her office, but not before grabbing her camera out of her bottom desk drawer.

༄༄༄༄༄

When Sarah and Jame were finished with their play, Sarah took her time getting dressed, trying to make it as sensual as possible, while Jame lay back on the bed with a sheet draped over her lap and her bare chest exposed, an amused look on her face. Sarah caught Jame's eye in the mirror and smiled. "Why are you looking at me like that?"

"How was I looking at you?"

"I don't know, maybe like how I look at my son. Lovingly, yet tickled at whatever he just said or did." Sarah shrugged as she reached down to tie her shoe, the sensuality gone from her movements now, as she wasn't sure how she could possibly make shoe tying sexy.

"I'm sorry, I didn't mean to put that thought in your head."

"Then what did you mean?" Sarah stood and walked to Jame's side of the bed, her arms crossed over her chest, a smile playing at her lips.

Jame sat up and swung her legs to the floor, then reached out and pulled Sarah to her playfully, her arms around her waist. Sarah laughed and, caught off guard, put her hands on Jame's shoulders to steady herself. "I've had girlfriends who asked less questions." Jame pushed up Sarah's shirt and kissed her stomach. Sarah squealed in surprise.

"Stop that, we don't have time to start again. Hey! That tickles!" She gently pushed Jame off her. "Was that your tongue?"

"You should know what my tongue feels like by now." Jame growled as she continued to kiss her way up Sarah's stomach, bringing her fingers up to slide under her bra.

Sarah moaned deep in her throat, then almost self-consciously found her gaze straying to the mirror. She wondered what Renee was thinking right now. She had a good feeling she knew what she was doing, and that thought made her smile. As Jame's lips finally found their quarry and were now paying attention to her left nipple, she let her mind wander to different lips and someone else's fingers on her midsection. What would that be like? Renee had far more experience than Jame. Sarah had a feeling that the older woman could bring her to new heights of sexual fulfillment. Too bad she was retired from taking clients, Sarah thought. Suddenly feeling self-conscious for reasons she couldn't explain, she took a step back and demanded clearly, "Stop."

Jame did so immediately, but not without looking up at Sarah with a confused expression on her face. "Everything okay?"

"Yeah, it's fine. I just need to go. My hour's about up. Gotta go be a mom." She afforded Jame a small smile and shrugged.

"Yes, of course. I'll see you next week."

Sarah glanced at the mirror before responding with hesitation. "I…I…might not be able to make it next week. I might have to do a thing…just a thing. We'll see."

Jame followed Sarah's gaze as it strayed to the mirror. "I don't think she's in there."

Startled, Sarah asked, "What? What are you talking about?"

"Ma'am. I don't think she's back there today. She's been in her office all day working on the budget. Her least favorite thing."

"Oh."

"You like it when she watches, don't you?" Jame looked at Sarah askance, interested in her answer.

Sarah's cheeks instantly flamed. "Well, it definitely adds something to the experience, not going to lie. Yeah, I guess I do."

"Do you wish it was her in here instead of me?" Jame didn't ask the question with jealousy or insecurity, only curiosity.

Feeling caught and as if Jame had read her mind, Sarah's cheeks reddened darker than before. Not knowing how to answer, her mouth hung open for a moment, before she could think to say, "I'm a curious person, can't help it. Nothing wrong with variety."

Jame smiled. "If that were true, you'd have tried other women in the house by now."

Sarah came forward and gave Jame a quick peck on the lips before backing away, lest Jame try to entice her to stay again. "And sometimes, variety is overrated. Now I really gotta go. Later." Sarah planted one more quick kiss, this time on Jame's forehead, before walking out the door. Once there was a door between them, Sarah leaned against it and sighed. She glanced at the door down the hall, the one that must lead into the room behind the mirror, and shook her head, laughing at herself.

≫·≫·≋·≪·≪

After Sarah closed the door behind herself, Jame stood and walked to the bathroom to clean up. Unlike most days, she hurried through the shower and dressed quickly, then grabbed her laptop from her bedside table. Ignoring the unmade bed, she promptly sat in her chair in the corner and pulled up her journal.

Sarah was more distracted than usual today by the mirror. Not that she played up to it as much, just that she couldn't seem to take her eyes off it for very long. Even during sex, I could tell her mind wasn't really here. Granted, that's not always uncommon. Some women come here to use me to work through the stress from their daily lives, and sometimes, I can see their minds wander, even though their bodies are engaged in something pleasurable. But this was different. Sarah wasn't distracted by her life outside this house, quite the opposite.

It almost seemed as if I had caught her in a lie when I asked if she would rather I be Ma'am. I think she thought that it would hurt my feelings if she said yes. Not at all. I know firsthand how good Ma'am can be, so I can only guess how Sarah must feel as she wonders about what I already know. And I understand that the thought of being watched can be a turn-on, that's why I haven't said anything about it before now. Who am I to say what Sarah should get out of our sessions? If touching me while imagining it were Ma'am is what she needs to do to work through whatever she's working through, then far be it from me to deny her that joy.

No, I don't know what she's dealing with in her real life, she hasn't yet felt comfortable enough to tell me her secrets. Today was the first time she mentioned having a son, but I wouldn't have expected her to bring that up. This is not the place for that. She only talked about her ex that one time, and she didn't say too much. I have no idea how long she was married, and the idea of her having a child never occurred to me, though I suppose it should have. She wears no ring, but I've seen the callus on the underside of the appropriate *finger*, the kind only a long-worn ring can cause.

There's been more talk in the house about Ma'am and Sarah meeting for coffee, though the way the story has spread, you'd think it was more than that. What had probably just been a chance meeting in a public place has blossomed into a full-blown relationship of epic proportions. One of the women claims she saw them kissing in the park, then another one upped the ante and swore she saw Ma'am sneaking Sarah into the house a couple of nights ago. I'm sure it's just a bunch of bored women with nothing better to talk about, making up rumors to entertain themselves, as well as make Ma'am seem more human.

She does have an almost ethereal quality about her. She doesn't talk about herself at all, so we're left to wonder and make up stories to satisfy our own innate curiosities. It's only natural to want to know her better. Just as it's only natural for her to hold herself from us. She's not trying to be our friend, nor us hers. However, I almost hope there is some truth to the rumors. Sometimes, I think Ma'am is sad and lonely, Sarah, too, for that matter. It would be nice if they were able to find some sort of peace and love here, in this house, where normally love has no place. Maybe I'm more of a dreamer and less of the scientist I'd like to be. But who doesn't want to find love?

Jame read over her words, correcting what typos she saw, then saved it with the day's date and shut down her laptop. She sat in her chair for a while longer, looking across the room at the mirror, but not really seeing it. She, too, wished Ma'am was in the little room as she felt a sudden urge to go to her and give her solace, though she wasn't sure why.

Chapter Thirteen

Renee stood on her mother's doorstep, trying to control the trembling in her knees. She tried to tell herself that this was just another Tuesday, it shouldn't be any different than any other one, but it wasn't working. She had something to say to her mother, and her mother wasn't going to be happy about it. Well, that's too bad, I'm doing it, she thought. She straightened her spine, cocked her head back, and steadied her knees. Finally, she turned the knob and stepped inside. Her mother was sitting in her favorite recliner, pushed all the way back, the TV tuned to the same soap opera she had watched since Renee was in grade school. She glanced at Renee when she walked in.

"Hey. Ian's in his room. But you know that." Cecilia's face didn't show any signs of welcome, nor did she move out of her chair. Instead, she turned back to the TV, clearly done with the conversation, and, in effect, Renee.

Regardless of the chilly reception, Renee took a step forward, thinking with a sigh, *Where angels fear to tread...* Determination to complete her mission still intact, she spoke aloud, "Mother, there's something I have to tell you."

With withering sharpness, she asked, "What is it now, Renee?"

"I'm moving back. I already have a house. I

bought the old Henson place. You know, the big Victorian." She needlessly gestured behind her in a vague way.

Cecilia narrowed her eyes as she looked at Renee. "Of course, I know it. How could you afford such a place? Robbing banks now, too?"

"No, I'm not. I saved every penny I made. Even made investments. Some of them paid off."

Her mother scoffed. "What do you know about investments and money? You never wanted to listen when I talked shop at home, said accounting bored you to death."

"I read up on the stock market. Look, it doesn't matter. The point is, I'm going to be here now, and I can see him on a more regular basis. In fact, I was thinking…" Renee braved a step closer, but before she could get another word out, her mother stood and came toward her with her finger pointed.

"Don't you dare! Don't you even think about taking him away from me. He needs stability. He's staying with me!"

"He's *my* son! It may have taken me ten years before I could get to a place in my life where I could take care of him, but I'm there now! And I'm taking my son!" Renee turned to go up the stairs, but her mother stopped her by grabbing her arm. "Let go of me."

"You are not taking him to live in some house of ill repute. He needs to stay in a good Christian home."

Now, it was Renee's turn to scoff. "A good Christian home," she said with a chuckle she didn't mean.

"You will not mock the Lord in my house, Jezebel!"

Renee's smile was almost sad. "If only I were destroying prophets, but I'm not, I'm just trying to raise my son." She turned around again and was able to place one foot on the bottom step before her mother reached out for her again.

"Renee Elizabeth Berry, you so much as take him off my property, and I will sue you for custody. I'd get it, too, and you know it! I've only let things go this long because you were keeping your nose out of things and letting me raise him. This is his home. You can't just take that away from him. Despite what you might think, this has more to do with what such a move would do to him and less of what I think of the life you lead."

Renee took her foot off the step again. She now sounded defeated. "Okay, but you can't stop him from seeing me more often."

Cecilia crossed her arms over her chest. "You're damn right I will if you start taking him around all those…women."

"What makes you think there's going to be anyone else living out there?"

"Oh, please. I wasn't born yesterday. What else would you need all those rooms for? And if I can figure it out, it won't be long before the rest of the town figures it out, as well."

Renee couldn't suppress a cocky grin. "God, I hope so."

"You think they're going to let you stay? This town won't allow it. I don't know how long you think you can keep this fool idea going, considering it's illegal." Her voice went down to a whisper on the last word.

"Mother, I assure you, there's nothing illegal

about running a bed and breakfast. Perfectly legal." Renee smiled.

Cecilia closed her eyes and shook her head. "Child, I swear. You can take him for your regular Tuesday, but don't go filling his head with nonsense about living with you because it's not going to happen. We can talk about seeing you more. That's all!"

Renee sighed, the air gone out of the argument for her. "That's all," she agreed. Then she turned her head toward the stairs and raised her voice, "Ian Christopher Berry, get down here and hug your mother!" Immediately overhead, they heard the scurrying of ten-year-old feet as he ran from his room to the stairs. Renee and her mother smiled when he appeared at the top.

But their smiles were pale in comparison to the beaming one on his face when he saw his mother at the bottom. He made eye contact first, then he quickly came downstairs and practically swung himself into his mother's waiting arms, which made her stagger backward. "Hi, Mom!"

Laughing, Renee replied, "Hey, kiddo. Practicing your linebacking skills, I see. Good job, almost took me down." She kissed him on top of his head, then ruffled his unruly hair.

When he pulled out of her embrace, he immediately ran his hands through his hair. "Aw, Mom, don't mess with the 'fro. It's bad enough as it is."

Renee playfully put her arm around his neck and rubbed her hand rapidly through his hair. "I made these curls, I can mess with 'em if I want!" She and Ian were both laughing, despite his squirming to get away from her. Even her mother couldn't help but smile.

"Grandma, help! You gonna let her do that to

me?"

Cecilia stood by with her hands behind her back and a grin on her face. "Unless you ask properly."

"Ha!"

"Grandma!"

Renee stopped rubbing his head but kept her arm around his shoulders. "All right, I'll stop. Let's go spend some of my money."

"Yes!"

"Renee, you're going to spoil him."

"Well, if I do, I'm sure you can set him back on the path to righteousness. Come on, Ian." They made their way outside quickly without giving her mother a chance to respond.

※※※※

Renee drove through her old neighborhood, passing the old craftsman houses she had always admired and her mother had always coveted. Cecilia Berry, in her ever vigilant quest for respectability, had wanted one and had tried to put a bid in for one when they first moved to the neighborhood after the divorce, but her bid had been rejected, and she had never forgiven the Wisnaskys for "stealing it out from under her." She had been able to secure a nice but smaller colonial a few blocks down. It had a pocket backyard with a swing set and a small vegetable patch off to one side. The front porch was bordered by rose bushes laden with pink roses that bloomed in November, and there was a flowering white geranium hanging from a basket on the porch. When she finally pulled into the driveway of her mother's house, Renee sat in her car and looked at all that respectability for a moment, thinking, *She tried to give me an idyllic childhood, and I couldn't stand it.* Just as her thoughts began to lean toward sympathy for a woman who had never seemed to have any for her, not that she wanted it, she shook the mood off, pulled her key out of the ignition, got out of the car, and went up to the door and knocked.

After a minute, her mother opened the door. When she saw who was standing on her front porch, a look of confusion crossed her face, and she blurted, "Renee?"

"Yes, Mother, it's me." Renee lowered her Elton John sunglasses to show her eyes.

"What are you doing here?"

"I came to visit. It's Tuesday." Even to her own ears, the words didn't seem to hold much meaning, so her mother's further look of confusion came as no surprise.

"Ian doesn't live with me anymore, he moved out after college. I thought you knew that."

"I do, I came to see you."

"Me?"

"Yes. Is that okay?"

Cecilia shrugged as she moved aside to let Renee enter. "I guess. I don't know why you would want to visit an old lady. Nothing exciting happening around here. Nothing that would interest you, anyway. Might as well come on in, I'm just watching my stories." Cecilia walked away from the door and back into the living room to her favorite chair and turned down the volume on a soap opera. "Might as well have a seat." She gestured vaguely to the couch.

When she saw the couch, Renee had to chuckle. "Is this the same couch we had when I was a kid?"

"You know it is."

"Why do you still have it?"

"Well, not all of us can afford to go out and buy whatever. The rest of us have to make do." Cecilia kicked her chair back and extended the footstool, keeping her gaze on the television screen.

Renee sat back into the corner of the couch, ignoring the dig from her mother. She figured it was the first of many. She turned to the TV and tried to focus on the screen, thinking that if she couldn't gain her mother's interest enough to hold a conversation, just spending time with her would be enough.

Cecilia clucked her tongue at something that happened on the screen, it obviously not taking much for her to get back into her show. "Slut."

For a moment, Renee thought the unexpected insult was for her, until she looked at her mother and realized her gaze had never left the screen. She chuckled to herself, never having heard her mother utter that word. "Why is she a slut?"

"That woman, that one who's now putting her clothes back on, which, I don't know why she bothers, sleeps with everybody. The number of marriages that woman has ruined! But it's not all her fault. The men aren't exactly dragged kicking and screaming. They're more than willing to hurt their wives. I say they're worse than she is. I mean, it doesn't make what she does right, of course."

Surprised by her mother's somewhat liberal attitude regarding the character, Renee replied, "No, it doesn't."

Cecilia looked at her with narrowed eyes. "I suppose you've known a lot of married men."

Choosing her words carefully, Renee said, "I've

known a few. Difference being that I never lured them away from anyone. And I sent them back to their wives."

Cecilia clucked her tongue again but said nothing more. Another few minutes passed in silence, then, "Now those two, they're in love. Everyone can see it, but they're still trying to hide it. It's the worst-kept secret in Duncan Falls."

Renee laughed, thinking the comment was a little too close to home, but she decided not to react otherwise.

When the commercial came on, Cecilia spoke almost wistfully. "That's all I ever wanted for you, you know? To find love and be happy. To be happier than I ever was. That's all any parent wants for their children."

Touched and surprised by her mother's words, Renee said, "I've had love in my life. And I hope to again."

"When did you have love in your life?"

"A few years ago, when Ian was still in high school. There was a woman…but it only lasted a short while. But I'm hopeful for the future. Always hopeful."

Her show had come back from the commercial, but Cecilia now ignored it. "You never told me about this woman. Ian never mentioned her."

"There was never time. But I promise, the next time there's someone worth mentioning, I'll bring her by."

"Okay. Ever since I heard about you liking girls, I wondered at what kind of woman you would date. I supposed being in your line of work you didn't need a girlfriend."

Somewhat at a loss for words, Renee stumbled

through her answer. "Well, um, sometimes, having a partner is a beautiful thing."

"That it is." Cecilia turned back to the screen. "Now that one right there lost her memory last year. She was in a car wreck. She's married, but it wasn't going well. Her husband was one of Julieta's many suitors. Poor woman doesn't remember her husband cheated on her, and he's acting like nothing ever happened, of course. And then, Julieta threatened to tell his wife and is now blackmailing him to keep quiet. It's a whole big mess."

"Sounds like it." Renee settled into her corner, determined to finish out the show and maybe the next one, thinking the goings-on at the Dragonfly were nothing in comparison to what happened on her mother's favorite shows.

※ ※ ※ ※

After her second interview, Sarah left the bank and headed to her car, feeling confident that she had the job. The interviewer seemed impressed with her answers and never seemed to let his gaze roam to her chest, which was a good sign. The last interview she had been on, at a real estate office, the interviewer couldn't hide the fact that he was looking her over. When the interview was finished, she shook his hand and left as quickly as possible. Mr. Sanderson, however, seemed interested in what she had to say and didn't seem fazed by the gap years in her résumé when she had chosen to stay home and raise her son. If she was able to get this job, she wouldn't have to depend so much on Patrick's alimony and could start putting some money aside. Though the money she was spending at the Dragonfly could easily have been used to start a savings account, she felt she deserved to have some affection in her life. And Jame gave her what she needed. Besides, it wasn't something she was going to be doing long term.

As she approached her car, she hit the key fob to unlock the driver's side door. As she turned to get into her car, however, she noticed a familiar dapper figure walking farther down the sidewalk toward the coffeeshop, satchel slung over her shoulder. She hesitated for a moment, then shrugged and muttered to herself, "What the hell?" She closed the door and pushed the button to lock it again, then quickened her stride to catch up to Jame. When she reached her side, she asked with a smile, "Why do I keep running into you guys?"

Jame turned to her with a startled smile. "By 'you guys,' I assume you mean Ma'am and me. Unless you've been running into others from the house."

"Oh, yes, all the Dragonfly ladies just seem to love this side of the square. I can't help but trip over at least one of you every time I come downtown. It's a problem."

"I've heard it can be. So, I hear through the grapevine that when you do run into my colleagues, you go for coffee. May I continue that tradition?"

Sarah laughed. "You may. Why do you think I chased you down?" She linked her arm in Jame's in a casual way as they made their way around the square to the coffeeshop on the other side, the same place she and Ma'am had had coffee the previous week.

The coffeeshop currently only held six customers, all older men and women of the sort that could be found in small-town coffee shops everywhere.

Sarah was convinced they were the same customers who had been in the shop when she had come in with Ma'am. She briefly wondered what they thought of her having coffee with two different members of the Dragonfly. Then, she chastised herself: *What are you doing? Since when do you care what anyone thinks?* Instead, she looked each diner in the eye as she and Jame made their way to a table and smiled at each one, daring them to voice displeasure. When they reached a table, Jame hesitated next to her before going to her seat, and Sarah realized Jame was probably having an internal debate about whether to pull out her chair. When Jame sat without doing so, Sarah thought to herself, *Wise choice.*

"You know the rumors are flying around my house. I'm not sure, but I think you and Ma'am are married now. Is that the case?" Jame smiled across the table at her.

Sarah returned her smile. "Oh, yes, and we're currently honeymooning in Tahiti. It's fabulous!"

"Well, congratulations! Would that make you Mrs. Ma'am? I want to make sure I get your title right."

"You can call me Mistress Sarah. And I guess that would make me your boss, wouldn't it?"

Jame inclined her head in acquiescence. "I suppose it would. But aren't you that already once a week?"

Sarah giggled. "Yeah, I guess I am."

Jame's look sobered. "If you and Ma'am have started a relationship and you wish to stop seeing me, I wouldn't take it personally. In fact, I would wish you well."

Flustered, Sarah said, "Well, I'm not. I mean, we're not. I mean, we're not dating, we just had coffee that one time. If that means we're dating, then by that logic, you and I'll be dating when this is over."

"I don't know if the house could survive that much drama."

"It does seem to be its own little microcosm of drama there, doesn't it?"

Jame considered before answering. "It's often how I think a sorority must be, with lots of gossiping, petty jealousy, and way too much conversation about fashion. But friendships are also formed there, solid bonds that will probably last a lifetime no matter where we all end up."

"That's nice. Do you have that with any of your coworkers?"

"Not really. I'm not like them much, and they don't know what to make of me." Jame sipped the coffee the waitress had recently filled for her.

"How do you mean?"

"Well, we don't have the same interests, for one. Plus, a lot of them are small-town girls who haven't been around women like me. I don't fit their norm, and they can't relate to me. But to be fair, I can't relate to them, either. So, we just coexist in the same space, trying to respect each other and staying out of each other's way as much as possible." Jame shrugged as if not sure what to say next.

Sarah was convinced there was more Jame wasn't saying, and she wondered what Jame was leaving out of her description of life at the house. Did the women there really treat Jame with respect, or did they bully her because she wasn't like them? Everything Jame said and more importantly, what she didn't say, made Sarah think Jame must be very lonely, and she felt sad for her. "Do you talk to anyone?"

Jame looked at her thoughtfully. "I appreciate your concern, thank you. But I do have people I talk to online. Old friends. We get vacation days, and I go and see my people then."

"Do they know what you do for a living?"

Jame hesitated for the briefest of moments. "Well, my best friend knows, but no one else. I've chosen not to tell anyone else because I don't want my parents to know. They wouldn't understand. And who can blame them? So, instead, I tell them half-truths. I live in a lovely old Victorian, assisting a rich, older woman in the daily operation of her bed and breakfast." Jame gave her a gentle smile and a slight shrug.

Sarah grinned. "The Dragonfly serves breakfast?"

"It does! But not for the customers."

"Damn. Wanted to make sure I was getting my money's worth."

Jame inclined her head again, as was her habit when she was showing deference. "I certainly hope that you feel as if you are."

Sarah's look softened, and she reached a hand across the table to take Jame's, who looked at her in surprise. "Oh, no, of course I am. I was just joking. I swear, I definitely think you're money well spent."

Jame smiled. "I know that you do, dear Sarah. Please don't think I was implying that I thought anything less. I'm fine. You can let go of my hand now," Jame replied gently.

Sarah let go, looking flustered. "Sorry."

"Don't apologize, you're a big-hearted person, and that's a beautiful thing to be. I'm glad that you express that side of yourself. Especially with me and especially here." Jame looked around the café nervously.

Sarah followed Jame's gaze and noticed for the first time since they sat that they were being stared at and not so surreptitiously, either. Turning back to Jame, she said not so quietly, "Of course, I will express myself any damn way I please, in public or otherwise. You're my friend, and if someone's afraid to show affection to their friends in public, then the problem is them, not the public."

Jame's face seemed to light up at her words. "You consider us friends?"

"Well, yeah…I mean, it's not conventional, but yeah. I will always say hi to you in the street and drag you to the nearest coffeeshop. Consider me your friend, Jame…wait, I don't know your last name." Sarah laughed at herself.

Jame's smile grew bigger as she replied, "Annis, I'm Jame Annis."

"Well, I'm glad to know you, Annis, Jame Annis." Sarah held her coffee cup aloft and Jame did the same, toasting to their friendship outside the Dragonfly.

Chapter Fourteen

Ma'am stood at the window in her private sanctuary, looking out over the back of the grounds. These days, it was the only place she went when she wanted to hide from the rest of the house. The only one who ever dared find her here was Stella. From her perch on the top floor, she could see the guest parking lot, specifically put there for the utmost privacy. Beyond that, she could see the rose-covered arbor, which led out to the garden Stella so lovingly tended. In the middle of the garden sat a gazebo, which had been put there by the previous owners and had been part of the reason she had bought the property. She didn't go out there much anymore, but it used to be where she went to hide, back when the business was still growing, and she had time to get away. Beside her on the wall were pictures she had taken of Ian out there. He didn't go back there often, so she only had a few.

The sun was brilliant and high in the sky this early October afternoon. The leaves were turning, and the trees were dropping them carelessly all over the yard. Looking at them, she remembered Ian when he was twelve. She had gotten him to help her rake them, a huge task considering the size of the yard, but still one she preferred to do herself. He had worked diligently with her for a few hours, clearing the front and side yards, but when they reached the back, the biggest area, he had started to flag. She had built up a sizable pile and had been standing and wiping the sweat off her brow when she had been taken by surprise by a charging Ian grabbing her around the waist and tackling her into the pile, laughing the whole time. She had hollered out in alarm but soon was laughing herself. They took turns tickling and burying each other, in the process kicking the leaves out of their nicely raked pile. She had looked about her, noticing the leaves' dishevelment, picked up a large handful, and dumped them on his laughing head. She had said, "You're gonna help me clean these up, Bubba."

He had squealed and pushed her back into the pile, then proceeded to try to bury her completely. She had let him cover her body, then had risen out of the leaves as if she was Frankenstein's monster and chased him around the yard for several minutes until they both collapsed onto the gazebo floor, panting, out of breath, but still laughing through it. They never did finish the backyard that day. After catching her breath, she had looked at him with a smile and asked, "Who sees the backyard anyway?" They had gone inside to clean up and have a cold drink.

It was a moment she wished she had framed on her wall, but she hadn't had her camera with her that day. It'd been a long time since they had played in the leaves, and she wasn't sure if she'd be able to talk him into it now. She muttered to herself with a chuckle, "He might hurt me now." He wasn't a short kid anymore. Now he was taller than her by nearly a foot, broad across the shoulders, and solid. She sighed as she turned away from the window to go back to the small writing desk she kept in her room, though she had nothing that needed doing there. She felt aimless today, not sure where to go or what she should do when she got there. As she sat, her bedroom door opened, and Stella came in with several envelopes in hand.

"Mail call." Stella smiled as she crossed the room and placed the mail on the corner of Ma'am's desk.

Ma'am gave her a brief smile in return. "Thank you." She blindly picked up the top envelope and opened it, vaguely noticing that it was from the city water department.

Instead of leaving, wishful thinking, Stella stood where she was, looking Ma'am over with interest. "What's wrong with you?"

Ma'am looked up in surprise. "What? What do you mean? Nothing's wrong with me."

"Really?"

"Yes, really."

"So why do you look like your dog just died?"

Ma'am looked up at Stella, tired amusement playing at her lips. "Because somewhere, someone's dog has died. And that makes me sad."

Stella replied with derision. "My, aren't you the sympathetic one."

"That's me," Ma'am confirmed as she reached for another envelope.

"I suppose it couldn't have anything to do with a certain someone canceling her appointment today, hmm?" Stella crossed her arms over her chest and looked down at Ma'am with great skepticism.

"No one makes appointments, they just come by."

"Really?"

"Yes, *really*. Now will you leave me be to pay bills? Someone has to make sure the lights stay on around here."

"I don't know why you don't hire an accountant."

Ma'am narrowed her eyes at her old friend. "I've told you before, accountants are unscrupulous liars who will just rob you blind. Besides, it's not difficult, just tedious."

"You just think that because you've always been lazy and bad at math."

"Who are you—my mother?"

"If I was your mother, I would have told you a long time ago to stop moping up here like Boo Radley and just talk to the woman! What are you—twelve?"

"What do you know about Boo Radley?"

"Don't try to sidetrack me. You never want to talk about this."

"That's because there's nothing to talk about. Now leave me be. Shoo." Ma'am gestured for Stella to leave, but it didn't work, she stood her ground. Ma'am sighed heavily. "What do you *want* from me?"

Stella grinned. "For you to admit you might actually like a woman, that you want to maybe have more than coffee with her, but you're too scared to ask because you haven't asked a woman out in years. Instead, you stay holed up here, satisfying your sexual needs with your employees but run away when it comes to something more than that."

Ma'am sat looking at her a moment, stunned at the honesty. "Wow. Okay, that was more truth than I expected."

"I'll always tell you the truth because I'm your friend. Now stop being a big stupid idiot and do something about it."

Ma'am looked at her with a plaintive expression. "But what if she says no?"

"Oh, my god! You *are* twelve!" Stella turned to leave, exasperated. When her back was turned, she muttered, "Impossible. Why do I try? Why do I even try?"

"Stella?"

Stella turned with her hand on the doorknob. "Yeah?"

"Thank you."

"Anytime. You big dummy."

Ma'am laughed as Stella left. Stella's accusation of her being twelve made her flash on a memory of Ian with his first crush. The girl in question had been a cute, geeky girl with short, tight brown curls who dressed in matching trousers and polo shirts that were always painstakingly tucked in. She also had braces and freckles. Whenever Ian spoke of her, which he tried not to do often, or was around her, he stammered, tripped over his feet, and seemed at a loss for words. She remembered trying to hide her laughter at the poor boy. Was she really that bad? She thought back to the other week when she and Sarah had run into each other on the square and the time before that at the botanical gardens. Both times, she had felt at a loss for words, trying to be charming but feeling as if she had failed miserably. The last encounter had been better. They had talked as if they were old friends. It had come easy, which surprised her. When they had parted ways, Sarah had hugged her, which was even more surprising. The feel of her stayed with her but not in a sexual way. The hug was a real one, strong. It wasn't a casual hug you would give an acquaintance, something you might do instinctively instead of a handshake. It held a promise of genuineness and true friendship. It was the proffered friendship that gave her pause. She had no reason to think, no reason to expect that Sarah thought of her as anything more. If even that.

Trying to put the hug and the conversation with Stella out of her mind, Ma'am opened another envelope on her desk, this one offering her a credit card she never asked for with exorbitant interest rates. She put that on a pile to be shredded and reached for another envelope.

※※※※

"So, to what do I owe the honor of this visit?" Danni asked as Sarah sat across from her at Danni's kitchen table, both hands around the coffee mug in front of her.

"Nothing. I just realized I hadn't seen my baby sister in a while."

"Uh-huh." Sarah stuck her tongue out at her, and Danni blew her a kiss. "What I meant was, it's Wednesday. Don't you usually have other plans on Wednesday?"

Sarah shifted uncomfortably in her seat. "I have, but that doesn't mean I can't change my plans. Besides, if I get that job, I'll have to stop my...current activities anyway."

"You going to be okay with that?" Danni asked with concern.

"Well, yeah. It's not like I'm in a relationship. That's precisely why I started going out there, so I could have something that was just on my terms, all about my needs, and easy to get out of. No strings attached."

Danni laughed. "Since when are you able to do

something that's no strings attached?"

"What? What are you referring to?"

"You've never had a casual relationship in your life, why should now be any different?"

"Because I'm paying for it," Sarah replied matter-of-factly.

"Sure, okay."

"I am!" Sarah protested.

"Well, duh! I know that, nimrod."

Sarah stuck her tongue out again.

"You keep doing that, and I'm going to bite you." Danni grinned at her.

"You're weird."

"Yeah, but it's a good weird."

"Mm-hmm." Sarah didn't seem convinced.

"Anyway, I've been meaning to talk to you about that. It seems that your, uh, activities have not gone unnoticed."

"Yeah, I know. I mean, I know this is a small town, but geez! It's not like I'm the only one to ever go out there."

"You might be the first woman."

"No, I'm not. Jame has other clients, some who've been going out there longer than I have. I'm just the first one not ashamed of it."

Danni nodded almost absentmindedly. "No reason you should be ashamed. Very sex positive, as the kids are saying these days. And being sex positive is very trendy."

"What I was going for."

"I think you're mocking me."

"I guess the tests were wrong, you're not dumb after all." Sarah grinned evilly.

"Don't be mean, or I'll tell Mom."

"Why stop now?" Before Danni could launch a protest, Sarah turned serious again. "I don't mind being sex positive, but I do worry that Patrick will try to use this against me."

"Oh, god, do you think he would?"

"Well, I don't think *he* would, but if he's as much ruled by his dick as I think he is…"

Danni finished the thought for her. "Then he might let the new girlfriend talk him into using your new hobby to get custody."

"No, I don't think he'd ask for custody. That'd mean he'd have to be responsible. But he might ask to pay less child support. I could totally see him doing that."

"What kind of asshat doesn't think the woman who raises his kid deserves fair compensation?" Before Sarah could respond, Danni answered her own question. "Oh, the one you married."

"That would be the one."

"So, if I understand what you're not saying, you're really here today because you want to scale back your visits to the house because you think your ex-husband is enough of a douchebag to take you to court or something."

"Yep, that's pretty much it."

"You're an idiot."

Sarah's eyes widened in shock. "Excuse you? You know I would do whatever it took to protect my son."

"Yeah, I do. But if you were really worried about that big, dumb starfish, you wouldn't have started going out there in the first place."

Sarah looked confused and mumbled the word "starfish."

Danni rolled her eyes. "You have a five-year-old, you should know who Patrick is. Anyway, that's not my point."

Sarah smiled and shook her head in embarrassed understanding. "No, I get your point. And to answer the question you're not asking, yes, there's probably another reason I didn't go to the house today."

"Yeah, I know. I mean, I have an idea."

"I'm sure you do."

"Only because I know you. And I know that you can't do 'no strings attached.'"

"You said that already."

"Still true. Admit it, you like the cute little butch."

"I *do*, but…not in that way."

"Not in that way. You sound like a kid."

Sarah grinned, then flipped her off. "I know way more cuss words now than I did when I was a kid."

"Just because your vocabulary's grown doesn't mean you have."

"Whatever."

"Queen of the comeback." Danni glanced across the room at the clock on the microwave. "Not that I'm trying to get rid of you, but what time does P.J. get out of school?"

Sarah looked at her phone, saw the time, and swore. "Shit! In less than half an hour. I gotta go. See ya later, sis." The sisters stood and hugged. "Love you."

"Love you, too. And try not to worry about…all this shit."

"I know. Bye. Maybe next time we can talk about your drama instead of mine."

Danni scoffed. "Please, that could take days. Anyway, go get that nephew of mine. Hell, bring him back if you want, and we can visit longer."

Sarah looked thoughtful. "I just might. Anyway, I'm going." She waved over her shoulder as she hurried out of the kitchen and saw herself to the front door.

Danni picked up Sarah's nearly empty cup and took it to the sink to wash it out, hoping Sarah would take her up on her offer.

༄༄༄༄

Since Jame had some unexpected free time, she spent it doing homework for her online class, as well as writing in her journal.

Sarah canceled today. Not a major surprise, as she warned me last week that she might. Also, not a surprise considering the state of her emotions as of late. I'm not even sure if she knows how she feels, but I think I'm beginning to. Her and Ma'am both. Both have been distracted to the point that they're not really present, even when they're standing right in front of you. Something must give between them soon. I've never seen Ma'am be so unsure of herself. At least that's how I'm reading her. When she talks to us women, she doesn't have the same tone, the same commanding presence she used to. If she's not careful, the women might see her vulnerability and try to take advantage.

If what I think is starting to happen is what's happening, then I wish they'd get on with it. They're not at their best. One way or another, one of them needs to make the first move. I mean, they're both old enough to have done this whole relationship thing before, they should know how it works. Instead, they're no better than adolescents, unsure of themselves, embarrassed, and happy/miserable. If this were a movie I was watching in the theater, I'd have yelled at the screen several times by now, "For god's sake, just kiss her! We all know you want to!" I don't know whether to laugh at their foolishness or throw my hands up at this point.

With a deep sigh, Jame saved and closed out of her journal before shutting down her computer. She wasn't sure why she was losing patience with them. She supposed she should see the alleged budding courtship between Sarah and Ma'am as cute or something, but she just didn't have it in her to find things like that cute. She wasn't against it, why would she be? She tried not to judge them against what she herself would do if she were them, knowing that if she wanted to be a good psychotherapist, she wouldn't impose her own viewpoints onto her patients. But she was human, after all, and it was hard not to. Again, she chastised herself for her impatience on their behalf and tried to see things from a romantic point of view. But it eluded her.

She decided to go down to the kitchen for a snack, maybe something salty, her biggest weakness. As she reached the bottom of the stairs, the doorbell rang, so she answered it. She was surprised at the visitor. "Sarah! I didn't think you were coming today."

Sarah instantly blushed and started to stammer. "Well, I originally wasn't, but I…I changed my mind."

Jame gave her a welcoming smile. "Of course. You're in luck, I'm not currently spoken for."

"Oh, that's unfortunate." At Jame's confused look, Sarah rushed on. "Sorry, what I meant was, unfortunate for you. I think. I meant, I don't want to see you."

"Oh."

"God, that came out wrong. What I mean is, I want...I'm here to...I mean..."

"You want to see Ma'am."

"What? Yes. That's it. I'm sorry. I used to know how to put words together. Form sentences, even."

"I understand. Let me see if she's available. You can sit out here, if you like." Jame gestured to the many available chairs and couches in the sitting room.

Sarah looked around at the women who were sitting downstairs and decided she'd rather stay where she was. "I can wait here."

"All right. I'll be right back." Jame inclined her head instead of giving her a full-on bow, then turned and walked down the hall to Ma'am's office, feeling Sarah's gaze on her. She heard Ma'am's voice giving her permission to enter, then turned the knob and went inside.

Ma'am was at her desk, working at her computer. She was wearing reading glasses, something she rarely let the women see. She didn't look up from the screen when Jame entered. "Yes?"

"Ma'am, Sarah is here."

Ma'am stopped typing for a moment, then resumed. "Does she want to meet with you now, does she need to pay?"

"No, I don't believe so. She asked to speak to you, but I don't think she wishes to spend time with me."

Ma'am stopped typing again, this time eyeing Jame over the top of her glasses. "Then what does she want?"

"She didn't say."

Ma'am took her glasses off slowly and looked

lost in thought for a minute. Finally, she said, "I wonder what she could want." She sat there puzzling over it, seeming to forget Jame was in the room. Jame cleared her throat. Ma'am quickly put her glasses back on, resuming the pose of the studious businesswoman once again. A not altogether unattractive pose. "Send her in."

"Yes, Ma'am." Jame went back into the hallway. When she did so, she saw that Sarah was standing only a few feet from Ma'am's office door with her hands behind her back, trying to look casual but not quite succeeding. "You can go in now."

"Thank you." Sarah gave Jame a small nervous smile as she passed her on her way in.

Jame wanted to reassure her, tell her that she'd be fine, but it was out of her hands now.

❧ ❧ ❧ ❧

While Sarah had sat in her car in parent purgatory, as she liked to think of it, waiting for P.J. to come out of the school building, she had been thinking over the conversation with Danni. Maybe Danni was right, maybe she was being an idiot. Even if the rumors made it back to Patrick, they wouldn't be enough for him to use against her. And she always put her son first—always. When the child support checks came in, she paid all the bills, bought groceries, paid for anything that P.J. might currently need, made sure to do something fun with him, and then, and only then, did she see to her own needs. As she had told Danni in the beginning, going to the Dragonfly had never been something she planned to do long term, it was just something she needed right now. She thought of it as her therapy. Only spending time with Jame, being treated as if she were special and beautiful and desirable, was better than sitting on a couch, telling some bored stranger her problems for a fifty-minute hour.

A moment later, P.J. bounded into the backseat, slinging his backpack onto the floor on the other side. As he was buckling his seat belt, he said, "Hi, Mom."

Sarah turned and smiled at him. "Hey, kiddo. How was school?"

"Good."

"Yeah? What'd you do today?"

"Learned a whole bunch of stuff."

"Like what?" She turned back around to focus on inching forward in the line.

"Stuff about words, and we practiced writing and just all kinds of stuff."

Sarah smiled. "Sounds like a lot of stuff."

"Yeah. Mom, I'm hungry. Can we stop and get a snack?"

Sarah was finally free of the line and made the first turn she could to try to get out of the traffic. "I tell you what, why don't I drop you at your Aunt Danni's house? She's always got good snacks. Would you like that?"

"Yeah! You think she'd let me play her games?"

Danni, still a kid at heart herself, had the best sugary snacks and the best game system. She had been sharing both with P.J. since he could crawl. Any time Sarah needed a babysitter and Danni was available, P.J. never gave her any grief about going. "She always does. And I won't be gone long, maybe only an hour or so. Okay?"

"Okay."

Sarah knew she could leave him there all night

and he would be fine with it. She made the turn that afforded her the quickest route back to Danni's place, not sure if she was doing the right thing but determined to do it anyway.

When Danni opened the door to them a moment later, she was happy to see that Sarah had taken her up on her offer. She spoke to P.J. first. "Hey, Squirt." She looked at Sarah and said, "I'm glad you came back."

"Hey, Aunt Danni. Do you have any cookies?"

"Don't I always have cookies?"

P.J. grinned. "Yes!"

"Okay then, don't ask silly questions." She smiled and ruffled his hair.

"Actually, I need you to look after him for a little bit. I need to go do something. I won't be long."

A slow smile crept up Danni's face. "Ah, okay. Sure, go do your thing. You know where to find us. Come on, P.J., let's go raid the cookie jar, then kill some bad guys!"

"Yeah!"

"No violent games!" Sarah admonished.

As they were walking into the house together, Danni directed her next words to P.J. "Your mom is no fun at all." PJ giggled.

"P.J., keep your aunt out of trouble. I won't be long. Love you."

He yelled back that he loved her, too, but he was already walking away from her.

Sarah looked at Danni. "Wish me luck."

"Not exactly sure what you're up to, but I wish you the best. May your quest be successful."

Sarah gave her a dubious smile. "Sometimes, I forget you're a gamer, you seem so normal. Then you say things like that."

"You're stalling. Just go."

"Okay, okay. I'm out of here." She kissed Danni on the cheek, then hurried back to her car and drove east.

❧❧❧❧

Sarah stood before Renee now, trying not to shift from foot to foot and wishing she knew what to do with her face. She settled on a smile. "Hello. I hope I'm not catching you when you're too busy."

Renee stood, quickly taking her glasses off and haphazardly throwing them on her desk. "No, no, I wasn't that busy. Just paying bills. Doing payroll. Have a seat." She gestured to the chairs in front of her desk, not moving from her spot of safety.

"Okay." Sarah took a seat, feeling a little underdressed in her jeans and T-shirt, the clothes she had worn when she thought her day was going to consist of nothing more than hanging out with Danni. It wasn't how Renee was dressed that was throwing her off. Renee was also dressed casually in worn jeans that hugged her hips and a button-down shirt with rolled-up sleeves, her reddish-blond hair loose about her shoulders. It was the office itself that was making her feel uncomfortable. The chair she sat in, as well as the one beside it, was leather, the walls were dark wood, and there were shelves of books behind the desk, to say nothing of the desk itself. It was a large wooden thing, the whole place feeling like an English study, instead of the converted bedroom in an old Victorian house in the Midwest that it actually was. She decided to focus on Renee instead. Renee was looking at her expectantly but also curiously.

Finally, Renee found her voice. "Were you wanting to see Jame or perhaps someone else?"

"I'm not sure I'm going to be seeing Jame anymore."

Renee's face was unreadable. "Is something wrong?"

"No! No, nothing's wrong. I've always enjoyed myself." She felt herself blushing again but charged ahead anyway. "I mean, Jame has been...Jame is... good at her job."

Renee bit back her smile. "I'm glad to hear it. My ladies aim to please."

"Oh, she did. I just, um, think that..." Sarah realized she was stumbling and babbling and admonished herself to take control. This wasn't who she was. She sat up in her chair, steadied her gaze, and said calmly, "I think you and I need to talk."

Renee sat back in her chair and looked Sarah over with interest. "What do you mean?"

"Well..." Sarah stopped talking and looked around them at the imposing office. "Actually, can you come out from behind that desk? I feel like I'm being interviewed or something. I'm not here on business, I'm here as a friend. And I want to talk to you that way." She stood and held her hand out across the desk, imploring. "Come on, let's go." Now Sarah smiled at her and cocked her head toward the door.

Curious, Renee stood with a building smile and took Sarah's hand and walked around to the other side of the desk. "Okay, I'll bite. What'd you have in mind?"

Feeling more confident, Sarah smiled flirtatiously. "Hold off on the biting, we'll see about that. For now, I want you to show me that gazebo I see every time I pull up. It looks like a fabulous place for a chat. Or whatever."

"Well, yes, yes, it is. Okay, let's take a stroll." They exchanged smiles, then Renee gestured to the door. "After you."

Sarah started to walk to the door but stopped and turned with a grin. "You know, I used to think the whole chivalry thing was sweet, but I've started to rethink the whole 'after you' business."

"Oh?" Renee asked, intrigued.

Sarah leaned in and half-whispered, "Yeah. I think letting the woman go first was just an excuse to look at our asses."

"You weren't supposed to know about that."

"Too bad. Why don't you go first?"

"So you can look at my ass?"

"Fair is fair," Sarah replied with a grin. Renee inclined her head, making Sarah briefly think of Jame as she passed in front of her to walk out the door. On her way by, Sarah whistled.

Renee turned around at the door. This time, it was her turn to blush. "You're going to turn a girl's head."

"We'll see."

They linked arms as they walked down the hallway and into the kitchen and out the door that led to the backyard. They passed Marie on their way. She said nothing, just watched them go by. Once they were outside, Marie pulled out her phone and sent a quick text to Stella.

Chapter Fifteen

Without a table between them, Renee and Sarah seemed to be sitting awfully close to each other, though they were probably about the same distance apart as they had been in the café, Renee reasoned. They sat facing each other in the gazebo, one leg on the bench, one on the floor. Renee couldn't stop smiling, even if, she suspected, she was making Sarah nervous. "So, you got me out of my office, what are you going to do with me?"

Sarah returned her smile but raised an eyebrow. "Hmm, I don't know, I'll have to think about that."

"Well, you definitely have my attention."

"Don't I always? I don't know, I was just thinking that we could get to know each other better. I mean, it's obvious there's…something."

"Yeah, 'something' is a good way of putting it," Renee agreed. "I'm kinda surprised you feel that way, though, considering the botanical gardens."

Sarah looked down a moment and sighed. When she looked back up, she was contrite. "I know. I wasn't sure what you wanted from me. I thought that you thought that…I don't know, that I was…"

"Easy?" Renee asked gently.

"Yes!"

"And now you don't?"

"No, I don't. At the café you were…you were genuine with me. And I really appreciated it. You were flirtatious but not in an aggressive way, just an honest one. If that makes sense."

"Yeah, it makes sense. So…"

"Yeah, so." Sarah took Renee's hand, which had been resting on the railing, and let their fingers loop together. "So now, my new friend, I want to ask you some things that I didn't get a chance to ask you in the café."

"Now I'm the one getting interviewed?"

"Yeah." Sarah laughed playfully and turned and brought up her other leg so that she sat on the bench and faced Renee cross-legged. Renee mimicked her style with a mischievous grin. "You're making fun of me!" Sarah lightly slapped her on the knee.

"I am not! I'm just trying to match you. You seem more adept at this than me, however," Renee replied as she struggled for a moment to mimic Sarah's posture. "I guess I'm not as in shape as I thought."

"Don't be ridiculous, you're gorgeous." Before the blush could rise in her cheeks, Sarah rushed on to fill her embarrassment with humor. "I'm also a lot younger than you." Sarah gave her an evil smile, which made her eyes appear as if they were closed.

"Ten years isn't so much these days."

"True. So, anyway…"

"Question time." Renee finished for her.

"Yes. I've been most curious…what makes someone stay in this business for so long, especially when it's illegal?"

"Oh, I'm sure it's the same for everyone… money. There's a lot of money to be made in pleasure. And as for legality's sake, I'm hoping that eventually the rest of the country gets its head out of the Bible and follows Nevada's lead and legalizes it. Well, it's only legal in a few counties there and only in places that look like where they shot *The Hills Have Eyes*, but it's a start." Sarah laughed, which Renee appreciated, but she went on. "What a woman chooses to do with her body is her business. Just like other things that can be bad for us, it should be regulated. Sorry, touchy subject." Renee suddenly looked embarrassed and brushed a loose hair off her face.

Sarah looked thoughtful. "No, I agree. It's bullshit. So, why here, of all places?"

Renee's face suddenly lit up. "My son was here. His grandmother was raising him, and I wanted to be closer to him, so I bought the house I've always loved since I was a little girl and set up shop. Seemed as good a place as any."

"What was it like working in this town before?"

Renee looked at Sarah with suspicion. "This really *is* an interview. Who are you really working for?"

Sarah laughed, then said in mock seriousness, "I'm working undercover with the police, trying to bust this thing wide open. And you just blew my cover."

"Such a shame." Renee wanted to kiss her, but she waited. It was too soon. She would wait for the right moment. Instead, she leaned back, cleared her throat, and answered Sarah's original question. "I didn't. I worked in Chicago. I saved up for years until I could move back. I wanted to do things different, make sex work a safe, viable option for women. And I do that."

"I know, and I'm glad." They sat smiling at each other for a moment, still holding hands, until Sarah took a deep breath and let it out slowly. "Okay, this is weird. I'm over here feeling all tingly just listening to you talk about your views on sex work."

Renee laughed. "If this is impressing you, then I have high hopes for the future."

"Do you?"

"I do. For instance, I want very much to just sit out here and talk to you for hours. Until the sun goes down and the moon comes up. What do you say?" Renee looked at her hopefully, but the look of hesitation on Sarah's face was unmistakable. "Something wrong?"

"Nothing, not really. I just told my sister I would pick my son up in an hour or so. I try to keep my promises to him. I mean, to everyone, but especially to him."

The rising fear in Renee's chest started to subside. "I understand completely. So, let's make the most of the time we have."

"Ooh, that sounds promising."

"I think so. Now it's my turn to ask you something."

"I'm an open book. Go for it."

"What made you fall in love with your husband?"

"*Ex*-husband." Sarah was quick to correct her, to which Renee smiled and inclined her head. "And wow, what an interesting question."

"You don't have to answer if it makes you uncomfortable."

"No, I'll answer. Just because I married him doesn't mean I loved him. I wanted to love him, he was the father of my son, but I just never could."

"Why'd you marry him?"

"I got pregnant, and I was hoping that maybe something would change between Patrick and me. Horrible reasons, I know, but it's the truth. I liked him, don't get me wrong, I was just never passionate about him. I think maybe I was afraid to do it by myself. But I know I can stand on my own now, and that's my goal from here on out. So, good news for you, I'm not looking for a sugar mama." Sarah grinned and pointed at Renee's chest.

"What about some sugar?" Renee smiled sweetly at her as she reached up to take the hand pointed at her sternum.

Sarah rolled her eyes. "Lame." Nevertheless, she leaned in for the kiss Renee was offering her. Finally, after weeks of teasing, she was able to kiss the woman on the other side of the mirror. She had always known it would be intense, but she wasn't prepared for the rightness of it. The instant feeling of coming home. It was a feeling she had never had with Patrick or anyone she had dated before him. Jame was a sweet kisser, passionate, but kissing Jame wasn't like this. It felt new and familiar at the same time. It was hard to describe it any other way, so Sarah didn't try to make sense of it. Instead, she put her free hand on the back of Renee's head and pulled her closer, causing Renee to moan into her. After several moments, they separated, and each took a deep breath before dissolving into giggles, as if they were schoolchildren up to no good.

"I don't know about you, but I feel like a teenager, experiencing her first kiss."

Sarah looked at her skeptically. "I bet you say that to all the girls." Before Renee could protest, Sarah asked, "Wondering if you did it right?"

"Among other things."

"Oh, you did it right. You did just fine." Now both hands free, Sarah put her arms around Renee's neck and went back for more.

They sat out there for another hour, before Sarah, feeling guilty, said her goodbyes. When she left, Renee walked back into the house through the kitchen, a faraway, serene look on her face. Stella and Marie were there, watching her.

Finally, Marie spoke. "Well, hello. For a moment there, I thought we were going to have another guest for dinner."

"No" was all Renee could bring herself to say.

Stella couldn't keep the grin off her face. She pulled out her phone and showed the picture on it to Renee. "See, I got a picture. It's not as good as you can do with your fancy camera, but I figured you'd want a record of the moment."

Renee took the phone from her. Stella had captured their first kiss, just as Sarah's hand had reached up to Renee's neck. "You must have been watching us a long while to get this." She gave the phone back to Stella, lightly shoving it against the other woman's chest.

"Someone had to make sure you didn't chicken out."

"I'm going upstairs." Without another word, Renee left the kitchen and headed up to her sanctuary. Once her back was turned, Stella and Marie high-fived.

꧁꧂

As she always did when leaving the Dragonfly, Sarah checked her makeup in the rearview mirror before pulling out of the drive. Thank the goddess for smudge-proof lip gloss, she thought. Although Renee didn't leave any marks on her, her cheeks and neck were still a little flushed, which was how her body responded to passion. It'd been a while since she'd seen the blush rise on her face like that. Even Jame, for all her attentiveness and youthful enthusiasm, to say nothing of her determination to please, hadn't been able to make the blood rise that much. It was more than passion, and she knew it. She said aloud, "No, we're not going to think about that," then she put the car in gear and pulled out of the drive.

When she arrived at Danni's place, she knocked once, then walked in without waiting for an answer. She could hear the loud video game from where she was standing and knew they wouldn't be able to hear her. When she walked in, P.J. and Danni were shoulder to shoulder on the couch, intent on the game in front of them on Danni's big-screen TV. Sarah had lost interest in video games years ago, despite Danni constantly trying to cajole her into playing. She had never been good at them, lacking the hand-eye coordination that the games seemed to require. When she couldn't get the characters to do what she wanted, she would get frustrated and stop playing. Even though she hadn't played in years, she recognized what they were playing and was happy to see that Danni had listened to her about violent games. She even recognized some of the characters currently racing around the track from other games she had grown up with.

"Dude, you totally cut me off!"

P.J. laughed as Danni teased him. "I'm going to beat you, Aunt Danni!" As he drove over the finish line, he stood and raised both arms in the air. "Yes! I told you!"

Sarah laughed, which got the attention of the

other two. "Good job. I could never beat her." Mother and son exchanged a high five.

Danni tossed her controller on the couch beside her, then switched off the TV. "That's because you have no skills. It's pretty sad, your five-year-old has more skills than you." Danni smirked and shrugged, then she turned to P.J. and offered her hand for a high five, as well. "Good job, little man."

"Yes! I am the champion!"

"One race, you won one race. Don't gloat, it's so rude." Danni tousled his hair, and P.J. took a step closer to his mother so that he was out of her reach.

Laughing, Sarah stepped up and hugged P.J. "Your aunt's right, though, don't be a sore winner. Okay?"

P.J. looked up at his mother questioningly. "What does that mean?"

"It means, if you win, don't make the other player feel bad for not winning." Sarah then bent down to whisper something in his ear.

Upon hearing what she said to him, he smiled at her, nodded, then walked back over to Danni and extended his hand with a smile. "Good game, Aunt Danni."

Danni looked back up at Sarah with a building smile and shook P.J.'s hand. "Thank you." Then, she stood and picked him up, quickly turned him upside down, letting his arms dangle. "You're just too cute. You're just too cute!" She tickled him, and he couldn't stop giggling.

Sarah watched them play, thinking for the umpteenth time that Danni should have children of her own. Instead, she was still too busy being a kid herself. Danni didn't just *play* video games, she composed music for them. She kept irregular hours and worked from home, which made her the perfect babysitter. She had also begun trying to teach P.J. music, for which Sarah was grateful. Finally, she interrupted them to say, "Don't get him too wound up, I still need to feed the beast and give him a bath before bedtime."

"Fine." Danni put him back on his feet reluctantly, then held her arms out for a hug. "Thanks for stopping by, little man. Always a pleasure."

He hugged her back with enthusiasm. "You're welcome, Aunt Danni. Love you."

"Love you, too, Pajamas." She squeezed him tight as he giggled at the nickname. When she stood and let him go, she finally looked at Sarah. She narrowed her eyes and searched her face. "There's something different about you."

Sarah felt the color rise to her face, which was ridiculous, she knew, as Danni was only teasing. "No, there's not. Come on, P.J., time to go." She put her hand on his shoulder to try to usher him out, but Danni was still talking and teasing her.

"Yes, there is. I know what it is," she said in a sing-song, mocking voice, a large smile on her face.

"Shut up."

"Mom, you said it's not nice to say 'shut up.'"

"Ha!"

"It's only okay to say it to your sister." Sarah stuck her tongue out at Danni, who just laughed.

"I don't have a sister."

"I know." Sarah smiled at him and tried to walk toward the door again.

"You know that's bad parenting, right? What if he has a sister someday?" Danni followed them to the door, seemingly unable to stop teasing Sarah until the very end.

Sarah rolled her eyes. "Well, it won't be from me. And if his father has one," Sarah leaned in to whisper, "I won't stop any sibling rivalry."

Danni looked shocked. "That's terrible!"

Now in her normal tone, Sarah replied, "You know I wouldn't do that. Besides, I really don't think Patrick wants any more." She suddenly put on a fake smile to indicate she was done with the subject in front of P.J. "Anyway, thanks. I'll see you later." Sarah turned to leave, but Danni touched her arm. She should have known she wasn't going to get out that easily.

"You going to tell me?"

In lieu of an answer, Sarah just gave her a coy smile and a wink, then stepped away from her and walked out.

Danni stood with her mouth open. "Oh, my god! No way!"

Still not answering, Sarah kept up the smile and now shrugged, as if the whole thing was no big deal, thinking, *Let her infer what she wants.* What she said was, "See you later." She gave Danni a finger-curling wave, then walked with P.J. to her car.

Danni was still standing on her doorstep watching them leave, shaking her head, when Sarah pulled out of the drive.

Renee took the back stairs off the kitchen that led up to her sanctuary. She didn't allow any of her employees to use these stairs as she considered them part of her privacy. When Ian had started coming to the house, she made him use the back stairs so he wouldn't have to walk past the women of the Dragonfly, lest he become educated far too soon, a fate that would have surely drawn her mother's wrath.

When she reached the third floor, it wasn't of her son she was thinking. She kept going back to Sarah's smile; she couldn't get it out of her mind. Or how her eyes almost appeared closed when she was being mischievous. Or the blush that rose on her cheeks and neck once they started making out and was still present when she left. It was nice to know that she could still make a woman blush, especially when that woman didn't work for her.

For want of something better to do, Renee opened her laptop, thinking she needed to do something useful, instead of sitting around mooning over her date as if she was still in high school. Did women in their forties still moon? She didn't think so. She couldn't remember a time when she ever had. From her first high school crush to her most recent girlfriend, she had kept a calm focus. The closest she had come to mooning was her recent, but brief, infatuation with Jame. After their initial weekend in St. Louis, once she had Jame signed on, she had lost interest in her for the longest time. She had gotten what she wanted out of that weekend, and it was time to get back to business. Once Jame started working, it took her awhile before the feelings of lust that she had in the beginning with Jame had come back. When they did, the feelings were so powerful that she had been able to convince herself that they were something more. She leaned back in her chair, feeling like a damn fool for thinking that Jame had been doing anything more than treating her like another client.

On the face of it, the Sarah thing could also just be about lust, she knew that. But something told her it wasn't. There was a connection there that she hadn't had with anyone in a long time. It wasn't forced, it was natural. She had meant it when she'd said she wanted to sit out in the gazebo and talk with Sarah for hours. She wanted to hear her stories, share her own, and make out under the stars. She also wanted to take it slow, not rush things as she had with Ann.

Ann had worked for her briefly, after she had picked her up in a bar during a trip to Chicago. She had gone up there to see a show, not to recruit women for the house. When she had seen the tall, leggy blonde checking her out, she only had the rest of the evening on her mind. The next morning, thinking she would never see Ann again, she had told her what she did for a living, just not where. Instead of being turned off and possibly disgusted, as Renee had hoped, Ann had been fascinated and had asked her several questions. Renee answered as best she could without giving too much away. Ann had recently left her job as a copywriter and was looking for a new one. When Renee had tried to explain that working for her may not be the career she was looking for, Ann insisted she was only looking for something temporary that would make a nice chunk of change. After thinking it over, she had agreed to hire the other woman, making sure she knew that the sex they had that weekend would not be repeated. Ann agreed.

After working for her for a couple of months, Ann had beckoned to Renee, who she knew was watching her through the mirror, to come into her room. Renee had hesitated only for a moment. That was the beginning of what she had tried to convince herself was a real relationship. She had even introduced her to Ian after they had been dating a month. Ann had been polite but uninterested in the teenager. Realizing this, Renee knew there was no future for them and had told Ann that their budding relationship was over. Ann had tried to threaten her with exposure, saying she would call the cops and get her shut down. Renee had just laughed and said, "You do that. The sheriff will be back on Thursday around two. He likes biker chicks, so dress appropriately." Ann had stormed off, cussing. Renee could only laugh, both at the woman's antics and at her own stupidity. Ann left that afternoon, to where, Renee had no idea.

She trusted Sarah, but the past had made her prudent. She would wait before she introduced her to Ian and would think long and hard before she introduced her to her mother, though it wasn't out of the question. And she didn't have to worry about Sarah wanting to work for her. But still. She was a firm believer in all things in time. It had taken many years before she was able to have more of a hand in raising her son, as well as getting off her back and behind a desk. Those things came to her because she was able to wait for them, because she knew the right time to make her move. Now that things with Sarah were moving along, she would steady the reins and enjoy the ride.

Chapter Sixteen

A couple of days after Ma'am and Sarah had their make-out session in the gazebo, Jame decided it was the perfect time to ask for her vacation. Like regular jobs, they were given time off, but unlike other jobs, they didn't have to put in a two-week notice and hope their boss approved it. It wasn't as if they had a peak production season. Jame likened it to asking your parents for permission to go to a party. It was easier to do when your parent was distracted. With Sarah and Ma'am spending more time together, that meant that Ma'am wasn't around the house so much, and when she was, she was easily distracted. She still did the basics, setting up the appointments and keeping the books, as far as Jame knew, but she didn't have the same hard edge anymore. She even smiled at the women in passing and didn't seem to care when they giggled behind her back about her finally getting laid.

Jame figured that maybe if she spent a week with her family and friends, by the time she came back, things would have settled into the new normal at the house and the women would be able to accept the changes in Ma'am, and Ma'am, for her part, would have stopped acting like a smitten teenager having her first crush. It was worth a shot, anyway.

When Jame had gone into Ma'am's office to ask for time off, it was the Saturday after the gazebo incident, which was how she thought of it. Sarah had just left after staying for a private dinner that Marie had made especially for her and Ma'am. Even though Sarah had stayed until the sun went down, which Jame knew because she saw them sitting out in the gazebo watching it together, Ma'am had gone into her office afterward instead of up to her room. Jame briefly wondered why they didn't go on a date already, somewhere that wasn't the house, but then, when she realized how much she was starting to care, she stopped herself, remembering that she really didn't care what they did. She just knew she needed time away.

Ma'am sat behind her desk, looking at something on her laptop, her glasses nearly on the edge of her nose. Jame had long ago figured out that Ma'am had gotten no-line bifocals over the summer, but it wasn't her place to notice, so she never said a word.

Without looking away from the screen, Ma'am asked, "What can I do for you Jame?"

Jame stood in front of her desk, her arms behind her back, her head steady and her eyes focused. "Ma'am, I was just wondering if I could take my vacation next week, starting Monday."

Ma'am took her gaze off the screen long enough to glance down at the appointment book on her desk, then briefly took in Jame standing before her. "Sure. Since Sarah's not a regular anymore and the librarian said she was skipping this week, that only leaves two other regulars, and I can either convince them to meet with someone else or have them reschedule. Go ahead. Monday, you said?"

"Yes."

"Okay, done." Ma'am picked up a pen and drew

a line through Jame's name for the week and made notes about rescheduling or switching Jame's other clients. Then she looked up at Jame and gave her a warm smile. "Have a good time. And see if your mom will make those cookies again, they were wonderful." Ma'am held the smile for a moment longer, then turned back to her screen, effectively dismissing Jame.

Jame stood there, somewhat surprised at how quick and easy it had been. She replied, "Yes, Ma'am, I'll ask. Thank you."

The last time she had gone home, her mother had sent her back with homemade chocolate chip cookies, saying, "Give these to that nice lady you work for. I know she's rich and can buy much better cookies than I could ever hope to make, but still." Jame had assured her that Ma'am would like them, and apparently, she had.

Jame left the office with a smile of her own, pleased that she was going to get to see her family and friends; it'd been months. She went upstairs to pack, also anticipating the three-hour drive to the small town downstate her family lived in. She hadn't occasion to drive much since she moved into the house, as most things she needed were within walking distance. So, her beloved 1968 Chevelle had to sit in the driveway most of the time. She and her father had rebuilt it together while she was in high school after rescuing it from a junkyard not far from where they lived. Together, they had rebuilt the engine, replaced the upholstery to as close as they could get to the original, then painted it dark blue with white rally stripes on the hood. It was her baby, and she hated that it stayed parked most of the time. Although, every week, she made sure to take it for a drive, just to "blow the cobwebs out," as her father liked to say, but it wasn't the same as taking it for a long drive. She was looking forward to taking the backroads home, not caring if it made her drive longer.

≈≈≈≈

Jame pulled into the driveway of a modest house in a town not unlike the one where the Dragonfly sat. Only instead of a town square, it had a Main Street, replete with buildings over a hundred years old, whose architecture Jame had always admired. On the drive to her parents' house, she passed the old movie theater, which had closed before her parents had been born. The letters from the marquee had been lost to time, but there was still an old poster in the window from the last movie played there. To get home, she turned down a side street, the only brick street left in town. It ran in front of the bank and used car lot. She turned left and went over the train tracks. Just before the still-functioning train tracks, she had crossed over the long-defunct streetcar tracks, which hadn't run through that area since the mid-fifties when the company switched over to being a freight business only and the trolley cars were parked for good. Some of the tracks could still be seen poking through here and there; though the company had removed most of the line, it had missed some.

There was nothing picturesque about the town. It would never be used as the set of a movie showing idyllic small-town life. Instead of tree-lined streets and craftsman-style houses, which all movies and TV shows everywhere seemed to think small towns consisted of, her town was full of trailer parks and dilapidated houses and yards full of cars on blocks. There was a road that ran on the east edge of town the locals called Rezzie Road, though its official name was Reservoir Road, as it led to the local supply of fresh drinking water/main drunken teenage party spot. Jame had never hung out there and had only driven around it a few times. Just off Interstate 55 on the way into town was a long-closed truck stop on the south side of the road and the Dairy Queen on the north that came in in the early nineties, just before Jame was born. According to her parents, it had been met with a lot of enthusiasm from the locals. She had never seen what the big deal was about it, it was just soft serve, but she knew she was in the minority in that view.

Her parents' house was one story, small and white, with a miniscule front porch, with enough room for a glider and a side table. Originally, the house had only two bedrooms, but her father had built another one on in the back for her brothers to share. They had always been jealous of the fact she had her own room. She had countered with, "Well, at least yours has an outside door. You can come and go whenever." And they did. Her father's reason for the back exit, he said, was because when the boys left, their room was going to be a sun porch. But that never came to pass, as her father never got around to completing the project. For now, it still held the bunk beds her brothers had slept in until they went off and joined the Army, as well as all their heavy metal and sports posters. The street signs her oldest brother, Rick, had stolen from near the school were still hanging on the wall by the back door. Someone years ago had thought it wise to name two cross streets Peters and Johnson, perhaps not realizing the amount of giggling that would cause teenage boys and other immature people.

No one was home when she arrived, which wasn't surprising, being a Monday. She knew her father was still working somewhere on the road crew, probably filling potholes, and her mother was working at the same factory job she'd had for years, making fan motor parts or assembling them. Jame had never been sure which. Her mom had stayed at home until Jame, the youngest, had entered first grade, then she had gone to work to help make ends meet. As a result, her mother now had a noticeable stoop to her back, and she was constantly rubbing her hands as the arthritis had long since taken hold.

When Jame entered the house, everything looked the same. Her father's "fat man's chair," as he referred to his recliner, was starting to look a little worn on the arms. The remote was still sitting on the arm from when he was last sitting there, probably the night before. There was a multicolored crocheted blanket on the back of the floral sofa that Jame's grandmother had made. The TV, an old square, heavy boxy one, was sitting in the ugly blond pressed wood entertainment stand, surrounded by her father's Harley-Davidson figurines and the same dusty DVD player they'd had since she was in grade school. The white walls were covered with school pictures of her and her brothers from every year. A wedding picture of her parents graced the wall above the TV. She smiled, liking the fact that it never changed. She closed the door behind her and went into her old room, which she couldn't get into until she closed the front door.

Just like the boys' room, her room was the same as it had been when she had been growing up. Pictures of her idols were still on the walls: K.D. Lang, Gina

Gershon from that one good movie she did, and a portrait of B.F. Skinner with his wild white hair and the quote, "Education is what survives when what has been learned has been forgotten." Since she had taken her favorite comforter with her when she left, her mother had covered her bed with an old quilt that her great aunt Ida had made especially for her when she was eight. It had been made from old scraps of material: blouses, paisley-patterned handkerchiefs, and flannel shirts. During a washing accident when she was in high school, the white parts had been dyed a pale pink, which she had initially hated but had come to accept. She had loved the blanket, as Aunt Ida had been her favorite, and she saw the quilt as containing something from every member of the family. She sighed, kicked off her shoes, laid on top of the quilt, and put her hands behind her head. She smiled and said, "I needed this."

When the front door opened a few hours later, Jame awakened from the nap she hadn't realized she needed. "Shit, what time is it?" She pulled her phone out of her pocket. It was after four. Realizing she had been sleeping for the last three hours, she sat up and stretched. As she was doing so, there was a knock on her door. "Come in," she said with a yawn.

The woman who walked in was a little shorter than Jame with collar-length mousy brown hair that was starting to gray, and a kind face that was now smiling at Jame as she came into the room. "Hi, honey. I saw your car when I came in. I'm glad you're home."

Jame stood to embrace her mother and kissed

her on the cheek. "I'm glad to *be* home. Sorry I was asleep when you came in. Apparently, I needed a nap."

"Oh, that's all right. I know you had a long drive. I'm sure that tuckered you out. Are you hungry?"

"It was only a few hours, not that long." Jame thought about it for a moment, then replied, "Yeah, I am kinda hungry. What leftovers you got?" Jame followed her mother to the small kitchen at the back of the house. It had undergone an upgrade since her childhood. Now it had a few more cabinets and a new countertop, as well as new paint on the walls. There was room for a modest table that all five of them could sit around, which they did every night at dinner, a tradition her father insisted on. The bathroom was off to the right and the door to the boys' room on the left. Jame took a seat at the table as her mother went to the fridge.

"Well, we still have some of that chili I made last night. That's all I got right now. With it just being the two of us, I only cook a couple of nights a week. I just make big batches of things, and we eat the same thing for two or three days. Your father doesn't seem to mind. Of course, I think that man would eat an old shoe if I covered it in ketchup and told him it was meatloaf." Her mother busied herself preparing Jame something to eat, chuckling to herself.

Jame smiled. "I'm sure that's not true. Your meatloaf isn't that bad."

Beverly Annis turned around from the counter and narrowed her eyes at Jame. "My daughter, the comedienne. I'd hush if I were you, I could make you warm this up yourself." Despite her words, she reached up to get a bowl out of the cabinet and proceeded to spoon some leftover chili into it to be microwaved.

Jame just smiled at her. She knew her mother's MO was to feed her every time she walked in the door. At least, the first time. After the initial meal, Jame was on her own. She wanted to protest, have her mom sit while she got her own food, but she knew it would do no good. So, she sat there and let her mother make her something to eat, but once the food was in front of her, she insisted her mother sit and talk to her. Her mother obliged but only after pouring herself a glass of sweet tea.

"Does that woman not feed you?"

Jame smiled around her spoon. "Yes, she has a great cook who makes old-fashioned stuff." Which was true. Marie cooked some of the same dishes her mother made, which was perfectly fine as far as Jame was concerned, but some of the women were from the city and used to eating different things. Jame would never admit to her mother that Marie's biscuits were the best she'd ever eaten.

Her mother looked impressed. "A cook, huh? Fancy. Would have been nice having a cook around here when you and your brothers were growing up. The boys especially. I've never seen anyone eat so much in my life. I swear, they both had tapeworms."

"Good thing I never had that problem." Jame grinned as she shoveled more of her mother's chili into her mouth. Her mother had also made hot dogs the night before and had warmed one up for Jame to put in the bowl. Jame had filled the bowl with crackers until there was no juice left, then chopped the hot dog into bite-size pieces, just as she used to do growing up.

"Oh, please...you ate so much, sometimes, I was convinced you were really a boy." Her mother glanced at Jame's attire: tennis shoes, jeans, and a button-down men's shirt, all expensive and all from the men's section. "Looks like I wasn't so far off." Beverly reached over and ruffled Jame's short hair. "But I gotta admit, you do look handsome. If that's what you're going for, that is. What are you going for, anyway?"

Jame blushed under her mother's teasing. "I wasn't going for anything in particular, but I'll take handsome."

"Are there any girls up there in that town?"

The blush became deeper as Jame swallowed and asked, "Girls?"

"Don't play dumb with me, Jamie Lynn, you know what I mean. Girls…of the dating kind."

"Oh, those kind."

"Yeah, those."

Jame immediately flashed on Ma'am and Sarah, though they were dating each other now, and though Jame knew both biblically, she knew they were not exactly what her mother had in mind. "Not really. I'm too busy working to have time for that kind of thing." Though evasive, it was still a true statement in its own way.

Her mother, seeing the hesitation in Jame, mistook it for reluctance to tell her the truth. "Are you sure there's not someone you're leaving out? Or are you just having, what do you call them, casual relationships, now?"

Jame laughed. "Let's just say I haven't met anyone to bring home to mother yet. But you'll be the first to know when I do."

"I'd better be. So, how's your boss?"

Jame caught herself from saying Ma'am as that

would be hard to explain. "Ms. Berry is doing well, as far as I can tell. Oh, and she wanted me to ask if you could send me back with more cookies. She said they were great."

Beverly beamed at this news. "Of course. How long are you staying again?"

"Until Saturday, then I really need to get back."

"Then I'll have plenty of time. And you can go with your father and me to the Fall Festival potluck at the country club. I hear this year they're going to have a Beatles tribute band." Beverly couldn't help but smirk at the mention of the band.

Jame laughed. "Yeah, because nothing says 'Fall Festival' like four middle-aged men in flannel shirts and pot bellies singing "Hey Jude" off-key."

Her mother joined her in laughter. "I hear the pharmacist does a passable impression of Paul, only he plays a banjo instead of a bass."

Mother and daughter were laughing together at the table when Ben Annis, Jame's father, walked into the kitchen. "Well, the prodigal daughter returns."

Jame smiled up at him. "Hey, Dad."

As he was getting a beer from the fridge, Ben couldn't help teasing Jame. "In my house less than a day and already eating me out of house and home. Don't that rich lady feed you?"

"That's what I asked her, she claims yes. Says there's a cook and everything."

"Ooh, fancy. Must be nice. Don't expect there to be servants in this house. In this house, you want something, you get up and get it yourself." He held the beer aloft in emphasis.

"I know, Dad."

"All right then. I'm going to my chair." With

that, the big man left the kitchen to take his place in his recliner, where he'd be until dinner, then he would return after the meal was over until bedtime, to watch TV.

Jame looked up at her mother but didn't say anything, long used to her father's attitude, which pushed the boundary between humor and rudeness. Instead, she stood and went to the sink to rinse her now empty bowl. She looked out the window into the backyard, instantly thinking of the dog she had growing up, an old overweight beagle and collie mix they had named Molly, though she forgot why. They got Molly when Jame was five, and she was already a few years old then. Molly lived until Jame was nineteen, when old age caught up to her. She came from people who didn't take their animal to the vet to be put down; instead, they did it themselves. Jame had been working at the coffeeshop when she had gotten the call from her mother that her father and one of his buddies had taken Molly out to the woods and "put her out of her misery." She had cried more than she ever thought it possible to cry over an animal. Afterward, she told herself no more dogs.

She put the now clean bowl in the strainer, then dried her hands on the dish towel sitting on the counter. Suddenly, she turned around and said, "I'm going for a walk. Last time I was here, I wanted to but didn't. I'll be back for dinner."

Her mother stood from the table. "Okay, have fun. Place hasn't changed much since you left."

"Didn't think it had." Jame left the kitchen, walking through the living room to get to her room where she had left her jacket. She didn't say a word to her father as she passed him, and he was engrossed in an old episode of the original *CSI* and didn't say a word to her as she walked by. Jame retrieved her jacket and walked out the door. She stood on the front porch for a moment and looked around, deciding which direction to go first. She decided it didn't really matter, as there wasn't much to see in the town of five thousand, and headed right, toward Main Street.

※※※※

Jame walked down Main Street, whose downtown section was six blocks in total. Along the way, she passed the Catholic church and the school that sat next to it, the one grocery store still left, and the auto parts store that had been in the same yellow building since before she was born. A couple of blocks down, she passed the old Rexall Drug Store, whose pharmacist was behind a high, raised counter in the back. Her parents never used that one, they used the Kelley Drugs across the street. Her mother claimed their prices were better, but Jame suspected the real reason was because the Rexall guy was a douche, but her mother was too polite to say so.

Instead of walking the entire length of Main, Jame turned when she came to the large complex that held all the city offices, including the police and fire departments, the city water, and, at the far end, the one-story library. Jame had spent a lot of time there growing up, reading everything she could. It was short on psychology texts, but she read all the classics and the books on local history. Because of her reading habits, she knew the current name of the town had been the result of a misspelling made by whoever it was who had filled out the paperwork to be incorporated.

She had always found that factoid amusing.

She walked a block off Main and came to a corner bar named Trinie's. She had never met Trinie, as the original owner had died a long time ago. It was now run by her son, who Jame knew. She walked in and looked around, taking in the massive antique mahogany bar and mismatched stools. There was a jukebox on one wall that played CDs and a pool table that took up most of the other side of the room with worn-out felt and sides that had no bounce left in them. She knew that because she had spent a lot of time around that table growing up. The owner's daughter had been her best friend since childhood, and the bar had been their playroom. The patrons were all people who knew and respected her family, and during daylight hours, when they were allowed in there, there were only ever one or two hardcore day drinkers who did nothing more than sit at the bar and watch TV, paying the girls no mind. And if they had, they would have had to answer to Louie, the owner, who tended bar during that time and was a big man with no compunction about knocking out someone if he thought they were mistreating his daughter, Rose.

As Jame was walking up to the bar, the door leading to the kitchen opened, and a young woman about Jame's age came out dressed in a black T-shirt with the bar's logo on the upper left side, faded jeans, and a short haircut similar to Jame's, only with less style. She had a bar towel in her hands that she casually threw over one shoulder and a cigarette behind her right ear. Jame smiled when she saw her. "Could you be any more of a throwback, Frankie?"

Frankie, who had grown up as Rose but had started shortening and going by her middle name in high school, took one look at her best friend and grinned. "Hey, if it isn't Joe Cool." Frankie came around the bar and greeted Jame with one arm extended for a shake, the other encircled Jame in a half hug. "Looking sharp, man. I think your clothes cost more than my car."

"What can I say, it takes a lot to look this good."

"Whatever, asshole. So, you need a drink before hitting the homestead, is that it? I would." Frankie went back around the bar, and Jame took the empty stool at the end farthest away from the TV, where there was one person sitting and watching the news, an older gentleman named Charlie, who was a regular.

"Nah, just stopping in to say hi. I went home first, took a nap. After Mom came home and fed me and Dad came home, I decided I needed a walk."

Frankie nodded knowingly. "Well, the least you could do is spend some of your ill-gotten gains at my bar."

"The least you could do is give your best friend a free drink."

"Oh, please. Do you see me walking around town in a shirt with a label in it? I don't think so."

Jame grinned. "Your shirt has a label, one with dancing fruit."

"Hey, don't knock the dancing fruit, they make a fine shirt." Frankie opened the cooler and pulled out a glass bottle of Coke and popped the top, then slid it across the bar to Jame, who accepted it with a grateful smile. "So, how's your mom? I haven't seen your parents in a while."

"They seem okay. I don't think they go out as much as they used to."

"So, how's that hot sugar mama you work for?"

Frankie grinned.

Jame had sent her a picture of Ma'am once, one she had secretly taken when Ma'am hadn't been looking. She had taken it with the sole purpose of showing Frankie. "She's good. She has a girlfriend now, I think. At least, it looks like things are heading in that direction."

"Gotta be hard to date in that line of work. What about you?" Frankie leaned in and spoke softly so her voice wouldn't carry down to Charlie. "Are there even other dykes in that town?"

Jame leaned in, as well. "Some, definitely some." She couldn't help the grin as she thought of the town librarian or her other regular clients.

"I don't mean your customers, idiot. I mean, you know, *chicks*."

Jame sighed. "I don't know, probably. Between work and the classes I'm taking, I haven't had much time for dating. Besides, it's not something I'm going to worry about until after I leave there. Kinda difficult, you know."

"True. Besides, you have the best of both worlds right now, man. All the pussy you want and no hassles to deal with. Plus, it obviously pays well." Frankie gestured to Jame's clothes.

Feeling embarrassed now at Frankie's second mention of her attire, Jame just shrugged it off. "I suppose so."

"Man, what I wouldn't give to be in your shoes right now. I wouldn't have to pull beer all day for Charlie down there or play bouncer on the weekends. But at least I get to throw out guys from our football team. That's fucking fun."

Jame looked at her skeptically. "You are *not* a

bouncer. You couldn't kick anyone's ass."

"Fuck you. I am too a bouncer. Besides, it's not necessary to kick anyone's ass. When I raise my voice and grab them by the ear, they fucking listen to me."

"Because they're scared of your dad."

"Beside the point."

Jame stayed for about an hour before she stood to leave, knowing her mother would have dinner on the table by six, and she had said she would be back. As she walked home, she couldn't help thinking about Frankie's reaction to her clothes and her life in general. Every time she came to visit, Frankie would make a comment about how much she envied Jame, and it was starting to get to her. Jame wanted to tell her how isolated she felt in the house, how the only friend she had there was a woman who, up until recently, paid to have sex with her. She knew Frankie thought her life was somehow idyllic, better than her own. Jame knew she had little to complain about. She did make a lot of money, probably more than even Frankie realized, and she did get to sleep with several women a week without commitment or drama. And she didn't have to see her parents or people she went to high school with every single day. Feeling lucky, Jame walked up the three steps to her parents' front door, knowing she was going to leave before Saturday.

Chapter Seventeen

The same Saturday Jame was in Ma'am's office asking for time off, Sarah was home with a sick P.J., the second time he'd come down with something since the school year had started. That evening, instead of the date she and Renee had planned, Sarah was sitting on the couch with a feverish P.J. asleep on her lap, a decorating show playing on the TV, and texting with Renee like they were in high school. It was an interesting way of getting to know each other, but Sarah felt it was more honest, as it allowed her to reveal things she might be too embarrassed to say in person. And with P.J. so close, she wasn't about to engage in flirting over the phone. At ten o'clock, she tapped P.J. on the shoulder and said softly, "Hey, bud, I think you need to go sleep in your bed now, okay? It's getting late. Come on."

He rubbed his eyes and sat up and mumbled, "Okay."

Before he could get off the couch, Sarah said, "Hold on, let me check your temperature." She leaned over and kissed his forehead, letting her lips linger there a moment. "You're not as warm as you were, it's going down. Let me get you one more dose of cough medicine before bed, okay?" She stood from the couch and went in the bathroom and took the children's cough syrup down from the medicine cabinet, then filled the cup to the etched line.

"Do I have to? It's gross." Nevertheless, he groggily followed behind her.

"I know it is, sweetie, that's how you know it's medicine. At least your medicine has a little flavor in it. When Mommy gets sick, they leave out the fruit flavor and keep all the gross. Enjoy it while you can, kid." She handed him the cup, and he downed it like a champ. When he was done, after shaking his head in disgust, she took the cup from him and rinsed it in the sink before replacing it on top of the bottle. "Okay, I won't make you brush your teeth tonight, but let's wash off the cough syrup stickies, then it's off to bed with you." After washing his face, which also served to cool him down a little, Sarah walked with him to his room and tucked him in. "Night, munchkin, love you." She kissed him again before standing to leave.

"'Night, Mom." He was already closing his eyes and settling in.

Sarah turned out the light and went back to the living room and settled back in on the couch with a smile on her face to continue the conversation.

On Monday, she kept P.J. home from school to be on the safe side, but by midday, she knew he would be well enough to go back Tuesday. When Renee texted to ask about him and if Sarah would be able to come for dinner, she didn't hesitate to say yes before even knowing if Danni could watch him or not.

When Sarah did call her, Danni asked, "Did it ever occur to you that I might have a life?"

"Not really, no."

Danni gave her a disgusted sigh. "Fine! Go, have fun, I'll just be here entertaining a five-year-old, who, sadly, is the best male company I've had in a while."

"That is sad. I almost feel sorry for you."

"Don't patronize me."

"Why are you so bitchy today, anyway? Did your character just die or something?"

"This isn't bitchy, you should know that by now. This is just mildly irritable. If you want bitchy, I can be bitchy." Dropping her voice to a sultry register, Danni went on. "I can be whatever you want me to be," she said before bursting out in laughter.

"You're twisted."

"You're the one paying prostitutes. Isn't that how you talk to them?"

"I'm not doing that anymore, and I'm hanging up now."

The last thing Sarah heard Danni say before she ended the call was, "Chicken!"

Later, when Danni came to the house, Sarah busied herself with giving Danni instructions about dinner and P.J.'s bedtime routine, then leaving as quickly as she could just in case Danni wanted to resume the previous conversation about prostitutes.

She was instructed to park in back, like always, then come in through the kitchen. Renee met her at her car and enveloped her in a hug, then gave her a welcome home kiss, but not a demanding one. Sarah hugged her back, lingering in the embrace, soaking in the warmth.

Renee kissed her on the cheek. "Come on, dinner's waiting."

They walked up to the house with their arms around each other's waists. "You know, someday you're going to have to take me on a real date, otherwise I'll think you don't want to be seen in public with me." Sarah smiled up at her.

Renee stopped in her tracks. "I just thought...

that you wouldn't want to be seen in public with me."

"What? Why do you…why would you…?"

Renee smiled. "Never mind, come on." She turned to usher Sarah inside, but Sarah held her ground.

"No, wait a second. I'm not ashamed of you or afraid of what anyone thinks. So, just stopping thinking that, okay?" Sarah reached up and caressed Renee's cheek.

Renee smiled. "Okay. I should have known better."

"Yes, you should. Now you promised to feed me." Sarah took Renee's hand and resumed walking.

"Yes, I did." Renee let Sarah lead her into the house as if she was in charge.

When Sarah opened the back door, she stopped in the doorway. The room was alight with candles, and there were fresh red roses from the garden on the table. Marie looked up and smiled at her as she placed their plates containing filet mignon on the table next to glasses of the dark red Syrah wine, which Sarah only knew because she had tried it for the first time the week before. "Oh, my gosh. This looks amazing." She turned to Renee, who stood next to her smiling. "Forget what I said about going out, this is wonderful. Thank you."

"I'm glad you like it."

Sarah didn't reply, she just kissed her. Neither noticed when Marie left the room.

༄༅༄༅

"Marie is a goddess. This is, by far, the best steak I've ever had. You are so lucky you get to eat her cooking every night." Sarah took another bite of her steak and savored it, closing her eyes in the process.

"Don't let her hear you say that, she'll ask for a raise."

"Maybe you should give her one."

Renee smiled at her behind her glass. "Why do I have the feeling that you guys will gang up on me?"

"Only if we need to. Otherwise, I'm on your side all the way."

"Well, that's good. Don't need my staff thinking they can get my girlfriend to take their side over mine." Renee grinned and quickly glanced around, making sure the woman in question wasn't within earshot.

"Don't get ahead of yourself. You haven't asked me to go steady yet." Sarah's look was pure tease as she held Renee's gaze long enough to make her shift in her seat, which made her break eye contact and start giggling.

"I haven't?"

Sarah shook her head.

"Well, I have been remiss." Renee took Sarah's hand in hers. "Sarah Burgess, will you be my…I'm not even sure what word's appropriate at our age."

"When you figure it out, you let me know. In the meantime, yes, whatever that is, I'll be that." Sarah couldn't help laughing at their exchange.

"Good."

"So, what's the story with you and Marie, anyway?"

"What? What do you mean?" Renee was taken off guard by the sudden change in topic.

Sarah shrugged. "I mean, she's not just your cook, is she? You have a history, don't you?"

Back in control, Renee replied, "I do believe

you're fishing."

"No, if I was fishing, I would have been more indirect. I'm simply asking."

"I appreciate that you come right to the point. I hate it when someone talks around the thing they really want to get at, never really coming right out and asking what's on her mind."

Sarah leaned across the table toward Renee and grinned. "You're stalling."

Renee grinned back. "You noticed. Okay, there is history there but not the one I think you're alluding to."

"What am I alluding to?"

"You think we were lovers."

"Were you?"

Renee laughed softly. "No, never. She and Stella are more like my family. I've never thought of them that way."

"How long have you known them?"

Renee leaned back in her chair and considered Sarah for a moment. Then, seeming to come to a decision, she said, "Seems like forever. They were the first friends I made when I was still a working girl. They'd already been in the business a few years. They looked out for me. They kept me safe. When I stopped turning tricks, I asked them if they wanted to come with me, and they said yes."

"So, now you take care of them." Sarah smiled.

"No, they still take care of me. Not only do they cook and clean for me, but they keep me out of trouble still. They let me know when I'm about to do something stupid, just like always."

"Oh, gosh, I hope they didn't say anything against me."

"No, in your case, the something stupid would be if I didn't make a move to let you know how I felt. Stella was especially vocal about that."

Sarah laughed. "Remind me to thank her later."

"I will."

Sarah hesitated before asking her next question. "Can I ask you something?"

"You can ask me anything."

"I've been curious…and if you don't feel comfortable answering, I'll understand, but I just want to know more about you, and I think this is something I should know. I mean, if we're going to, you know, date."

"You don't have to be this nervous. I know what you want to ask. And it's okay."

"It is?"

"Yes."

Renee paused before continuing, and Sarah didn't speak, she just waited for the answer she now wasn't sure if she was ready for.

"When I was seventeen, a man by the name of Cecil Montrosse became the youth pastor at my mother's church. He was young, in his mid-twenties, funny and seemed to understand us teenagers. He listened with a sympathetic ear to all my teen angst about my mother. He started to want to spend a lot of time with me, just hanging out, then it felt like dates. I had known I liked girls since junior high, but I hadn't told anyone yet. Not in this town. So, he didn't know. Not that it would have mattered." Renee paused and took a sip of wine before continuing.

Sarah reached across the table and took her hand.

Renee squeezed it gently and continued.

"During one of our counseling sessions, that's what my mother called them, he told me that he knew of a job in Chicago that would hire me that paid well. He said if I wanted to leave my mother, who I was convinced I hated, the job paid well enough to live on my own. He said he even knew some girls I could room with until I made enough to get my own place. He was offering me a chance to run away from home and make good money doing it. Who wouldn't want that? So, I said yes. We waited until the next month when my mother had scheduled a small trip for herself to go see her sister for the weekend. I begged off, said I had homework. She believed me and said she was proud of me for caring so much about my schoolwork." Renee shook her head at her mother's naïveté.

"He trafficked you."

"Yes. But I wasn't held prisoner. I was free to leave. I knew that. It was my choice to stay."

"Why? Why did you stay?"

"Remember what I said the other day? There's a lot of money to be made in pleasure. I learned quickly how to make the most of it. Marie and Stella kept me safe, as I said. They told me where to make the most money and what neighborhoods to stay away from. The three of us shared an apartment so we could save as much as possible."

"Did you have a pimp?"

"Yes. A man named Johnny Elliott. He went by Johnny E. Real imaginative guy, ol' Johnny."

Sarah's face was becoming more troubled as Renee spoke. "Did he ever…I mean, was he ever mean to you?"

"He never hurt me, if that's what you mean. He ruled by threats and intimidation, mostly. He slapped some of the other girls around, though, the ones who mouthed off. I kept my mouth shut and did what he said. It was a job to me. One I didn't plan to stay at forever. After ten years, I had enough saved and had made some good investments. Some really good investments. Plus, I was only with Johnny for two years, then Stella and Marie and I left and did our own thing. We went high-tech."

Sarah smiled a little at that. "High-tech?"

"You might say we diversified our portfolio. We took our business off the streets and into an escort service we started. It's amazing how much the price goes up when your garden variety prostitute puts on a fancy dress, gets her hair done up nice, and starts calling herself an escort instead of a hooker. Suddenly, you're classy enough for men in suits. And eventually, you have enough money to do whatever you want."

"Like give other women a safe place to work."

"Exactly."

"So, whatever happened to the youth pastor?"

"For a while there, he was the pastor at my mother's church. He took over when Pastor Brian retired. I didn't move back until after he was reassigned to Georgia. As far as I know, that's where he is now. With a wife and three children."

Sarah shook her head. "Bastard. I really want to murderate him."

Amused, Renee asked, "Murderate?"

"It's a word. I think I heard my sister, Danni, use it when playing video games. I think it means to murder with extreme violence."

Renee laughed. "As opposed to gently murdering someone."

"Yes!" Sarah joined her in laughter.

"Well, I've had a lot of time to think about it, and I don't bear him any ill will. As I said, I made my own choices. Did he prey upon a teenage girl's vulnerability? Absolutely. Were there other victims, other girls he manipulated into becoming prostitutes? I would bet anything. But I can't blame it entirely on him. I stayed. I'm still here, just in a different way. No, he shouldn't be allowed to have influence over young girls, but I've made my peace with him. Hating him would do me no good." She downed the remainder of her wine, then took Sarah's hand. "I think that's enough history for now. Come on, I want to show you something. It's upstairs."

Grinning, Sarah replied, "Said the spider to the fly."

Renee stood from the table. "Dear Sarah, I'm not trying to fill your head with flattery to trap you. If I'm ever lucky enough to get you to stay in my bed, you can come and go as often as you like."

Sarah eyed her shrewdly before replying. "That's what they all say."

"As always, it's your choice."

"Of course, I'll follow you, weirdo. Lead the way."

Renee gestured up the back stairs. "Follow me."

As she was following Renee up the stairs, she said with humor, "Wow, this really is a winding staircase just like in the poem."

"Having second thoughts?"

"Not on your life."

※※※※

Sarah entered the room on the third floor. She

ignored the four-poster bed on the other side of the room. The first thing she noticed were all the pictures of a young boy at various ages, as well as a few of Renee, though there weren't many. There were several on each wall, though the walls weren't covered. She was drawn to one of the boy when he appeared to be in middle school or junior high. He was wearing a baseball uniform, bent forward with his hands on his knees, watching something off camera. He looked eager and ready to run, as if he was on the verge of flight. Sarah walked up to it and touched the frame, then turned to Renee standing near her, smiling. "Is this your son?"

"Yes, when he was twelve. I caught him as he was standing on third about to steal home. He hated when I took pictures of him while he played. I told him he was lucky that I wasn't one of those parents that got into fights and embarrassed him. He said I embarrassed him in other ways." Renee sighed as she continued to look at the picture.

Sarah took her hand. "Embarrassing our children is one of the joys of parenthood. How else are we supposed to repay them for being little shits?" She grinned to show she was only teasing. Renee smiled.

"Very true. And that was the beginning of his shitty phase. I'm still waiting for that to end."

"How old is he now?"

"Twenty-five."

"Oh, god, I have all that to look forward to." Sarah covered her eyes.

"Yes, but there are good things, too." Renee pointed to another photo. In this one, Ian was older and wearing a cap and gown, holding his diploma proudly in one hand, his other arm around an older woman. "Like, when you get to watch him graduate as valedictorian of his high school class and he stands on the podium and says, 'I wouldn't be here without the strength and determination of the two strongest women I know, my mother and grandmother.' Or when he tells you he wants to study to be a victim's advocate so that young children have someone to turn to."

"You did well, Mama." Sarah pulled Renee to her and wrapped her in a hug after kissing her on the cheek.

Renee accepted and returned the hug, relaxing in Sarah's arms for a moment, more than appreciating how tightly Sarah held her. Finally, she pulled back and placed a kiss on Sarah's lips before stepping away. When she did so, she gave her a small smile. "It would be wrong of me to take all or even some of the credit for that. My mother raised him. I was more like the rich relative who saw him once a week and spent money on him, did all the fun things he wanted to do, then left before I had to take responsibility. I wasn't a parent to him, more like an older sister. I didn't do anything to earn his respect or his love."

"Baby, you gave him a chance. And you protected him. And he obviously loves you." Sarah gestured to more of the pictures on the walls. In all the ones where he was looking directly at the camera, he was smiling. He was looking at the photographer with such deep affection that it was undeniable. "He wasn't smiling for the camera. He was smiling for his mother."

Renee took another look at the photos through Sarah's eyes. She saw the playfulness he always seemed to have dancing in his soft and warm brown eyes, the corners of his mouth in a wide smile. This was the boy she remembered playing with in the leaves. This was the boy who gave her house a name. This was her son. "You're right. I guess this is easy to forget sometimes when he's looking at you with such resentment or accusing you of exploiting young women." Renee sighed, the moment of nostalgia over.

"He said that?"

"In various ways. He doesn't think anyone's here of her own free will. He can't accept it. Sometimes, I think he's too altruistic for his own good. I think he's on a mission to save me and save the women of the Dragonfly from me." Renee turned to Sarah in earnest now. "I have never, I would never have anyone working for me who didn't want to. I—" Sarah stopped her by lightly covering her mouth with her hand.

Feeling awkward about doing so, Sarah quickly removed her hand from Renee's lips but jumped in before Renee could start talking again. "Shh, I know that. You don't have to convince me." She replaced her fingers with her lips, placing another light kiss there, then took Renee's face in her hands and smiled, trying to change the mood. "Was this what you brought me up here to see, or did I just sidetrack things?"

Renee returned her smile, grateful for the change in subject. "You didn't sidetrack things. I wanted to share my son with you anyway. But you're right, this is not why I brought you up here." Sarah raised an eyebrow and looked at her expectantly. "Not that, I mean, not yet. Just a moment." Renee stepped out of Sarah's embrace and walked over to her desk and pulled open the middle drawer. She took out a white picture frame, then walked back over to Sarah looking a bit sheepish. "There's one more picture I've thought about putting on my wall, but I wanted to make sure you were okay with it. But this one isn't for my wall, it's for yours." Sarah looked at her quizzically, and Renee silently handed her the frame.

What Sarah saw was the photo of her and P.J. that day at the botanical gardens. Renee had caught them laughing together. P.J. was watching the butterfly fly away, and Sarah was watching P.J. Renee's camera captured a side of her she had never seen. The play of the sun on her hair made it appear as if there was a glow about her. She looked almost angelic. Sarah couldn't help but stare in awe. "Wow. Your picture... you make me look way better than I am. Wow. I just...I love this." She hugged the picture to her chest and looked up at Renee with a smile of pure joy.

"Sarah, my camera didn't make you look any different than you are. You're just beautiful."

"Lame," Sarah whispered as Renee leaned closer and kissed her. This kiss was different than the others. This one had intent and purpose. Sarah knew exactly what Renee wanted, and she wanted it, too. Blindly, her arm reached out and set the photo on the desk. Sarah heard it knock something over but didn't bother to look. Instead, she put both arms around Renee's neck and kissed her back with the same intention. The same purpose. A part of Sarah's mind was thinking that they were too far away from the bed to just tumble down on it, and the desk just seemed an uncomfortable rendezvous point, no matter how many movies and TV shows tried to make it seem otherwise. Instead of relishing the feel of Renee's lips or her exploring fingers, Sarah couldn't help but giggle at the images coming to her. Of the items on Renee's desk tumbling to the floor in their wild frenzy to get it on on her desk. Of the spilled pens and pencils poking her in various places. Of a stray sticky note attached to the back of her shirt. That broke the dam, and she had to step away from Renee. She couldn't help laughing, and the confused look on Renee's face made it worse.

"Something wrong?"

Trying to get herself under control, Sarah stepped closer to her again and put her hand on her chest. "No, baby, it wasn't you. You were great. Really great. I just…I just had this image of us doing it on the desk and…and…" Sarah started giggling again, then took a deep breath to get herself back under control. "The whole thing just made me laugh. I'm sorry, I didn't mean to ruin the moment."

Renee put her arms around Sarah's waist, bringing her back to her. "Not at all. Your laughter could never ruin the moment. Besides, we can still pick it back up again."

Sarah looked into Renee's eyes and caressed her cheek and sighed a contented sigh. When she had been trying to control her laughter, her gaze had strayed to the picture of her and P.J. on the desk, and she realized she couldn't stay, not tonight. "I would love to…but I can't tonight. What kind of mother would I be if I stayed here, having…fun with you while my son was home sick? But ask me up here again, and I'll come to your parlor."

"I'll keep that in mind. And you always have an open invitation to my sanctuary."

"Sanctuary? So, that's what this is?"

Renee nodded.

"It's not your lair? I'm almost disappointed."

"Trust me, that is one thing you will not be."

"You think you're all that, huh?"

Renee shrugged. "Baby, I haven't just been around the block, I tore it down and rebuilt it."

Sarah laughed. "What does that even mean?"

"I don't know, but it sounded good, right?"

"I think it sounded like you have a lot to live up to. I'll be expecting a lot."

"Good, you should."

Later, they kissed goodbye under the full moon. When Sarah pulled out of the drive, Renee stood there a while longer, looking up at the Hunter's Moon. For her, the hunt was over. She knew what she wanted, and she could wait as long as she needed to.

Chapter Eighteen

On Wednesday, Jame was luxuriating in the fact that she didn't have any reason to get up early. Not that they had any early morning customers. Her job wasn't exactly a nine to five. She normally woke up before the other women while the house was quiet to do her homework and take a brisk walk, the only exercise she really cared to engage in. For the second morning in a row, however, she had been able to stay in bed with her favorite quilt snuggled up to her chin. It smelled like her mother's favorite lavender-scented detergent, a smell that took her back to childhood. The smell blended well with its artificial pale pink color, she thought, with a smile. She loved her job, but sometimes, she needed a break from taking care of everyone else's needs. If only her parents had a deep tub like the ancient clawfoot one at the Dragonfly, this vacation would be complete.

With a stretch, she reached over and grabbed her phone off the nightstand to check for messages. There was one from Frankie from around two in the morning. She probably texted after the bar closed, Jame thought. The message read: *Hey Stud, you're here until Saturday, right? We need to go out Friday. HMU.* Jame liked the idea. It'd been awhile since the two of them had been out together. They always crossed the river to St. Louis, the closest thing they had to a city with a gay district. Then she remembered she had plans for Friday. She texted back, *I can't. I promised my p's I'd go to the Fall Fest. Why don't we go together?*

The Fall Fest? Gosh, if we leave early enough, we can watch the parade too.

I feel that you're being sarcastic.

You think? Come on, I hardly get to see you since you ran off and started working at the Best Little Whorehouse in the Midwest. Don't make me pull the best friend card.

Jame paused before she responded. She never thought of the house as a whorehouse or a brothel. It was just the Dragonfly. Somehow, talking to Frankie always brought it home to her what she was and what she did for a living. Despite her Victorian surroundings, she wasn't living out the plot of a Jane Austen novel or even a Brontë romantic tragedy. When her reign at the Dragonfly was over, there would be no coda that would simply state, "Reader, I married her." Now frowning, she finally responded. *Sorry, the parent card beats the best friend card. Besides, you work in a bar. Hell, you live above one. Why would you want to spend your off time in another one?*

And you work in the sex trade, yet I assume you still have sex for free when the chance arises.

Actually, no. Why would I? If you don't want to come to the fest that's up to you, but I'll be leaving Saturday morning.

Fine. Who knew my best friend was such a loser?

Love you, too, asshole.

Just as Jame put her phone back on the nightstand and sat up in bed, there was a knock on her door. Confused, as both of her parents should have been at work, she said, "Yes?"

Her father opened the door and poked his head

in. "Get dressed and meet me in the garage." With that terse message, he started to close the door behind him, but Jame called him back.

"Dad, wait." He opened the door wider and looked at her expectantly. "I thought you had work today."

"It was raining this morning. Can't fill potholes in the rain. It's cleared up now, but I still have the rest of the day off. Now get your lazy butt out of bed and meet me in the garage. Grab some coffee if you really need it. You look like you need it." With that, he smiled, then closed her door.

Confused, Jame shook her head and shrugged, deciding she had nothing better to do. She wasn't sure what he had planned, but she dressed in a pair of old jeans she found in her closet, as well as a baggy flannel shirt she hadn't worn since high school, making sure to put on an undershirt, as the detached garage wasn't heated.

When she opened the back door in the garage, she stopped in the doorway. She saw her father standing in front of the most beautiful car she'd ever seen with the hood up, putting in a quart of oil. "Oh, damn."

Her father craned his neck to smile at her. "Thought you'd like it. Your brothers never seem to appreciate beauty like this."

Still in awe, Jame walked closer to the machine and reached her hand out to caress the fender. "Of course not, they're Neanderthals. Dad…where did you get this? I mean, a real 1955 Chevy Bel-Air."

"Yes, ma'am, it is. Bought it from a guy I worked with last spring. It's your mother's favorite colors, shoreline beige and gypsy red." Ben Annis smiled proudly as he closed the hood and wiped his hands on a blue paper towel.

Jame was too busy gazing lovingly at the car to realize her father had called her ma'am. If she'd been paying attention, she would have been amused. Finally, she found her voice, "So, is this Mom's car?"

"Mostly. On the weekends, she's the one who drives it. Although, I'll drive it to the next car show. She says those things make her nervous. Your mother likes taking the backroads. She has a need for speed." He smiled, thinking of it.

"A lead foot, you mean."

Her father laughed. "That too." Ben reached in his pocket and pulled out a set of keys. "Hey, bigshot, catch!"

Jame raised her hand instinctively as he tossed the keys in the air. She grinned. "Really?"

"Don't question it, just drive."

"All right!" Still grinning, Jame quickly opened the driver's door and got in but not in such a hurry that she failed to notice the restored leather interior or all the chrome on the dash, the huge steering wheel that looked as if it would be more at home piloting a bus instead of a car. She ran her hands over the grooves on the back of said steering wheel, then looked at her father. "Where shall we go?"

Ben looked at her with a smile of his own. "The Mother Road," he said, then he pulled a pair of aviator sunglasses out of his pocket and put them on.

"Gotcha." As Jame turned the key and put the car in reverse, her father reached up to the visor and pushed the button that would open the garage door, then leaned forward and turned the knob on the radio. It was tuned to the oldies station. When the familiar refrain to Roy Orbison's classic *Pretty Woman* began to play, Jame tapped out the opening beat on the steering wheel, then backed out of the garage.

≈≈≈≈

Jame and her father decided to drive the forty-plus miles to St. Louis via the section of Route 66 that coincided with Route 4. They cruised on that until they hit Interstate 70, then took a short jog on that, until finally landing on Interstate 55 and rode that the rest of the way into St. Louis. She already knew where he wanted to go. Every time they took a joyride together to St. Louis, he made sure to stop at a place on The Hill, the Italian neighborhood, at a restaurant famous for its fried ravioli. Jame found a place to park, appreciating the stares the car was getting. She trusted that the car would be safe while they ate.

After gorging themselves on pasta and garlic bread, making sure to get some to go for her mother, Jame and her father headed home, this time with her father driving. It was on the drive home that Ben mentioned her clothes. "That lady, your boss, she must pay you well."

Not sure how to respond, Jame replied vaguely, "Yeah, I guess so. Why do you say that?"

"The clothes. I think the outfit you arrived in is worth more than my whole wardrobe."

Embarrassed, Jame replied, "Not really. Outlet mall all the way. I just have good taste."

Her father took it in stride. He laughed. "Well, that's true. I don't know from clothes. I get a new flannel, I'm happy."

"Well, a good flannel is a good thing, too. I still

have my flannel."

"Don't you mean my flannel? My flannel you stole from my closet in high school."

"You know, after a while, Mom just started giving me your old shirts. She said not to tell you."

Ben grinned. "I know."

Surprised, Jame laughed. "Of course, you did. I used to steal jeans from Rick, and Tony still doesn't know what happened to his belt."

Ben laughed with her. "I think he's figured it out. The last time he called, he said, 'Tell that brat I want my belt back.'"

"Damn. I was hoping he would never figure it out." Jame fingered the buckle of the leather belt she wore, remembering the women who had slowly pulled it off her or the one who asked to be spanked with it. Jame had refused, one of the few times she had ever refused a client. She knew how much that belt would hurt. Tony had snapped her with it a few times growing up. She never agreed to anything that would inflict pain. Ma'am had asked her why. Ma'am hadn't been upset with her for not pleasing a client so much that she never came back. Instead, she wanted to know why. All Jame could say was, "I don't want to hurt anyone." Ma'am had let it go.

"At least now you can afford your own stuff and your life of thievery is over."

"Very true." They rode in silence for a while. Jame looked out the window at the flat, drab landscape. The fields were all harvested now and would lie empty until the spring. She had always thought she lived in the most boring section of Illinois. It was like living in a sepia photograph, everything had a yellow and brownish hue to it. At least farther north where the

Dragonfly sat, there were vivid green hills and valleys. Even the fields there seemed to have more symmetry and color, a beauty of their own. The area she had called home for the first nineteen years of her life could have served as the cover of a John Steinbeck novel.

Her father seemed on the verge of speaking, but the words took a few moments to come out. Finally, he said, "You know, I've been hanging out at Trinie's on Saturdays."

"Yeah, you always have. This isn't new."

"Right. Ever since Louie took it over when his mother died."

"I know. You and Louie used to hang out there and play pool when you were kids, like me and Frankie, right?"

"Yeah, that's right. Some habits never change, I guess."

"Why are you telling me this?" Jame looked across at her father, curious. What he was telling her wasn't news. Louie and her father had been best friends their whole lives, she knew they hung out. She felt he was leading up to something but wasn't sure what.

"Well, you know one thing men like to do in those places is talk. Mike Byers will tell anyone who'll listen about the time he met Al Pacino when he and the wife went to Disneyland. Swears up and down he saw him toss his cookies on the Pirates of the Caribbean. Or Paul Vincent, who can't shut up about being drafted by the Bears in high school, but he blew out his knee before he graduated and lost his chance. They're just stories. Who knows how true they are? Probably not much, but we listen to them anyway. Nothing much new happens around here to talk about, nothing interesting, at any rate. One guy goes on vacation or tries something new, he'll ride that story for decades."

"Yeah," Jame said with caution.

"You remember Rudy Duvries?"

"Yeah."

"I suppose you know his son, Charles. You went to high school together, right?"

"Yes. He wasn't actually a Rhodes Scholar, as I recall."

Ben chuckled at her words. "Nope. Hasn't changed, either. I only mention him because he's been telling a story at the bar about that time a few weeks ago when him and a bunch of his buddies went upstate to this brothel."

Jame froze. She didn't say a word, she just waited for her father to continue. She could feel him glancing at her, waiting for her reaction.

"He said he saw you there. He said you were working there. Said you were all duded up in men's clothes, taking women upstairs. Said you were a, a…well, I'm sure you can guess what he said." Ben changed lanes and sped up, passing several people who seemed surprised at what the old car could do.

"What did…what did you say?"

"Nothing. Before I could say anything, ol' Frankie came over and punched him. Damnedest thing I ever saw." Ben started laughing. "He wasn't expecting it and fell off his barstool. She told him to keep his mouth shut about things he knew nothing about. Then everyone started teasing him about getting flattened by a girl. He left not too long after that. Frankie says she barred him. She's a good friend to you."

"Yeah, she is."

"It almost seemed like she might know something, so I asked her if what he said was true."

"What'd she say?"

"She said what you did was your business, and if I wanted to know, then I had to ask you."

Good ol' loyal Frankie. That hadn't been the first time she had punched someone to defend Jame. Growing up, Frankie had taken it upon herself to be the one who stood up for Jame when anyone made fun of her for being different. As time went on, it was easy to forget things like that. "Are you asking me?"

"Yeah. I guess I am."

"You won't tell Mom?"

Ben exhaled for a moment and looked off to the side. He was silent, then he turned to her and asked, "How could you do that, Jamie Lynn?"

"For med school. I'm saving everything I can. Way more than I was making at the coffee shop."

"So, that lady, she's not your boss in the conventional sense, huh? What do you call it? A madam?"

"Yes." It seemed surreal to be having this conversation with her father. He wasn't supposed to know.

"And you're really going to go to school?"

"Yes, I promise. I'm sorry, Dad." Jame couldn't read him to be able to tell if he was disappointed in her or not, but how could he not be? She was his only daughter. She felt she had already disappointed him when she had come out to him, now this.

"Jamie, honey, just tell me you're safe there and that you don't have to do anything you don't want to do."

"Oh, god, yeah. Ma…Ms. Berry has rules in place." Jame stopped, not sure what else to say that wouldn't be too much information for her father. She settled on, "She runs a tight ship and keeps us all safe. In every sense. And healthy. And I can always say no, and she doesn't get upset about it."

Ben nodded along to her words, and he seemed to be more settled in his mind about it all. "That's good. So, uh, so, how long are you going to be doing this?"

"Not much longer. A year or two, tops. I have a plan."

"Good, good."

"Are we okay?" she asked worriedly.

"Yeah, we're okay. I can't say this is the life I wanted for you, and I really hate that this is the choice you made, but it's your choice and you're safe. And she takes good care of you."

Jame smiled at that. "She does."

"Good. No, I won't tell your mom."

"Thanks."

"Yep. I think I owe Frankie a beer, though." Ben looked at Jame and grinned.

"Yeah, me too." Jame turned, unable to say more, and put her arm out the window and rode the wave of wind for several miles.

Thursday night, Jame told her mother that she wouldn't be able to stay for the Fall Fest, her boss needed her help with an unexpected rash of bookings that weekend.

Her mother handed her a plastic container with

several dozen cookies. "Well, good thing I made these early. I had a feeling this would happen. Last time you were here, you only got to stay three days. I'm sure she's a nice lady, but why give you the time off if you're just going to get called back early?" Beverly shook her head as she turned back to the stove to finish preparing dinner.

"I know. Sometimes, things happen she doesn't expect. She'll love these, by the way, thank you for making them. Did you make any for me?" Jame asked, amused that her mother had affixed an old Christmas label to the container that said, "To: Renee Berry, From: Beverly Annis (Jamie's mom)."

Her mother turned around, wielding a plastic cooking spoon as a weapon. "You'll get cookies at Christmas. Jamie Lynn, there are three dozen cookies in there, and every last one of them better reach your boss if you know what's good for you."

Jame laughed. "Yes, ma'am!"

On Friday, Jame slept in, relishing her old quilt, then packed her things and headed for the highway. Before she left town, however, she had a stop to make. It wasn't quite noon yet, but there was already a car parked in Trinie's small parking lot. Jame pulled in two spaces over and went in the back door. It looked the same as earlier in the week. Charlie was at the end of the bar watching a rerun of *Bonanza* on a local channel that had played shows like that since she was a kid, if not longer. Frankie was at the other end of the bar reading the local paper, which only came out on Thursdays. She looked up when the back door closed. A smirk crossed her face when she saw Jame walk in.

Frankie put down her paper and immediately grabbed a bottle of Coca-Cola out of the freezer, popped the top off with the opener attached to her belt, then slid the bottle across to Jame, who had just sat in front of her. "Bored or leaving early?"

Jame returned her smile. "Yes." She took a swig of the Coke and gave an appreciative sigh. "Why does it only taste good in glass bottles out of a bar cooler?"

"Don't know, but it's the same with beer."

"Hear that."

"So, the Fall Festival's just not enticing enough to keep you in town, huh?"

"'Fraid not."

Frankie gestured to herself. "What about me? Aren't I good enough to blow off your parents for?"

"Sorry. I gotta get back. There's a party tomorrow. I need to be there." Jame shrugged as if it was out of her hands.

"Bullshit! You can't fool me like you can fool your parents, Annis. I know you just couldn't stand it any longer and had to get away. Three days seems to be your limit for staying here."

The corner of Jame's mouth lifted in a smile. "I've been here since Monday."

"Whatever, coward. Go, go back to your posh digs upstate. Leave the rest of us here in the boonies." Her words were harsh, but she couldn't suppress her grin.

"One would think you're not going to miss me. That almost hurts."

"Not as much as your face." Jame and Frankie burst out laughing. Charlie heard them and turned in their direction but didn't say anything.

Jame reached into her wallet and pulled out a fifty-dollar bill and pushed it across the bar. "I forgot to pay the other day. Also, I want to buy you a drink, and then Charlie can drink on the rest of this."

Frankie froze, looking from Jame to the money on the bar, then down at Charlie. "Why?"

"I'm told I owe you a drink. Also, it'd be nice if just once Charlie didn't drink away his V.A. check." She glanced down the bar to the man in question. He still watched the western.

Frankie took the money, then said loud enough for Charlie to hear, "Hey, Charlie, looks like my friend Jame likes you. Your drinks are on her today."

Charlie raised his mug aloft in a toast. "Thank you, Jamie Lynn."

"No problem, Charlie. And thank you for your service." She lifted her bottle in the air and nodded. The older man returned her nod but had no other words. After taking a drink, he returned his attention to the TV.

Once Jame's attention was back on her, Frankie asked cautiously, "What do you mean you owe me a drink? I drink for free, remember?"

"Symbolic."

"Symbolic of what?"

Instead of answering her question, Jame asked one of her own. "Why didn't you tell me he knew?"

Frankie didn't say anything for a moment, she just held Jame's gaze. Finally, she looked down at Jame's bottle instead of her eyes and shrugged. "Like I said to him, it wasn't my place to say. It was between the two of you."

Jame nodded in thought, considering her words. "It caught me off guard, though."

"I'll bet it did."

"Did you really knock him off his barstool?"

"Goddamn right I did! No one trashes my best

friend and gets away with it. That's *my* job."

Jame chuckled and said, "Thanks, asshole," then extended her hand across the bar.

Frankie grinned and shook it. "Anytime, loser."

Jame downed the rest of her Coke, then stood. "I should be hitting the road."

Frankie came from around the bar. "Seriously, dude, we need to hit the bars together. Next time you're in town, no excuses. You and me in the city. I won't take no for an answer. Or any other bullshit excuse you can come up with."

Jame clasped Frankie's hand in hers. "It will happen. Now hug me goodbye before I'm compelled to say something nice to you."

"Right." Frankie held her tightly for a moment, then stood back and let her go. "Oh, here," she went back behind the bar and opened the cooler and pulled out another Coke, opened it, then handed it to Jame. "One for the road."

"Thanks. See you at Christmas." She held the drink up to Frankie as she headed toward the door and waved to Charlie, who returned the gesture. Once in the car, she pulled out of the parking lot slowly, though there was little to no traffic. She drove the two blocks to Main Street over the brick road that always made it sound as if you had a flat tire, then turned east toward the highway. Once she passed the Catholic school and Main turned residential for the next mile, she sped up and didn't take any time to enjoy the view.

Chapter Nineteen

"So, Ms. Big Spender is finally taking you out on the town, huh? 'Bout damn time." Danni smirked at Sarah as she stood in the bathroom doorway watching Sarah applying makeup.

Sarah smiled. "Yes, but I haven't minded hanging out at her house. It's made it easier to get to know her. We talk for hours, and she's told me a lot." She finished with her eyes and put the cap back on the mascara, then placed it back in her makeup bag. Then, she rooted around until she found what she was looking for, her favorite shade of burgundy lipstick.

"That's all you do out there is talk?"

"Yes! Well, we kiss." Sarah paused in her ministrations a moment as a look of sweetness crossed her face as she thought about her times with Renee. She shook herself out of it, then finished with her lips, smacking them together and checking her reflection in the mirror. "This isn't about sex. We're working on something here. We'll get to that when we get to that. Be patient. I'm the one who should be worried about that."

"Apparently, thinking is all you're doing. You should have sealed the deal by now."

"Sealing the deal, as you call it, is easy. Building something that has potential to last, that takes work."

"Especially with women, amiright?" Danni grinned and raised her hand for a high five.

Sarah clasped hands with her, then replied, "My own sister, a misogynist."

"Am not!"

"Are too!"

"D2!"

As the sisters were falling into giggles from their old routine, P.J. came out of his room and stood next to Danni, who put an arm around his shoulders. "You look pretty, Mom. Where you going?"

Sarah felt warmed by his words. "Thank you, sweetie. I'm going to have dinner with a friend. You're going to keep an eye on Aunt Danni for me, okay?"

P.J. looked up at Danni. "Did you bring your toys?"

Danni laughed. "Which ones?"

"You know the ones."

"Yes, I brought the game system. But only after dinner. Mom says."

P.J.'s face lit up. "I know, we can have pizza for dinner and eat while we play!"

Sarah laughed, and Danni looked thoughtful. "Hmm, I like the way you think, kid. I'll take it under advisement. Now run along for a bit so I can tease your mother some more before she leaves."

"Mom says it's not nice to tease."

"That's right."

"You know, if you're going to insist on teaching him manners, I won't be able to relate to him at all." Danni ruffled his hair and kissed him on top of his head.

Before Sarah could reply, P.J. threw his arms around her waist in a hug. "I hope you have fun, Mama. Love you."

Sarah hugged him back. "Love you, too, little

man." P.J. loosened his grip and ran back to his room. Sarah smiled after him.

"So, anyway…"

"No, no anyway. I'm going on my date, we're going to have dinner and a good time, and however it ends is how it ends."

"For your sake, hopefully with a walk of shame."

Sarah grinned. "There is no shame in my game, sister."

Danni looked surprised as Sarah walked past her.

After another hug from P.J. and a wish of good luck from Danni, Sarah left for the restaurant. She had insisted on meeting Renee there, rather than having her pick her up because she wanted a more casual setting to introduce Renee to P.J. Also, she wasn't completely sure Danni wouldn't embarrass her.

The restaurant Renee had invited her to was on the square, one that Sarah hadn't had much occasion to go to very often, as it was more on the upscale side. Nevertheless, she parked nearby and checked out her reflection in the rearview mirror before getting out of the car. As always, her makeup was subtle and light. She paid the most attention to her eyes, as she'd frequently been told they were her best feature. She checked the corners for stray eyelashes, which she constantly seemed to do when she wore mascara. Everything looked fine. The burgundy on her lips made them look fuller, and she smiled at the thought of leaving lip prints on Renee's collar. Finally, she exhaled, then got out of the car, locked it behind her, and made her way into the restaurant.

The stick-thin hostess who greeted her was dressed all in black and looked barely old enough to drink. She smiled at Sarah and asked, "Do you have a reservation?"

"Yes, my…it's in my date's name, Renee Berry."

"Of course, let me see. Yes, I have that right here. She's waiting for you."

The smile never wavered from the younger woman's face, making Sarah wonder if, by the end of the evening, the other woman's face hurt from the effort.

Another young woman dressed in black approached the podium and said to Sarah, "Follow me, please."

"Thank you." Sarah nodded and followed her through the restaurant until they arrived at a table for two near the far wall. Renee stood as Sarah approached and kissed her on the cheek. Sarah took in the collared men's shirt that she was now used to seeing Renee wear, thinking dark green looked good on her, and the slacks hugged her frame well. As always, Renee wore her reddish-blond hair down, and it fell about her shoulders with natural waves. The subtle lights from the restaurant made her eyes glisten. As they sat, she said, "You look fabulous, and I feel very lucky to be here with you." It appeared that Renee blushed at her words, but it was hard to tell in the low light.

"Thank you. And you are as beautiful as always. I like you in dresses."

"You just like looking at my legs."

"Is that wrong?"

"No. But there's more to me than that."

"Oh, I'm aware. Trust me, my eyes don't just linger on your legs. I take in all of you." Renee reached across the table for Sarah's hand.

"Well, good. And I will feel free to return the

gesture."

"I hope so. Though I hope you know I'm more than just a pretty face." Renee smiled, and her words made Sarah giggle.

"I'm slowly figuring that out about you, though the face isn't too shabby, either."

Renee inclined her head. "I'm glad you approve."

The banter and the flirting continued throughout the meal, and Sarah could appreciate the fact that she felt an ease with Renee as if they'd been friends for many years. Yet it was more than that. She could feel the sexual tension building as the meal went on and tried to convey her feelings to Renee with frequent touches and soft looks. It'd been awhile since she had given out these signals, and she hoped she hadn't lost her touch.

When the meal was over, Renee looked across the table at her and asked, "Would you like to accompany me back to the house?"

Sarah smiled warmly, thinking, *I can still do this*. What she said was, "Yes, I would." They stood to leave, Renee walking behind her with her hand on the small of her back, close behind. When they reached Sarah's car, Renee took her time kissing her as a prelude to what was to come. Sarah responded to the kisses with the same passion but stopped when she realized how close she was coming to making out on the town square. She put her hand on Renee's chest and took a breath. "Save some for home."

"Home," Renee repeated. "Yes, I'll save some for home. I'll follow you out."

Sarah nodded and replied, "Okay." With a final, less passionate kiss, they separated, and after checking her lipstick in the mirror, Sarah backed out of the space and drove around and out of the square with Renee following close behind. What she hadn't seen while she and Renee stood kissing next to her car were Patrick's parents leaving the restaurant. They stopped in their tracks when they saw her, completely shocked.

※※※※

Friday was one of the busiest nights at the Dragonfly, so all the women were either downstairs waiting for a customer or already upstairs with one when Renee and Sarah arrived. Their ascent up the backstairs went unnoticed, which was fine with Sarah. She didn't want to see them, least of all Jame. Tonight, she didn't want to think about the afternoons of sex they had shared, as it had no place. That had been to fulfill a temporary need, and she was glad Jame had been so gentle with her; it had been what she needed at the time. But tonight with Renee was about something more. Hopefully, something more permanent.

When they reached her room, Renee seemed to hang back, almost shy. The light here was better than the restaurant, and Sarah could see Renee's eyes more clearly. They were looking at her so tenderly, it was almost hard to take. She gripped Renee's collar playfully in both hands. "Oh, no, you don't, don't go all tender on me now. You've already romanced me. All those weeks you spent watching me should have told you what I want."

Renee's eyes now showed surprise. "Yes, I suppose you're right."

Sarah cocked an eyebrow. "Well?"

Renee didn't say another word. Instead, she

lunged forward, capturing Sarah's mouth with her own. Sarah, her hands still gripping Renee's collar, pulled Renee to her. A moan escaped her as Renee's arms went around her. She loosened her grip now and, instead, unbuttoned Renee's shirt, pulling it frantically out of the slacks when she was done. Renee took her arms away from Sarah long enough to let the shirt fall to the floor. Sarah quickly slipped out of her dress and was about to remove her bra, but Renee reached up and stopped her. Sarah smiled and dropped her hands and let Renee remove the garment for her. Renee dropped to her knees, kissing her way down Sarah's chest, until she reached her nipple, where she let her tongue linger, while her fingers caressed Sarah's thighs. Sarah gripped her fingers in Renee's hair and put her head back and closed her eyes. After lingering for a while on her nipples, Renee moved on and kissed down her stomach. Before Renee could go any farther, however, Sarah gently pushed her back. Renee looked at her confused.

"Everything okay?"

"Baby, everything is fine, but I'd rather be on the bed." She took Renee's hands and pulled her to her feet, and Renee stood and smiled. Sarah put her hands on Renee's face and kissed her gently.

With her arms around her waist, Renee took a couple of steps back, bringing Sarah with her, until they were standing at the foot of the bed. They discarded the rest of their clothing there, then Sarah lay down and looked up at Renee with merriment.

"You finally got me here, big talker. What are you going to do with me? Can you live up to the hype?"

Renee laughed. "Oh, I think so. But before I do, maybe you could do something for me."

"Oh?"

Renee positioned herself on the other side of the bed, barely within Sarah's reach. "Start without me. I'll be on the other side, watching, like before."

Sarah raised an eyebrow. "Really, that's what you want?"

"Yeah, that's what I want."

"Okay," she whispered. Sarah put her head back on the pillow and closed her eyes and let her fingers travel slowly down her stomach. As she came closer to her clit, she heard Renee take a breath. Her fingers found her clit and rubbed, slowly at first, working it up to attention, while her other hand strayed to her nipple and squeezed. Her fingers worked faster, and she moaned, arching her back. Her clit throbbed, and she rubbed it between two fingers.

Renee leaned over and covered Sarah's mouth with her own and gently cupped her hand over Sarah's until they were both moving in unison over Sarah's clit. Together, they moved faster until Sarah cried out, but it was muffled by Renee's kiss. Renee moved her fingers down until they were inside, while Sarah kept working her clit. Renee shifted so that she was lying half on top of her as she moved her fingers in and out. Sarah moved her face aside to take a breath. Renee moved her lips to Sarah's neck and left small kisses there. Sarah's orgasm rose to a crescendo, and Renee stilled her hands as she felt Sarah's muscles tense inside her. She rode the wave with her and slowly moved inside her again once Sarah's body relaxed.

They rode the wave together several more times until Renee knew Sarah was completely satisfied. After a brief respite, Sarah pushed Renee on her back and looked down at her captive with a satisfied grin, holding Renee's wrists against the mattress. "It just occurred to me that the boss needs to be put in her place, and I'm just the woman to do it."

"I think I stopped being the boss when we walked in here." Renee twisted her wrists, testing Sarah's grip.

"You got that right." Sarah glanced at Renee's right wrist. "Already trying to get free? Hmm." Sarah turned back to her with a thoughtful expression.

"What are you thinking?"

"I'm thinking you're moving too much. Hold that thought." Sarah rolled off Renee and let go of her, then went to the bedside table, opened the drawer and rummaged through it.

Renee leaned over to watch, amused. "Why are you snooping through my things?"

"Because the bedside table is where most people keep their..." She pulled out a pair of handcuffs with a keyring attached and smiled. "...these." She pushed the drawer closed with her hip and twirled the cuffs on one finger as she walked back to the bed.

Renee was already leaning away from her. "I wish you hadn't found those."

"That's really a moot point now, isn't it?" Sarah removed the key and set it carefully on the table behind her, then turned back to her quarry. "Now then, as for you..."

Renee reached out for her, pleading. "No, just let me please you some more. Put those away."

Sarah studied Renee's face, deciding if there was real fear there or if this was just the game Renee wanted to play. She saw the light dance in Renee's eyes and the slight upturn of the corner of her mouth and knew this was a game Renee was more than willing to play. "What would please me is if you would raise your hands above your head. I think you know what I'm getting at."

Renee said nothing, she dutifully raised her hands as instructed, holding them close together.

The headboard was solid. There was nowhere convenient to attach the cuffs, so Sarah clasped Renee's wrists together and pushed her arms back until they were leaning against the oak. As she did so, her nipple grazed Renee's mouth, and Renee took advantage of the opportunity and drew the nipple into her mouth, flicking her tongue across it. The movement made Sarah inhale at the sudden touch. A moan escaped her as Renee continued to work her magic. Sarah grabbed the headboard, pushing more of herself into Renee's mouth, and leaned her head back. She couldn't help but sway back and forth with the rhythm Renee was creating. After several moments, Renee moved her head slightly so she could give equal attention to the other nipple. "Oh, god." Sarah licked her lips, then pulled back so that she could meet Renee's lips with her own. She let her lips wander to Renee's neck, then her collarbone, down to the soft tissue above her heart. She lingered there, drawing the skin into her mouth until she knew her mark would be left behind. Renee moaned and squirmed underneath her but kept her arms raised as if they were being held in place by something other than Sarah's wish. Sarah continued her exploration down Renee's body until she reached her clit, and she opened her eyes and looked up to meet Renee's, which were looking at her with such love and trust it almost took her out of the moment. She smiled up at her but said nothing, then she closed her eyes and continued where she left off, but now with a different focus. It was about more than just getting Renee to a place of bliss. It was more than learning how loudly she could moan. It was about loving her so much in that moment that Renee's joy became her joy, and when, after several minutes of Sarah's attention, Renee screamed Sarah's name loud enough to be heard downstairs, Sarah rolled with her and cried out her own wordless cry of pleasure.

As Renee's body shook with the aftershock of her orgasm, Sarah crawled back up to lie at Renee's side, and it was only then that Renee brought her arms down. Sarah contemplated leaving the cuffs on a little longer, but now she just wanted to snuggle against her, feel Renee's arms around her. She leaned over and grabbed the key from the night table and took off the cuffs, dropping them blindly to the floor. Finally, when she felt Renee's arms around her, she snuggled up to her and settled in.

Later, as Renee was falling asleep, Sarah leaned over and kissed her on the corner of her mouth. She whispered, "I have to go home."

Renee moaned and clasped her arm. She mumbled, "No, stay."

"I can't. P.J. is expecting me to be there in the morning. Next time, I promise."

Renee grumbled in displeasure but said, "Okay." She shifted her head slightly, and Sarah leaned down to kiss her goodbye.

"Sleep now, baby. I'll call you later." Sarah kissed her again, then eased her way out of bed and dressed quickly. She took one more look at the woman sleeping on the bed and smiled before she left the room, closing the door gently behind her, and made her way out to her car.

When Sarah got home, Danni was asleep on the

couch, curled up on her side, her arms underneath her. Sarah smiled and took the throw off the back of the chair and laid it on top of her.

Danni opened her eyes as Sarah turned out the light. "You're home. How'd it go?" she mumbled.

"I'll tell you in the morning. Go back to sleep."

"Okay." Danni pulled the blanket up to her neck and closed her eyes again, asleep before Sarah could close her bedroom door.

※※※※

The next morning found Sarah in the kitchen making pancakes when Danni woke up on the sofa. P.J. was sitting on the floor near her, playing the video game she had brought over the night before with the sound turned down. She stretched, then looked down at him. "You're playing without me, no fair."

P.J. giggled. "Morning, Aunt Danni."

"Morning, Sprout."

"Why are you still here?"

"Because I fell asleep, duh!" She reached over and tickled his neck, and he laughed and scrunched up his shoulder to avoid her fingers.

"Stop it! You're going to make me crash!"

"Aww, that would be too bad. I guess I shouldn't do this, either." Danni now attacked him with both hands.

Sarah stood in the doorway between the kitchen and living room watching them play. "Did you just seriously make my child lose on purpose?"

Danni stopped tickling him and looked up at Sarah. "He hasn't lost yet, he's just not first. Besides, I didn't do that to make him lose, I just couldn't resist attacking him. Just something about him makes me want to tickle him!" She went after him again, this time making him drop the controller and collapse into giggles.

"Well, if you two kids are done playing, there's chocolate chip pancakes on the table."

Danni stopped tickling, and she looked from Sarah to P.J., and a look of delight crossed her face. "Ooh, chocolate chip pancakes? I'm so in! Come on, we can play more after breakfast."

As Danni and P.J. walked past her, Sarah asked Danni with a smirk, "Don't you have a home?"

"I do, but it doesn't have chocolate chip pancakes."

"Or a five-year-old you can relate to."

"Hush. I know what time you came home last night."

Sarah made P.J. his plate and set it in front of him, then poured him a glass of milk. "How could you? You were asleep."

"Well, I know it was after two when I went to sleep, and you came home later than that." Danni sat at the table and made herself a plate, stabbing three pancakes from the plate in the center of the table, then smothered them in syrup.

Sarah worked at hiding her smile. "Well, never mind that, the point is I slept here last night." She looked down at P.J. pointedly before meeting Danni's gaze, who seemed to understand.

"That's true. I'm surprised you're up this early. Something must have given you a renewed sense of energy." Danni grinned as Sarah glowered at her.

"Shut up and eat your pancakes."

Danni chuckled as Sarah turned to pour herself a

cup of coffee. As she was stirring, there was a knock at the door. She looked up in surprise. "What the hell?"

Danni made a move to answer the door for her, but Sarah held up her hand. "Don't worry, I got it. Maybe it's the mailman or something." She walked through the small living room to the front door and looked out the small window. "What the hell?" she repeated. She opened the door and asked the man standing there, "What are you doing here? This isn't your weekend."

Patrick McArdle stood looking at her with nothing but contempt. His words were clipped with anger. "Can you come out here, please? I don't want P.J. to hear this." He stood with his hands on his waist, his jacket unzipped over his flannel shirt. His heavy boots made a clomping noise when he walked across the porch to stand as far from the door as he could, expecting her to follow him.

Sarah hollered into the house, "Danni, I'll be back in a minute, I just need to talk to someone," before she closed the door behind her. Once it was closed, she asked, "What's wrong?"

He turned to face her and practically spit out the words. "What the hell do you think you were doing last night? Do you think people aren't going to know? I mean, I had heard the rumors, but this, to know it's true? I don't even know what to think, Sarah."

"What the hell are you talking about?"

"My parents saw you...my own mother saw you...kissing and making out like some teenager... with that...that...whore!"

Sarah didn't think, she reacted. She smacked him hard enough to leave her handprint on his cheek. Before he could respond, she moved closer to his face and hissed, "You call her that again, and it won't be your face I go after. You have no right to lecture me on who I date, much less call her names. At least I was civil when you told me about that slut you live with."

Patrick rubbed his cheek, smarting at the impact. "No right? He's my son!"

"This has nothing to do with P.J. He wasn't there."

"I should hope not, but it's only a matter of time before you take him out to that house full of hookers." Sarah moved as if to strike him again, and he flinched. "Everyone knows. We've all known about the place for years. It's no secret. And we know who she is. It's bad enough that you had to go and turn queer, but did you have to do it with her?"

"I didn't *turn* anything, you idiot. And you have no right to speak about her. What's it matter what she does for a living? And what fucking business is it of yours?"

"I don't want my son exposed to that kind of lifestyle, that's what. And if you keep it up, I'll take him away from you."

"He hasn't been exposed to anything, nor is he going to be, and you have no grounds to take him. You would lose."

"Really? Are you sure? As I said, in this town, hell, in this county, everyone knows who she is. And not everyone approves of it. Child neglect, child endangerment, I'll do whatever I have to do. Don't push me."

"Don't threaten me. I'm not doing anything that would hurt him. You should know me better than that."

"I thought I did. But who you are now, how

you've been acting, this is a side of you I've never seen. And I don't like it. And I don't like it for my son."

"*Our* son."

"Whatever. Bottom line, you stop hanging out with prostitutes, and I won't sue you for custody. I can provide him with a stable home, I make a good living, and Ciara and I are engaged. What have you got? You don't even have a job. You won't be able to live on my money forever."

Sarah stood there seething, taking in his words. She wanted to refute them, but she couldn't. She never received a call back on the bank job, and she had no other interviews lined up. "I *love* him."

"You think I don't? Think about it, you choose. Him or her. It's up to you." He stared her down a moment, then turned to walk away. Before he left the porch, he turned back around. "You know, I've never slept with a whore, always wondered what it was like."

"Really? I thought you had." Before he could speak again, she cut him off. "Get off my porch." She turned and went back inside. She heard his boots going down the steps as she closed the door. She leaned her back against the door and covered her face with her hands.

Danni came in from the kitchen and put her arms around her. "I'm sorry, baby girl. It was all I could do not to come out there and rip his dick off and smack him with it."

Sarah laughed into Danni's shoulder and wiped her eyes with the back of her hand, then she looked worriedly at Danni. "Do you think he means it? Do you think he can do what he said?"

"Let him try. He has nothing to get you on. Nothing. So, you were caught snogging the town madam, so what? Big fucking deal. There's nothing he could take to a judge. Nothing. Okay? Don't let him worry you."

Sarah took a couple of deep breaths as she let Danni's words sink in. "I hope you're right."

"Of course, I'm right. I'm always right."

Sarah rolled her eyes.

"Rude."

Sarah laughed, grateful to Danni, and gave her a quick hug. P.J. came out of the kitchen wiping his wet hands on the back of his pants.

"Ready for a rematch, Aunt Danni?"

Danni turned in his direction and smiled at him. "Whenever you are, Andretti."

"Who?"

"Never mind." She gave Sarah's hand a squeeze before stepping back and joining him on the sofa.

Sarah left them to their fun as she walked into the kitchen to clean up the breakfast she didn't get to enjoy. She put the uneaten pancakes in freezer bags, then put them in the freezer on top of the bag of frozen spinach, then she scraped the plates into the trash before putting them in the sink to be rinsed off. Her phone buzzed in her pocket, indicating she had a message. She wiped her hands on a nearby towel and pulled her phone out of her pocket. She saw that the text was from Renee, but she didn't open it. She slipped the phone back in her pocket and turned on the tap to heat the water.

Chapter Twenty

"Yes, that was a dozen red roses. The card? The card…um…how about, 'I miss you.' No, wait, does that sound too needy? I think it's too needy. How about, how about, 'All my love, Renee.' Sounds kinda lame, I know, but that's the best I can do. Thank you." Renee gave the woman on the phone her credit card number and Sarah's address and hung up feeling as lame as Sarah always teased her of being. She wasn't good with expressing herself with words. She felt so inadequate. What could she say to the person who she hadn't had any contact with in nearly a week? It wasn't for her lack of trying. She'd called and texted several times, but they all went unanswered. Maybe there was a reason, maybe she was busy. It just didn't seem like her. What had she done to make Sarah run away from her like this? Had the sex been that bad? Had the possibility that they were moving toward something more permanent and solid sent her running for the hills? Had she come to her senses and remembered who Renee was?

Renee knew she couldn't offer Sarah normalcy. What did she expect—that they would just settle down and raise her son together? That Renee would go to PTA meetings and bake cookies and have birthday parties full of children? Sarah had every right to want those things, but maybe she realized she would never get them from Renee. Renee had proved that she wasn't a good mother when she sat on her own mother's couch and gave her baby away.

Nor was she the marrying type. She could bring home the bacon and then some, but she didn't exactly have the kind of job one could talk about at cocktail parties. Nor was she the type of girl one could bring home to mother. What Renee had been hoping for was a fantasy that could never be. She was surprised it had lasted as long as it did. She put her head in her hands, on the verge of tears. When the door to her office opened, she sniffed them back and sat up. She avoided Stella's gaze and mindlessly turned pages in the calendar in front of her as if she had a reason to do so.

Stella eyed her knowingly. She came up to stand beside her and leaned against the desk next to her. "Baby girl, what do you think you're doing?"

There was a strain to Renee's voice when she started to speak, so she cleared her throat to cover it up. "I'm a…I'm just checking something." She continued flipping pages.

Stella reached out and gently stilled her hand. "Stop it. You don't have to pretend with me."

Renee stopped but held on to Stella's hand. "Sorry."

"No sorry about it. Now how long has it been? Four days?"

"Six," Renee whispered.

"And you haven't heard a word?"

"No."

"So, she's ghosting you?"

Renee let go of her hand and sat back in her chair, then looked up at her confused. "Since when do you know current slang?" The corners of her mouth lifted in a slight grin.

"What? I know things. It's just dirty pool if you ask me. Letting you wine and dine her, then once she gets you in bed, boom! She vanishes like a ghost."

Renee chuckled. "I don't think ghosts go boom."

"How do you know? You ever met a ghost?" Stella crossed her arms over her chest and looked at her expectantly.

"Not to my knowledge."

"There you go then." Stella's look softened as she saw Renee's gaze become distant. "What else have you sent her besides flowers?"

Renee looked up at her, then quickly looked away. "What?"

"Don't pretend like you don't know what I'm talking about, Renee Berry. Answer the question."

"Am I on trial?"

"Maybe. I haven't decided yet."

"Why are you asking me this?"

"Because I've known you since you were a pup. I've seen you have crushes, and I've seen you get your heart broken. But this is the first time I've ever seen you in love. And it looks like you're on the verge of getting your heart broken worse than it's ever been before. I want to make sure you're not making a damn fool of yourself over some punk-ass bitch who doesn't deserve you."

Renee burst out laughing. Wiping her eyes, she replied, "You can take the girl off the streets... Just when I thought you had finally grown up."

"Being grown up has nothing to do with it. We're family, and you protect your family. Just say the word, and I'll cut a bitch if I have to. I still have my blade, the one I used to carry all the time."

"I remember. The switchblade. You even had a name for it."

Stella smiled. "Justice."

"Yep, that was it." Renee sighed. "As much as I appreciate your offer to commit a felony for me, hold off on that for now. Hope is not lost."

"Well, you keep hope alive, I guess." She patted Renee on the shoulder, then turned to go.

"Stella...thank you." Renee stood, and Stella opened her arms and enveloped her in a hug.

"That's all right, baby girl. I got you." She hugged her tighter.

Renee returned the hug, holding Stella to her. It'd been a long time since she had needed a hug like that from Stella. The last time had been when she had come back after leaving Ian with her mother. Stella had held her all night as she cried. Before she could stop them, the tears were falling and dampening Stella's shoulder.

"Shh, it's okay. I got you. It's okay."

≈≈≈≈

Later that afternoon, Renee took her camera with her as she strolled through the park. The leaves were popping up in more brilliant colors, and the ducks had all but left the pond, though there were a few hangers-on. She stood on the fishing dock and took pictures of the two ducks that were left as they swam side by side. She imagined they were a couple who'd raised many ducklings. Perhaps some of the ducks who came back every year were their offspring. She clicked off several shots of them before she moved on to the foliage.

It was a great fantasy, but she knew that's all it was. She had read somewhere, probably in one of Stella's nature magazines that she sometimes left on the kitchen table, that ducks don't mate for life. Every mating season, they find a new partner, do the deed, then they're on their way. They take what they need from each other and get on with their lives. Much like people, she thought. But ducks weren't at fault for that behavior, it was just how they were made. People didn't have that excuse, they knew better. At least, they were supposed to.

"Don't jump."

She smiled behind the camera at the familiar male voice, then pivoted so the camera was pointed directly at him. "Smile for the camera, son."

Ian put up his hand. "Haven't you taken enough pictures of me by now?"

She lowered the camera, still smiling. "Are you kidding? I still have space on my wall. Besides, I could never get tired of looking at this face." She pinched his cheek lightly, then on impulse, reached up and kissed him where her fingers had been.

He looked back at her in surprise. "You okay, Mom?"

She sighed, then patted him on the shoulder. "I'm fine." She walked to one of the two benches on the dock and sat. Ian joined her.

"Seems like something's on your mind. You look...distracted. Something you want to talk about?"

She looked out at the water, contemplating. Then she turned to him and asked, "Do you still hate me?"

"What? What are you talking about? I never hated you. Where is this coming from?"

"Just something I've been thinking about lately. I know you did in your teens. How could you not? I just gave you up for…for a life of debauchery. I would hate me." She held his gaze for a moment, but she couldn't look at him for long and soon turned away.

Ian moved closer and took her hand and spoke earnestly. "Mom, I never hated you. Sure, there were times when I didn't understand why I lived with Grandmother, and later, when you moved back, why I couldn't live with you. I was confused. I didn't know if you loved me or not." She turned around abruptly at that.

"Ian, no! I always loved you. Always."

"I know that. Grandmother told me all the time. She made me understand."

"Your grandmother? What…what did she tell you?"

"She said that sometimes mothers, no matter how hard they tried and wanted to, couldn't do all the mom things. Sometimes, she said, moms had to make sacrifices for their children, do things they didn't always want to do, just so their children could have the best life possible. She said you were doing things the best you knew how to give me a good life. And that even though I couldn't live with you, that you loved me as much as God loved Jesus." A grin played at the corners of his mouth, and it made Renee laugh.

"Because I gave my only begotten son? Great, now you're the Christ child. I hate to break it to you, son, but you weren't a virgin birth."

"I've seen the pictures of black Jesus, there's a resemblance," he teased.

"No wonder your grandmother loves you so much." She tweaked his nose, which made him laugh, and he put his arm around her. She rested her head on his shoulder.

"What's not to love?"

"True."

"So, we good?"

"Yeah, we're good." She sat up and looked him in the eye. "I've always loved you."

"I know."

"I'm glad that you do."

She squeezed his hand, then stood, her attention seemingly caught by something in the water. She raised her camera and took aim, then quickly turned and snapped a candid of Ian, then laughed at him.

"You're in a weird mood today. I'm not sure if I want to share a meal with you." He stood and shook his head at her.

"How about a glass of wine and a really thin tasteless cracker?" She smirked at him.

"I'm going to refrain from making jokes about white people food because my grandmother raised me better than that."

Renee linked her arm with his and started walking toward the ramp that led off the dock. "That's a shame."

"You had your chance, but you left me with her, and this is what happens."

It felt good to laugh with him as they strolled through the park arm in arm.

✧✦✧

Realizing she hadn't heard from Sarah all week, Danni sent her a text on Thursday. *Hey, just wondering if I need to be available this weekend for my date with the cutest five-year-old in town.*

No.

"Wow, that was short and sweet," Danni muttered as she sat back on her couch, sipping her morning coffee. She tried again. *You okay, sweets?*

I'm fine.

"Okay, woman, you're going to talk to me whether you like it or not," Danni declared to an empty room. *Sarah, I've known you long enough to know when something's bothering you. Is it Patrick? Has he said something again? Do I need to turn him into a castrato?*

LOL No. He hasn't said anything else. He should have nothing to get me on. I broke up with her.

"Son of a bitch!" *Oh, honey, please don't do that. Talk to Patrick. If you don't, I will.*

Don't talk to Patrick. What's done is done. I'm not losing my son over this.

She knew Sarah's mind was made up and she understood it, but that didn't change the fact she thought she was making a mistake. Sarah had never been happier in a relationship than when she and Renee were together. She left for their dates with the biggest smile. Patrick had never made her look like that. She was convinced that the only thing Sarah and Patrick had had in common was that they were both good-looking people, but Patrick was about as deep as a puddle. He hadn't had anything else to offer except a pretty face. Then, when P.J. came around, he was what they had in common, but it hadn't been enough to keep either of them interested. But Sarah had been determined to keep her vows, for her son. She wanted him to have a stable childhood. It was Patrick who couldn't keep it in his pants. Sarah didn't deserve this.

Danni thought about sending a string of invectives Patrick's way, or better, leaving a steaming pile from her neighbor's German shepherd on his front porch. But childish pranks were not going to solve this, no matter how satisfying it would be to see him stomp out the flames. She had a better idea. At least, she hoped it was a better idea. She stood and grabbed her keys and a jacket from their hooks by the front door and headed out to the east side of town.

Instead of pulling around back, Danni parked in front. She didn't think she'd be there long, plus she didn't give a rat's ass who saw her. As she was walking up to the porch, she looked up at the blue metal dragonfly on the overhang over the steps. It was such an odd thing to name a house of ill repute after. She knew that many cultures saw the dragonfly as a symbol of change and self-realization. She briefly wondered what truths one found out about themselves at the Dragonfly.

The one time she had come out here, she had just gone up and rang the doorbell, as if it was any other house. She figured why not. It *was* just a house. Who cared what went on inside? She recognized the person who opened the door and gave her a smile. "Hi. You're Jame, right?" Danni asked as she stood on the porch, hugging her arms to herself, regretting that she had only grabbed a hoodie. It felt as if it was just barely above freezing.

"Yes. Come in, you must be freezing." Jame opened the door, and Danni came in quickly, grateful.

"Thank you."

"Of course." Jame closed the door, then turned to a shivering Danni. "You're kind of early. Most of the women are still sleeping. The ones who aren't are having breakfast. But perhaps I could help you." Jame gave her a warm, sincere smile.

"Wow, you are charming, my sister was right."

"Your sister?"

"Sarah."

"Ah, yes. I'm sorry, I didn't get your name."

"It's Danni."

"Nice to meet you, Danni." Jame gave her a half bow.

"Yeah, don't do that. I'm not here for that. I need to talk to your boss. Is she awake?"

Startled but trying her best not to show it, Jame replied, "Yes, she's in her office. I'll go see if she's busy. You can wait out here if you like."

"Yeah, that's fine." Danni paced in the hallway while Jame walked past her down the hall, then knocked on a door, waited a moment, then walked in, closing the door behind her. While she was waiting, she looked around. The walls in the hallway were covered with framed photos of flowers and butterflies, some trees. They were quite beautiful. She wondered who took them. Then, she remembered the photo Sarah had showed her of her and P.J. in the park, and she realized the same person must have taken these photos. They showed a sensitive side to the woman that some, probably even her employees, wouldn't expect. Danni knew just the mention of her could make a huge smile appear on Sarah's face and a blush on her cheeks that was a shade makeup couldn't reproduce. She had to fix this.

Jame opened the door a moment later. "You can go in."

"Thanks." Danni walked past her into the room, and Jame closed the door behind her. The woman known in the house as Ma'am and to Sarah as Renee stood from behind her desk and offered Danni her hand.

"Hello. You can call me Renee. You're Danni, correct?"

Danni stepped forward to shake her hand. "Yes. I just need to talk to you a few minutes. There's something you should know."

"Is Sarah okay?"

"What? Oh, well, yes. I mean, she hasn't been in an accident or anything."

Renee let out a sigh of relief. "Good."

"No, she's fine, physically. Can I sit?" Danni indicated the chairs in front of the desk.

"Please." Once Danni was settled in a chair, Renee took her seat behind her desk.

"Okay, I've been trying to figure out how to say this, and I haven't really settled on the best way. It's a short drive out here, and I haven't had long to rehearse."

Renee squelched a smile. "I hope Sarah hasn't sent you out here to do her dirty work. Because if she has, you can save your speech. If she wants to break up with me, she can do it herself."

"She hasn't broken up with you?"

"Isn't that why you're here?"

"What? No!"

"She hasn't said anything to me since she left Saturday. Not one word. If she's not dead in a ditch somewhere, then it's obvious she doesn't want to see me anymore. It would be nice to know why, but I'm not going to force her to talk to me if she doesn't want to. Why did you come out here then?" Renee eyed her suspiciously. She saw some resemblance to Sarah in the eyes, but not much. Danni was a petite blond with a furtive, bouncy nature, either from too much coffee or a natural nervousness, Renee wasn't sure.

"Well, she told me...never mind. The point is, you deserve to know why, and that's why I'm here." Danni took a deep breath. "She distanced herself because of that waste of space Patrick."

"Her ex-husband?"

"That would be the one. He got wind of the two of you, and he threatened her. Said she had to choose between you and her son. Otherwise, he would sue for custody. I don't know on what grounds, but even if he didn't really stand a chance in court, he could make things unpleasant for a while. She didn't want to go through that. I guess she made her choice. I'm sorry." She meant it. She didn't know Renee, but anyone who could make Sarah look like that woman could deserved her respect.

"I guess she did. I wish she would have talked to me first. Told me about it, at least."

"I know. Maybe she thought you would talk her out of it. And if you did, she would have had a tougher choice. Look, I'm not going to try to justify her blowing you off 'cause that's not cool, but I know it was from fear. I just thought you had a right to know." Danni stood to leave.

"So, what did you think I would do with this information?"

Danni shrugged. "I don't know. Fight for her, maybe. I know she loves you, though she hasn't said that. I know my sister. There's a look she gets on her face when she talks about you. She smiles kinda shy-like, and she looks off to the side like she's thinking about you. It takes a while for that smile to fade. You did that." Danni eyed Renee as if examining her. "And I expect you do the same. With the women in this house, I'm sure you're the hard-ass boss you need to be, but that's not who my sister talks about. She talks about someone who's thoughtful and romantic, almost sweet. Someone who plays at being a big flirt but turns into a shy teenager who soaks up all the love."

Now it was Renee's turn to blush. "She told you all that?"

"Not all of it. The rest I just figured out. I should go."

"Thank you for telling me this." Renee extended her hand again, and Danni shook it.

"No problem. You needed to know. Now go get her, damn it!"

Renee laughed at Danni's parting words. Once Danni was gone, Renee went to the window and looked out. She could just make out the edge of the rose garden. "She *does* love me," she whispered as she imagined herself picking the last petal off one of the roses. "Now what?" she asked aloud. "Now what?"

Chapter Twenty-one

Renee spent the next several hours pacing in her sanctuary. She went to several pictures of Ian on the wall, remembering the moment each had been taken. She had never touched a real camera until she moved back and had been about to see Ian more often. Until then, she had only ever used the silly little 110 cameras that were all the rage when she'd been in high school. The cheap cameras never produced a good quality picture. They were often blurry around the edges, lacking detail, and everyone looked like they were harboring demons in their soul, the red eye was that horrible. But the fact that she had missed so much of his growing up, she wanted to capture the rest of his childhood on film. She had taken a couple of classes at the community college and learned how to take better pictures and eventually how to develop them. She bought an expensive camera and put a dark room in the basement. Her interest grew, and suddenly, she had more pictures of trees, birds, flowers, and Ian than she knew what to do with.

Now near her bed was a new section of photos. She had made a second print of the picture she had given Sarah of her and P.J., as well as another one she had taken of Sarah more recently. One day, while Jame had been gone, Sarah had come by, and they had walked in the garden. As Sarah leaned over to smell a bright pink rose, Renee had captured her as her eyes had closed and she was smiling. Renee sighed as she fingered the edge of the frame. She turned away from the photo, determined what her next move would be.

She left her room and hurried down the back stairs to the kitchen where Stella and Marie were sitting at the table, enjoying a cup of coffee and laughing together. They stopped when they saw her. She gave them a reassuring smile. "Family meeting. Now. In the main room."

Stella and Marie exchanged glances. Marie spoke first as she eyed Renee curiously. "Family meeting?"

"Yes. Now. It's as good a time as any, the house isn't busy. Come on." Without another word, she beckoned them to follow her out, and puzzled, they stood from the table and did so.

Renee walked through all the downstairs rooms, counting heads as she went. Most of the women were in the front room, as usual. Two were missing. She turned to Maria and asked, "Where's Stacey and Meghan?"

Maria looked up at her from her place on the couch where she sat thumbing through a magazine. "Upstairs, as far as I know. Meghan's sick today, and Stacey keeps going up to check on her."

"Okay. Can you go up and tell them both to come down here? There's about to be a family meeting, and I want everyone present and accounted for."

"Family meeting?" Maria asked, somewhat fearfully.

Renee smiled sweetly at her. "Yes, you heard me. A family meeting. Now go."

"Yes, Ma'am." She scurried off the couch and up the stairs. The rest of the young women looked up in interest, though no one dared ask her what was going on. They all sat quietly, waiting. She stood in the middle of the room with her arms behind her back, casually pacing, while she waited for them to return. Stella and Marie leaned against the wall, looking on in curiosity.

When the three others returned, Meghan was not looking her best. Her hair was disheveled, her eyes were red-rimmed and droopy, and the tip of her nose was red and sore-looking. As soon as she entered the room, she made a beeline for the couch and curled up in the corner. Stacey sat beside her, handing her Kleenex, and looked at Renee expectantly.

Renee walked to the edge of the room, near Stella and Marie, and took a deep breath. "Okay. Meghan, I'm sorry I had to get you out of bed, but this is important."

Meghan said nothing, just blew her nose loudly, then whispered she was sorry.

"That's quite all right. Now I've spent the day thinking. And pacing. But mostly thinking. I had a lot to think about and a lot to consider. I had to weigh my happiness against..." She looked at all of them in turn. "Well, I had to take all of you into consideration. And what I ultimately came to was that..." She turned to Stella, who seemed to know what she was about to say and gave her a smile and nod of encouragement. "...was that as of now, the Dragonfly is immediately and permanently closed." Exclamations of shock and surprise were uttered, some sounded angry. Renee put up her hand in a quelling gesture. "Don't worry, I will honor all of your contracts, and you're not being kicked out of your home. I'm giving you all sixty days to find new accommodations."

Through all the anger and mixed emotions, one

voice rose above the others to ask the question that was on all their minds. "Why?" Jame asked.

Renee turned to her, grateful she had been the one to speak. She paused so she could choose her words carefully. "Because...because I'm tired of giving up those I love."

Jame seemed satisfied with her simple answer and said nothing more.

Renee turned to her two oldest friends. "I'll honor your contracts, as well. We will always be family, and I won't leave you in the lurch."

Marie waved a hand as if her words were no big deal. "Contracts, hell, you're not getting rid of us that easy."

"She's right. Though maybe it is time you left the nest."

Renee grinned at Stella, her closest friend and sometimes surrogate mother. "Never too late, I guess."

"So, what are you going to do?" Marie asked.

"Isn't it obvious?" Stella asked. "She's going to fight for her woman, that's what. She's trying to be all respectable about it."

"You're giving up everything for a woman?" Marie asked, incredulous.

"No, I'm not. I'm not giving up anything. I'm just going to try being normal for once. See what that's like."

Marie scoffed. "Normal's boring."

"Well, I'd like the chance to find out. If you'll excuse me, I have some contracts to reread." She nodded to them as she left the room.

Marie shook her head in disbelief. "Never thought I'd see the day when Renee Berry would give up her business for a woman."

Stella watched Renee go. "It's not for the woman, it's for the boy."

"What boy?"

Stella took her wife's hand and kissed her. "Come on, I'll tell you all about it." She dragged her along as they went back to the kitchen. The murmurs of disbelief followed in their wake.

༒༒༒༒

Renee sat at her desk, glasses on, rereading the contracts and making out checks. She knew what she was doing was right, there was no hesitation or doubt in her mind. It was time. Just as she signed her name to the bottom of Stacey's check, there was a knock on her office door. She answered it without looking up. "Come in."

Jame walked in and closed the door behind her, then walked to stand in front of Renee's desk with her hands behind her back. "Ma'am, I realize you're busy, but I was wondering if I could have a moment of your time."

Renee smiled at her. "I just signed your check a minute ago, you're no longer my employee. Call me Renee. And you can stand or sit however you like." She set her pen down, took off her glasses and looked at Jame with curiosity.

"I'll try." She took a seat and crossed her legs, trying to be casual.

"Good, that's better. Now what can I do for you?"

"I don't want to get into your business, but I have to ask, are you sure about this?"

"Yes. I'm sure."

"What I mean is, what if…I mean, the rumor is…"

Renee interrupted her with a chuckle. "I've not known you to put much stock in rumors, Jame."

"Well, they're running rampant out there right now. The consensus seems to be that you're doing this to please Sarah. That maybe it was her idea."

The smile faded from Renee's lips. "No, Sarah has nothing to do with this. She's unaware I've made this decision. And furthermore, she would never ask me to make it. She's not like that."

"I'm glad. And I'm not surprised. About her, I mean. So, it begs the question, what *will* you do with retirement?" Jame smiled, trying to be at ease and have a casual conversation with the woman, who, up until a few minutes ago, had been her boss.

"I don't know. That's the part I haven't figured out yet. I'm still working on that. Hopefully, Sarah will be at my side. But even if not, I have options. Maybe I can finally be that college graduate my mother always hoped I'd be. What about you? How will this change your plans?"

Jame leaned forward in her chair, serious now. "That's what I actually wanted to talk to you about. When I was home, I reassured my father that I was still planning to go to college. But what if that's not the road I'm supposed to travel?"

Renee smiled at Jame's expression, but Jame ignored it and went on.

"What if I'm supposed to do something different? Help people in a different way? Ma'am, I want to buy the Dragonfly, keep it running."

The look of surprise on Renee's face was genuine. She hadn't expected that. "You want to what?"

"Hear me out, please. During the time I've been here, I've seen my role shift from being simply someone who gives others pleasure to that of someone who helps people become more confident in themselves, someone who can lend a willing ear or simply open arms to sooth them. I know sexual surrogacy is a far cry from my original goals, but I think my original goals were wrong. This feels right." Jame's face showed earnestness and determination.

"Jame, every girl in this house, hell, every hooker who's ever walked the street, knows that people come to us for more than just to satisfy their sexual needs. We're all therapists. You've just discovered the hidden truth about our profession. That doesn't mean you should throw away your future on sex work. Be a doctor. Fulfill your promise to your father. You don't want this." Renee sat back in her chair. "I'm sorry, the Dragonfly is not for sale."

Jame stood and leaned over the desk. "Ma'am… Renee…if you don't want to sell the Dragonfly, fine. But I know what I want for myself. I'm not making this decision lightly. And I will finish school, one way or another. Let me keep the Dragonfly running. And keep those women employed. Some of them have no other place to go. Few of them have savings. None of them have college degrees. Most of them have families they can't return to. Did you know Stacey's mother OD'd when Stacey was twelve and her father was never in the picture? Stacey was put in foster care until she aged out. Maria ran away from her abusive stepfather and a mother who blamed it on her. Kendra—" Before Jame could continue, Renee cut her off.

"I know. Why do you think I hired them? Over the years, I've hired so many women with stories like that, Stella used to joke that I should call this place Renee Berry's Home for Wayward Girls. I understand about their pasts, and I don't want to send them back there, which is why all of you are getting an additional bonus that wasn't part of your original contract. What they choose to do with that is up to them. Some decisions they have to make themselves." Renee stood and went around to Jame and caressed her cheek. "I'm glad that you care about them. You really are sweet."

"Then let me keep caring about them. Let me keep this place running."

"You're asking me to leave my home, the business I've built…"

"You said yourself, you don't want to lose anyone else you love. Go and focus on love while I stay and focus on business. You can keep the house if you want, just let me run the business."

Renee sighed and walked over to the window where she could just see the backyard and hugged her arms to herself. "I love this house, but this was never really a home, was it? Not for me. No matter how much I tried to make it one. I hid in here or upstairs, surrounded by pictures of my son, wishing for something that I gave up years ago."

"You have a son?"

Renee turned back around but stayed where she was. "I do. His name's Ian. He was raised by his grandmother. He's a young man now, about your age." She smiled to herself and shook her head, the first time she had thought about that. Then she went on. "He's a good man. A nice one. Through no fault of my own, I should add. I missed so much, and it was all my choice." Neither said anything for a moment, then Renee seemed to come to a decision. "Okay, I'll let you buy this place but on one condition."

Jame looked at her questioningly, and she went on.

"That you continue to employ Stella and Marie as long as they wish to be employed."

Jame smiled and crossed the room to her with an extended hand. "Deal."

Renee shook her hand. "Oh, and one other thing…don't let the job consume you. Make time and room for love."

"You have my word…Renee."

Renee grinned. "Feels weird, doesn't it?"

"A little bit, but I think I can get used to it."

"How about a hug for your old boss?"

"Or one for a new friend?" Jame asked hopefully.

"That too." Renee hugged her to her, not feeling any of the old stirrings from when she thought she had feelings for Jame. Interesting how things can change in such a short time, she reflected, when you meet the one person who changes your life in unexpected ways. She squeezed Jame tighter, then let her go.

☙ ❧

Sarah sat on her couch, trying to ignore the incessant texts from Danni. Danni meant well, but Sarah wished she'd just lay off. At least for a while. She knew she shouldn't have ghosted Renee when things heated up with Patrick, but she panicked. She just didn't see any way she could have Renee and P.J., so she chose her son, as she knew she always would.

She couldn't do what Renee had done with her son. She didn't judge Renee for her choices, but she knew it was a choice she couldn't make. After getting out of a loveless marriage, she was grateful that she at least had P.J. by her side and the house he would grow up in. That was all she needed, and she wasn't going to do anything to jeopardize that. She knew she owed Renee an explanation, an apology, something. But she wasn't sure how to form the words. If she was being honest with herself, she'd say that she was also chicken shit. She had a feeling that if she were face to face with Renee again, one look into those blue eyes, the love looking back at her, and she'd give in. She had faced down Patrick, had him on the ropes, and he was no longer a threat, but she just wasn't sure if now really was the right time to be starting a new relationship. It had happened so quickly, maybe they just needed more time.

There was a noise on her porch. It sounded like the unmistakable sound of the shuffling of boots, and she rolled her eyes in exasperation, muttering, "Damn it, Patrick, what the hell now?" But before she could get off the couch, she heard the sound of the boots retreating. Curious, she got up and went to the front window and pulled back the curtain, only to see the unmistakable leather-clad back of the woman she had just been thinking about. Renee stood at the top of the steps, obviously hesitating, her back to the window, so all Sarah could see were the black, worn boots, the faded jeans that hung loose at her waist, with a wallet in the back pocket, the black biker's jacket, the one with the zippers. She could tell the jacket wasn't zipped up, as it fit her too loosely. Her long, reddish-blond hair fell down her shoulders in a casual way, occasionally catching a light breeze. "Damn it, damn it, damn it. So not fair."

"You okay, Mama?"

Sarah turned from the window and saw P.J. standing in the middle of the living room, looking at her curiously. She spoke to reassure him and put on a smile. "Yes, baby, I'm fine. Go back to your room for a bit, okay? Mama's about to have company."

"Okay." He turned and left, going back into his room.

Pulling her black sweater around herself, Sarah opened her front door and couldn't help smiling at the startled look on Renee's face. Before Renee could say anything, Sarah asked, "So, you're just going to leave without even knocking on my door? What a waste of a cool jacket."

Renee looked down at the jacket, seemingly embarrassed. "What, this old thing?"

"Oh, don't act like you don't know how hot you look in that."

Renee cocked an eyebrow at her, her tone changing abruptly to one meant to tease. "You think I look hot in this?"

"Stop trying to be charming. Unless that's why you're standing on my porch. To be charming." Normally, Sarah would have smiled flirtatiously at her and either responded with flirting of her own or just played it coy and let Renee do all the work. Now, however, she wasn't in the mood for either. Seeing Renee standing before her, especially when she had seen her through the window with her back to her, unsure of herself, hesitating, made the guilt Sarah knew she would feel when she saw her again come flooding up to the surface. It was hard to look at her face without feeling like the worst person in the world.

"In a cool jacket?" Renee asked hopefully.

Sarah laughed softly. "Right." Her mood quickly

sobered, and she became contrite. "I'm sorry, Renee. I owe you an explanation." She couldn't take the look in Renee's eyes, so she looked down at her feet. The boots were old and scarred but holding up well. They looked as if Renee had walked miles and miles in them, yet they only showed a little road wear. They had gone the distance with her, and Sarah was suddenly wondering if she could live up to their steadfastness.

"No, you don't."

"Yes, I do. I'm sorry for the silent treatment. You didn't do anything to deserve that."

"Maybe, but…"

"No maybe, you didn't. I fell back on an old bad habit when I was faced with an impossible decision. That's not an excuse really, but it's the truth. There's more I need to say to you, but I'd like to do it inside, where it's not freezing. Can you just, can you just come in, please?" Sarah pointed behind her and cocked her head in the direction of her living room.

"P.J.?"

"What about him?"

"Aren't you afraid of me meeting him?"

Sarah looked at her confused, at first, wondering where Renee would come up with such a thought. Then, she realized. With a nod of recognition, she replied, "My sister called you, didn't she?"

"Well, she didn't call. She stopped by."

Instead of admonishing Danni—there would be plenty of time to do that later—on impulse, she reached out and touched Renee's jacket. It was almost as worn as the boots, but it was in better condition. She could tell Renee must take loving good care of it. It was as soft and smooth as only worn leather can be, and every time Renee moved or shifted, the jacket creaked as only old leather could. Renee silently watched her caressing the jacket, her gaze locked on Sarah's. Neither spoke for a moment, until finally, Sarah cleared her throat and said, "Get in here, it's cold." She stepped back and Renee stepped inside. Sarah closed the door behind them.

After they came in, Renee took in the room, then her gaze settled on Sarah once again. The look she gave her was one of concern. "I don't want to cause problems with your ex."

Sarah knew she meant it, that the last thing Renee wanted to do was to come between Sarah and her son, to do something that would cause them harm. This realization touched her, but she tried to play it off as no big thing, and she waved a dismissive hand. "Please. I can handle him. He did scare me initially when he came by, and that's why I went dark on you. I had a lot to think about."

"And what did you come up with?"

"That's he's a prick. But I knew that already. Also, I took my sister's advice and called a lawyer. According to her, there's really nothing he can do. My dating you doesn't put P.J. at risk. There was a concern about the Dragonfly, but I told her that he's never been there, and I didn't plan on taking him. She said unless I do something that would actually endanger him, there's nothing Patrick could do to take him away. As long as the company I keep isn't dangerous, the legality or illegality of your business shouldn't be a problem. So, I intially ghosted you because I panicked, but I haven't reached out to you because I was scared you were pissed at me, and you'd have every right to be. So, I guess what I'm saying is, I'm a coward, and I'm sorry, and I really hope you can forgive me. Okay, that was incredibly long-winded of me, I'm sorry. I'm suddenly nervous." Sarah stepped closer to her, still hugging the sweater around herself protectively.

"Well, first of all, I'm not pissed, though, you're right, I should have been. I was confused, then worried, then I guess I just accepted it. Okay, maybe I was a little pissed." She smiled and Sarah bit her lip, more in resignation than in humor. Renee went on. "But when Danni stopped by and explained it I understood what you were doing, though I wish you had talked to me about it first. Just don't make a habit of running away when things get real, you hear me?" Renee cocked an eyebrow.

Sarah was contrite. "I promise."

Renee smiled and brushed a stray hair off Sarah's cheek. "What are you nervous about?"

"What am I nervous about? I'm nervous that I completely fucked this up. That you don't want to date me anymore. Or even speak to me. That you hate me. I would hate me. I'm afraid that I just let the best thing that ever happened to me slip away because I was scared." She took a breath, then went on. "Maybe you haven't noticed, but I'm babbling here. This is the part in the movies where the guy always stops the girl from talking by kissing her." Now that the dust had settled, now that she had spoken her mind and gave voice to her fears, she suddenly felt better. The look on Renee's face helped. She used the love she saw looking back at her as something to anchor to and relax.

The look on Renee's face turned playful, and she grinned. "I'm not a guy, and I love listening to you babble. I think I could spend the next fifty years listening to you babble."

"Lame." Sarah smiled as she put her hand on the back of Renee's neck and brought her closer for a kiss, letting it linger, letting it make a promise that she was now bound to keep.

Renee put her arms around Sarah and kissed her back. When the kiss ended, she said with a chuckle, "You say 'lame,' but I hear 'I love you.'" Sarah chuckled but didn't disagree. Encouraged, Renee went on. "Also, you had every reason to be scared. I get that. As much as I missed you, as much as I wanted to come here and, I don't know, make some dramatic scene, drive up in a white Mustang, as a modern knight would, I also understood what you were doing. I mean, I hated it, but for selfish reasons. Fuck, now I'm the one babbling."

"It's okay."

"Anyway, you won't have to worry about that prick anymore. He won't have anything to hold over you."

"What are you talking about?"

"As of this afternoon, Jame is the new owner of the Dragonfly."

Sarah couldn't believe it. "Are you serious?"

"You sound almost mad. Why?"

"Because I am almost mad. Why would you do that? I would never ask you to do that, you love what you do." Sarah pulled away from Renee a bit, not sure how to process what she just heard.

"I know that, that you would never ask me to, I mean. But you can't love a business. I should know. I tried. It's not that fulfilling. I want you in my life as long as you want to be a part of it, which I hope is a really long time. I've enjoyed the business and even that house, but I feel more love standing in your living room than I've ever felt in the Dragonfly." Renee pulled her back against her and Sarah came back, reluctantly at first.

"So, you *didn't* give up the house for me? Because I would hate it if that were true. And that would be a big risk to take."

"I just thought it was about time I grew up. And part of that means being here for you, for P.J., being a part of your lives. If you'll have me."

"Didn't we settle that?"

"Did we?" Renee asked playfully.

"I thought so. What, do you need an engraved invitation?" she teased.

"That would be nice."

"Well, this is the best I can do." Sarah pulled Renee to her for a kiss.

When the kiss ended, Renee replied, "That'll work." They laughed together and kissed again.

There was a shuffle of movement behind her, and Sarah saw Renee's face flame. She worked to suppress her giggles at Renee's uncomfortableness at P.J.'s approach.

"Hey," Renee said sheepishly to him, ignoring Sarah's giggles, which she couldn't suppress after all.

"Hi," he said shyly.

Renee gave him a little wave. "Hi." She stepped closer to him and extended her hand. "I'm Renee. I'm a friend of your mom's."

He shook her hand like a gentleman and said simply, "I know."

"You do?"

"Yeah, Mama told me."

Renee looked from Sarah to P.J. "What else did she tell you?"

P.J. walked closer to his mother. "She said she hoped I got to meet you. Oh, and that you were someone special." Sarah put her arm around his shoulders and hugged him to her.

Renee smiled down at him. "Well, that was very nice of your mom. Your mom's special, too."

"I know."

Both women chuckled. "Do you think it's okay if I come around sometimes to hang out with you and your mom? Maybe take you two out to do stuff?"

P.J. shrugged. "I guess so. Do you like video games? My Aunt Danni makes video games and has all the cool ones!"

"No, honey, she doesn't make them, she just makes the music for them."

"Well, I haven't played any since junior high, but I'll play them with you if you like, though I'm not very good."

"Neither is my mom. That's okay, I can teach you."

"I would like that." Renee reached for Sarah's hand as she ruffled P.J.'s hair, then she put her arm around Sarah's waist and smiled.

Sarah returned the smile, thinking they looked like a family and cursing Patrick for trying to force her to miss out on this.

Epilogue

Jame's log:

It's been awhile since I've done a journal entry, and I realized there are some things I need to put down for the sake of posterity. Though, honestly, I don't know who, if anyone, will ever read these pages. I'm really just talking to myself. But that's all right. Later, when all I have are my memories, my journals will help me relive things I hadn't thought about in years. Enough of the maudlin stuff, there are plenty of good things happening.

It's been one year today that I shook Renee's hand and offered, or more accurately, begged, to buy the Dragonfly. A lot has happened since then. That's why I haven't written, I've been so busy. Since that fateful day, I've been busy learning all the things I didn't know about running this place. It was a lot. From doing the books and paying taxes to hiring and managing the women to dealing with the clients, there was much more than I would have anticipated. Renee has been patient and generous with teaching me things. She even stayed on for the first month so I could observe how she does things. She has an ease with people that I hope to be able to learn. She understands them far more than I could ever hope to learn in a classroom.

She and Sarah live together now in Sarah's house. Her ex doesn't like it much, I'm told, but there's nothing he can do about it. P.J. has still never been out here, and Renee is no longer associated with the place. She even started a whole new career as a photographer. She opened a little shop on the square called R and S Photography. Renee takes the pictures, and Sarah does everything else, I hear. Renee seems happier than I've ever known her to be. She laughs a lot now, and she doesn't seem as guarded as she used to. And she hugs me every time she sees me. I used to find it odd, but I'm used to it now, and her hugs are all-encompassing and warm. I have even started to look forward to them.

    I realized that there was one other person I knew who knew how to run a business, and that was Frankie. I gave her a call and made her an offer she couldn't refuse. She'd been running that bar of her dad's since high school, or thereabout, plus she's not afraid to bounce the jerks out. She does well with keeping order around here, and she gets along with the women. Not long after she got here, she met Julie, the girl next door. I didn't think Julie would be her type, she's too wholesome, but Frankie says I'd be surprised. I don't think I want to know what that means.

    Before Renee moved out, she had the idea to build a small cottage in the back for Stella and Marie amongst the roses. We finally finished that last month, and they seem to love it. As of now, they're still working here, but I don't know for how long. I fear I may only be able to enjoy their cooking and daily good cheer for a couple of more years as I think they're looking to retire soon. And they deserve it.

    I moved into the sanctuary on the third floor. It's twice the size of my old room, and Renee had it decorated in a style to match the age of the house. I've always preferred that. As far as the rest of the house, I *took out all the rooms behind the mirrors and turned them back into the closets they were meant to be. The women of the house greatly appreciated that. Besides, I have no desire to watch them work. I don't need to.*

My parents were disappointed, I think, when I told them I wasn't going to med school, but I think they've adjusted. My mother does like the fact I'm a business owner. She still doesn't know what the business really is, and Dad is keeping my secrets. They came to visit over the summer, and I canceled all appointments that week and told the women to pretend to be guests as if this was the B and B I had told Mom it was. Thankfully, they went along with it, and Mom had no idea.

Jame was interrupted in her typing when the office door opened, and Danni walked in. "Babe, come on, Sarah and Renee are expecting us like a half hour ago." She looked at her bare wrist and gave Jame a wry smile. "Come on, chop, chop."

Jame returned her smile and replied, "Okay, just a second. Almost done." Danni leaned in the doorway and sighed histrionically. Jame went back to her journal.

And, reader, someday I'm going to marry her. But that's another story.

She saved the document, then closed her laptop and stood. "Okay, I'm ready. Sorry to keep you waiting." Jame went to her and gave her a brief kiss, then took her hand.

"Apology accepted. Don't let it happen again."

Jame chuckled as they walked out the door.

If you liked this book?

Reviews help a new author get discovered and if you have enjoyed this book, please do the author the honor of posting a review on Goodreads, Amazon, Barnes & Noble or anywhere you purchased the book. Or perhaps share a posting on your social media sites or spread the word to your friends.

About the Author

Sam McAullif is a work in progress. They have published four previous novels of lesbian fiction, four erotic short stories, and a book of poetry all under the name T.L. Hayes. Follow them on Facebook or their author page, at tlhayesweb.com for all the latest news and the occasional blog, usually about books, but not always.

Other books by Sapphire Authors

Last First Kiss: A Passport to Love Romance – ISBN – 978-1-948232-95-1

Alessia Cavalii is a rising star in the competitive international wine scene, and one of only twenty-six female master sommeliers in the world. Her home is a renovated winery on the windswept coast of Italy, she has a career she loves, and she is finally free of a toxic relationship. But Alessia is hiding a dangerous secret—one that could, in a second, shatter the life she's built.

Parker Haven is a captain in the U.S. Army and stationed at the NATO military camp near Salerno. An investigator with the Military Police, she's pulled in to help solve a string of murders in the city and finds herself inexplicably drawn into Alessia's world. As the intrigue surrounding the case—and the alluring Alessia—spins more and more out of control, Parker realizes she may have to choose between her military career and the woman she's falling for. Do we ever truly know the people we love?

A storm's brewing on the horizon. Can Addie and Greyson weather it, or will it blow them over?

Blueprint for Romance: A Garriety Romance – ISBN – 978-1-948232-71-5

After the death of her husband, Dylan Lake's ability to trust in others is shattered. Her life is thrust into turmoil between caring for Emma, her seven-year old handicapped child, and working hard to make ends meet. Dylan doesn't have time to pursue a romantic relationship. Finding that one special person only happens in dreams. When fate keeps throwing Dylan and Kat together, Dylan finds her attraction to Kat something she can't ignore. Will her trust issues stop her from letting Kat into her and Emma's life?

Leaving her old job and moving halfway across the country were the scariest things Kat Anderson had ever done. Starting a new life and career takes priority over any foolish notion of a fairy-tale future of romance and love. Kat's attraction to Dylan is time taken away from building a new business.

Can Kat juggle love and duty to find her Happy Ever After?

Welcome back to Garriety, the town with an open heart, and home to some of the quirky and warm characters from Add Romance and Mix. Join Kat and Dylan on their quest for true romance with a little help from Kat's sister Briley and her family, along with a host of new characters.

To Be Loved – ISBN – 978-1-948232-79-1

A dead body, women and kids in peril, treachery at every turn—no problem for the close-knit sexagenarian friends of the Silver Series, Dory, Robby, Jill and Charlene! When a calm evening walk leads Dory to suspect bad news is happening right next door in her placid neighborhood, and when a waif comes under Jill's wing, routine life takes a vacation. And when a corpse points toward a suspect who's far from virginal in character, and seems to link to the waif and the bad news, well!

All bets are off.

The women rally to defeat evil and correct injustice, helped with a generous serving of karma from a very unexpected source. Along the way, they work with and for the police, sometimes in—ah, unorthodox—ways. But what are a few more gray hairs to law enforcement when the cause of justice is advanced? They encounter smugglers in the devil's oldest crime, street-smart kids wiser than their years, maids in distress, and unlikely allies in Skid Row. But the persistent four also marshal the vengeance of the angels, through their own.

Bobbi and Soul – ISBN – 978-1-948232-41-8

Bobbi Webster wants nothing more than to be the best family practice doctor for her home town in rural Oregon. To accomplish that, she's enrolled in a two-year fellowship in rural medicine at Valley View Medical Center in Colorado. Sparks fly when Bobbi meets the Reverend Erin O'Rouke, a petite, feisty priest who meddles in the treatment of Bobbi's patients. To make matters worse, Bobbi wants nothing to do with any religion, much less the woman she dubs, The Elf.

Erin serves as vicar at a small church where a few parishioners have stipulated that she must be celibate, reflecting their "love the sinner, hate the sin" tactic. After she clashes with Erin, Bobbi recognizes how a recent breakup of an abusive relationship has falsely colored her perception of Erin's world and work. Likewise, when Erin understands how Bobbi's emotional wounds make her vulnerable, her natural empathy moves her closer to Bobbi.

They find themselves drawn to each other, but how can Bobbi and Erin overcome so many obstacles to find love?

Faithful Valor – ISBN – 978-1-948232-85-2

Sometimes danger isn't found on a battleground—it's sitting at your front door. Nic Caldwell is back Stateside, working the job she was supposed to have before her most recent deployment, and living her best life at home. At least she thought she would be, except her PTSD is always in the background, dragging her back to her tour in Afghanistan. As she struggles to control her demons privately, her public life with Claire is almost picture perfect. However, a picture can't show everything hiding just under the surface.

Claire Monroe has the love of her life back in one piece—almost. She's trying to help Nic adjust to her new normal both physically and emotionally while also going back to school and raising their daughter, Grace. With all the difficulties Nic's re-entry poses along with the new challenges of being an adult student, she wonders how she can guide them back to their old life while building a new one for herself.

Cece Ramirez has decided that the Army has served its purpose and she is ready for a new chapter in her professional and personal life. Retiring from active duty and moving on to a new role as a police officer on a college campus, she realizes that she's traded camo, discipline, and rifles for book bags, bikes, and rowdy post-adolescents. While she and the students at Cal State Monterey Bay might be the same age, their pasts are vastly different, and the transition from soldier to college cop may not be as smooth as she hopes.

When a chance encounter at a near-base shopette challenges Nic's authority and leaves her and her family in potential peril, Cece and Claire must pull together to back Nic up in peacetime, and right at home.

Thr Dragonfly House

www.ingramcontent.com/pod-product-compliance
Ingram Content Group UK Ltd.
Pitfield, Milton Keynes, MK11 3LW, UK
UKHW042003230426
12048UKWH00009B/518